LOVE'S CAPTIVE

Thorn's gaze swept the room, then focused on Diana. "I do hope your accommodations please you."

"There is only one thing you can do to please me!"

His mouth twitched with a devilish grin. "I would go to great lengths to please you, my lady."

Diana gave him a steely look. "Then allow me to return to Sidhean."

"In due time."

"You have made a terrible mistake," she said. "If you seek your brother's return, you should have selected another means of barter."

He stepped closer. Raising his hand, he went to place it on her shoulder. But she backed away. "If you put so much as a hand on me, I'll kill you!" she spat, quickly producing the silver dirk.

"You flatter yourself, lass," he said at last. "One would think you deem yourself irresistible! Let me assure you that I do not find you in the least attractive. Now"—his manner grew brusque—"I suggest that you retire." He turned away, then gave her a last glance. "Keep your knife, if it makes you rest easy, Diana. I'll not be battering down the door to avail myself of your charms."

WHITE HEATHER

HELENE LEHR

LEISURE BOOKS **NEW YORK CITY**

This book is dedicated to the Colbergs:
Bill and Shirley; and Grace

A LEISURE BOOK®

June 1995

Published by

Dorchester Publishing Co., Inc.
276 Fifth Avenue
New York, NY 10001

Printed in the United States of America.

Chapter One

October, 1485

Somberly, Diana watched the weak sun splay across the glen, enhancing the colorful plaids worn by the gathered nobility.

The entire court was assembled there on that crisp day. Men and women who had not seen each other in months were clustered in groups, sharing the latest news and gossip.

At odds with the jovial atmosphere, Diana was subdued. If there had been a way for her to avoid this event, she would have, and most gladly. The queen's presence, however, dictated otherwise.

Nothing would be solved. Were six sheep worth the blood that would be shed this day? Diana thought not.

With a sigh, she moved closer to the queen in the event that Margaret might need her services.

She stood there quietly. Only King James and Queen Margaret were seated. The rest of the court stood about in various stages of anticipation, for what they were soon to witness would be no ordinary journey.

The battle about to take place at the invitation of the king would settle a dispute between two clans, one of which was Diana's own.

Even as she viewed her kinsmen with pride, Diana knew that the confrontation would not end the long-standing border dispute between the clans, which the king would not involve himself in, knowing that his siding with one clan would alienate the other.

This particular disagreement, however, centered around the minor matter of six sheep. The small, short-tailed animals had strayed onto the disputed territory and were now claimed by both sides.

When King James heard of the matter, he commanded the feuding clans of MacKendrick and MacLaren each to send ten men onto the field of battle.

Diana turned away from the babble of good-natured laughter and the placing of wagers as to the outcome of the ensuing fracas.

She was suddenly thankful that, despite the circumstances, her father, the Earl of Sidhean, was not among the men on the field; nor was

her brother Robert. Both had set out from Sidhean more than a week earlier, but had never
made it past Inverness, where the earl had
taken ill and been forced to return home.

Roused from her reverie, Diana viewed the
young woman who now came to stand at her
side. As with most noblewomen, Anne Mac-
Tavish had also come to court for two years as
a lady-in-waiting to the queen. At 16, Anne was
the same age as Diana, but several inches
shorter.

" 'Tis pride you must be feeling, lass, to see
your kinsmen ready to defend their honor."
Anne raised her head to smile at Diana.

"Aye," Diana said, then bit her lip. "Though I
fear some will not be returning to Sidhean."

Anne shrugged her plump shoulders and gave
Diana an amused look. "Och! Men will ever
fight," she noted, turning away. " 'Tis their curse
and charm all in one."

Diana made no response, having caught sight
of a knight belonging to the MacKendrick clan.
Although he was the hugest man she had ever
seen—at least six feet four inches tall—he was
perfectly proportioned. Beneath a coat of mail
that fell to his knees, his long and well-muscled
legs were encased in leather boots, which were
laced up to his calves. A lean torso flared upward to broad shoulders. At the moment, his
face was averted as he swung himself up on his
steed.

Diana couldn't help but admire the magnificent golden stallion the knight had just mounted. The large, deep-chested animal was bred for strength and agility, trained to carry a warrior in full armor without faltering.

Horses such as this destrier abounded at Sidhean, one of the finest keeps in the Highlands. But the color, the regal bearing, and the alert look in his eye set this prancing and pawing stallion apart from his contemporaries.

Then the knight turned in Diana's direction, and her breath caught in her throat as the force of his gaze accidently met hers. Beneath thick mahogany-colored hair streaked with burnished gold, his eyes were a vivid blue. The man radiated such a forceful arrogance; Diana wondered how anyone could best him.

As the skirling of the pipes rent the stillness, the knight turned to face his adversaries. He was not wearing a helmet. The men were to fight only with shield and sword. Maces, as well as claymores—those heavy swords requiring the wielder to use both hands—had been barred by order of the king.

Diana looked at Anne. "The knight on the golden stallion," she murmured. "Do you know who he is?"

Anne nodded. "Aye. That is Sir Thornton MacKendrick, the heir of the Earl of Dunmoor."

"His son?" she asked.

"Nay. The earl has no sons, even though he has been wed these past eleven years. Sir Thornton is his nephew."

Diana fell silent as the king gave the sign for the battle to begin. She watched as the combatants came together, each side shouting its battle cry with a ferocity that rang through the otherwise quiet glen.

The next 20 minutes seemed to pass in a blur of wheeling horses and flashing swords. Some warriors fell from their mounts and quickly got to their feet. Some fell and never moved again.

Even having been surrounded by Highland warriors all her life, Diana was astounded at the cold determination with which the golden knight fought. No man who approached him bettered him. On his face she saw no emotion. He did not display anger, vengeance, or even satisfaction.

When it was over, only two men were still mounted on their horses. Both were Mac-Kendricks. One of them was the golden knight. Squires rushed onto the field to aid those who were still alive.

Thorn angled his horse closer to his comrade, who was slumped in his saddle.

"Angus? Are you hurt bad?" he asked.

"Nay. 'Tis only a nick in my shoulder." The knight straightened up and smiled. "You're not to be worrying about me!"

Despite the reassuring words, Thorn's brow creased in concern. Angus MacKendrick, a distant cousin of his, was in charge of the men-at-arms. A seasoned warrior in his late thirties,

Angus was not a man to complain about an injury. Still, though bleeding profusely, the wound did appear to be superficial.

After a few more words with Angus, Thorn nudged his horse forward and approached the king.

"Sir Thornton," the king said when Thorn paused before him. "You have won fairly. 'Tis our judgment that the animals in question are the property of the Clan MacKendrick."

Thorn bowed his head in grave acceptance. Though he made certain that his manner was respectful, he held his sovereign in contempt. James's avarice would be the downfall of them all. Already there were rumblings among the noblemen and whispered meetings to oust James and install his son in his stead. Thorn knew that if that time came, he would fight at the side of the young Prince James.

The lad in question was standing behind his father's chair, and he now offered his congratulations, which Thorn acknowledged with another bow of his head.

Thorn then turned to pay homage to the queen and his attention was caught by the tall, willowy lass standing at her side. The first thing he noticed were her eyes. Framed by lashes that were just as black as her hair, they were gray, of such a pale shade as to be startling.

Gypsy eyes! he thought to himself, only now becoming aware that she was staring at him.

He was uncertain as to what to read into that

look, for he had never seen the likes of it before. It was not friendly; it was not hostile. Certainly it was not admiring. That was an expression Thorn was used to receiving from a woman, and had that been the case, he would have merely smiled and turned away. Though he wanted to turn away, he seemed unable to, as if he were bewitched.

"Sir Thornton!"

With difficulty, Thorn tore his gaze away from the lass and again viewed his king.

"The court physician will attend to your kinsman's wounds if you will assist him back to Holyrood."

"Aye," Thorn responded quickly, chagrined by his lack of attention. "My thanks, Your Grace."

The king inclined his head, then rose and left the field.

Soon after, the royal party began to make its way back into Edinburgh, at a leisurely pace.

As she led her horse onto High Street, Diana took little notice of the many shops that lined the cobbled thoroughfare, for it was densely crowded with citizens, peddlers, and vendors, all of whom scattered every which way when they saw the king's banner.

Raising her head, she could see the huge stone castle of Edinburgh, which overlooked the valley upon which the city sprawled. Just below it was Holyrood, the royal residence.

As they made their way up the solitary avenue that led to the palace, Diana was surprised to see Prince James angle his horse alongside hers.

"I've been told that you will be leaving us soon, Lady Diana," he noted.

"In about a fortnight, Your Highness," she replied. "As soon as my brother arrives to escort me back to Sidhean."

" 'Twas grievous news to learn that the Earl of Sidhean is ailing."

"Aye. From all accounts, my father is gravely ill." Her voice was somber.

"Your presence at court will be sorely missed." Jamie offered a grin. " 'Tis not often my mother's ladies are as fetching as you."

A smile curved Diana's lips as she viewed the young prince. Only 13, he exuded the Stuart charm, which was so sadly lacking in his dour father.

Though pleased with the compliment, Diana did not take it seriously. It was a well-known fact that even at his young age Jamie had an eye for the lassies.

"At least you will be here for the festivities this evening," the prince said. "I'll have your word that you will save the first dance for me."

"Gladly, Your Highness."

When they at last entered the courtyard, Jamie spurred his horse forward.

Assisted by a footman, Diana dismounted. Sensing she was being watched, Diana turned to see Sir Thornton MacKendrick staring intently at her. She leveled a look at him that she hoped was disdainful.

"You certainly have eyes for that one, don't you?"

Startled, Diana turned to Anne, whose lips were curved in a mischievous grin.

"Certainly not!" Diana tossed her head and moved toward the ornately carved double doors of the palace. "Like all MacKendricks, he is rude and without manners," she added as Anne hurried to catch up with her.

"He spoke to you?" Anne sounded shocked.

"Nay! He did not have to speak. The fact that he was staring at me was indication enough of his ill-bred ways."

"How did you know he was staring if you were not looking at him?" Anne giggled as they mounted the stone steps.

"I did nothing but convey my displeasure," Diana retorted hotly.

Anne was still grinning when they reached their room, which was not far from the queen's apartments. But she made no further comment. When they entered, servants had warm baths waiting for them.

A screen was positioned between the two tubs in front of the fireplace, offering them a degree of privacy while allowing them to chat companionably as servants assisted in their toilette.

Having disrobed, Diana sank gratefully into the warm scented water. Riding sidesaddle, as she was required to do while at court, left her muscles aching.

" 'Tis difficult for me to believe," Anne said as she stepped into the other tub, "that in less than three months I will be wed."

Diana leaned forward slightly as a servant scrubbed her back. "Are you looking forward to it?"

"Aye," Anne said enthusiastically. "Lord Hamilton is a fine man. As I told you, his keep is not far from Edinburgh. Doubtless, we will be at court more often than not."

Diana smiled. For herself, she much preferred the Highlands, and she was most anxious to return.

"And what about you?" Anne asked then. "Have you received word of a betrothal for yourself?"

"None," Diana answered as she stepped out of the tub. A maidservant quickly draped a towel around her shoulders. "However, I did not expect any news of that sort before I return to Sidhean. My father has given me his word that no contract will be set in motion without my consent."

Anne frowned. "Surely such an important decision should be left in the hands of your father. How will you know if you made the right choice?"

Diana laughed as she shrugged her arms into the robe held by the servant. "I'll know. When the times comes, I'll know."

16

A while later, they were both dressed. With a shared smile, they hurried to attend their queen, after which they all descended the stone stairs to the main hall to join the rest of the court as they assembled for the evening meal.

Except for an area in the center, which had been cleared for dancing, Diana noticed that the floor had been scattered with fresh rushes.

As she seated herself at the long trestle table, upon which were set plates of silver emblazoned with the king's crest, Diana reflected that she would not be present at too many more of these functions. The thought did not sadden her. While she had enjoyed and benefited from her two years of service, having been taught among other things how to dress and conduct herself as befit a noblewoman, Diana longed for the familiarity and warmth of her home and family.

She leaned back in her chair as servants began to place the food on the table. Tonight there was roast pheasant, leg of veal, and mutton, which had been heavily seasoned with mace and nutmeg.

The only utensil next to her plate was a silver spoon. Diana removed her dining knife from the waistband of her gown and began to eat.

When the lavish meal was at last at an end, the musicians began to play and the dancing began.

As promised, Diana danced with Jamie, who despite his youth was accomplished and witty.

Yet she found her eye straying unwillingly to the golden knight, who seemed to be watching her with an expression that unnerved her. After inadvertently making eye contact with him, she refused to look in his direction again.

Seated beside his cousin, Thorn watched the young lass dancing with the prince. In fact, though he very much wanted to, he could not bring himself to look away.

After a time, he felt a sharp poke in his ribs, and he turned to look at Angus. The man sat stiffly, and Thorn knew that, beneath his brown doublet, his shoulder was heavily bandaged.

"You keep staring at her," Angus said with a note of consternation. "Bonnie though she is, she is a MacLaren! One look at her plaid will tell you that!"

Thorn took a deep draft of his ale. "MacLaren or no, you must admit that the lass possesses a beauty that would leave a bard floundering for words." He looked at Angus. "Have you noticed her eyes? Gray as the mist in the morning."

"Eyes!" Angus made a sound of disgust. " 'Tis apparent she's not leaving you floundering for words."

Thorn smiled slightly. "They're extraordinary," he murmured. Her back was to him, and he took note of her slim waist. She was wearing a light woolen gown of green and black, the skirt decorated with tiny tartan bows.

Angus leaned closer. "Listen to me, Thorn! If

I have noticed your interest, you can be certain that the MacLarens have, as well! They'll not sit still for it! You know how hotheaded they are."

"You worry too much, laddie." Thorn chuckled. "The MacLarens cannot see beyond their cups." He downed his ale and again viewed the MacLaren lass. "Now, you must admit, Angus, a wench like that could really warm a man's bed when the snow covers the bracken."

"Aye." His cousin gestured toward a serving maid whose large breasts bounced with each step she took. "And so could that one!"

A hearty laugh erupted from Thorn. "Ah, the lovely Lili."

Surprise flashed across Angus's face. "You know her name?"

Thorn nodded. "She told me." He cleared his throat. "When she requested permission to, um, assist me in my bath before I retire."

Angus groaned, and when Thorn turned to him, he said, "No wonder she turned me down." His look turned accusing. " 'Tis only because you will one day be an earl!"

"There's no other reason," Thorn said with mock solemnity.

That response drew a grin from Angus, who shook his head slowly from side to side. "You're a rogue, Thorn."

As the evening progressed, the noise level rose to deafening proportions and the serving maids constantly replenished mugs with ale, whiskey, or wine.

The jokes grew bawdy and the laughter raucous. By midnight, Diana's head was aching. She longed only for sleep, and she was vastly relieved when at last the queen rose to take her leave.

As Diana got up from the wooden bench, she tugged on the hem of her gown, which had caught on the rough edge. Diana was halfway across the room when she heard a deep masculine voice call to her.

"My lady?"

She turned, and her eyes widened when she saw Sir Thornton MacKendrick striding toward her.

He was wearing a breacan woven in his clan colors of red and black. The belted plaid garment was draped elegantly over his left shoulder, the ends being secured with a silver brooch. His dress sword sported a jeweled hilt. His trews were of his clan tartan. His trousers fit as snugly as hose and outlined his muscular thighs and calves.

As he paused before her and offered what she thought to be a mocking bow, Diana could feel her cheeks grow hot with indignation that this enemy of her clan would dare to address her.

From the corner of her eye, she could see her kinsmen reach for their swords. She knew that only the presence of the king prevented a melee.

Mayhap, Diana thought, the knight was unaware that she was the daughter of the Chief of the Clan MacLaren.

"Sir?" she responded coldly. This close, Diana noted details about the man that were not so evident at a distance. His lashes were long and thick; his mouth was well-defined, his lower lip fuller than the top; his chin was cleft.

He extended his hand, palm up. One of the tartan bows that trimmed her gown looked very small in his large hand.

"I believe this was ripped from your gown."

One glance told Diana that the bow did indeed belong to her. Were she to take it, however, she knew her hand would come in contact with his, which she did not want.

Raising her eyes, Diana looked at the man again. She felt a flush stain her cheeks as she murmured, "You are mistaken, sir. The frill does not belong to me."

His gaze went to her skirt, then rose to meet her own. Seeing the amusement that glittered in those crystal blue eyes, Diana began to tremble with anger.

When the stranger spoke, his voice was so low that his words carried only to her ears. "Then you will have no objection, my lady, if I keep this as a remembrance of our first meeting?"

Diana gasped in outrage at his familiarity. First and last! she thought indignantly.

She fixed the knight with the coldest look she could summon. Whether the bow in his hand belonged to her or not, he had no right to approach her. Had her father been present, Diana knew that this particular scene would not have occurred. Yet it had, and she would have to deal with it.

" 'Tis no concern of mine what you do with anything you find whilst burrowing in the rushes, sir!" she said sharply. Then she arched her brow. "Upon reflection, 'tis the only proper place for a MacKendrick to be," she added, injecting a tone of sweetness into her voice. She was gratified to see his mouth tighten and his eyes narrow dangerously at the insult.

The man bowed, then walked across the room to join his clansmen.

Though Diana heard a few disgruntled murmurs from the MacLarens, no one made a move. But they—and she—had seen MacKendrick's skill with a sword. It would be death to challenge him.

When she reached the arched doorway a moment later, Diana paused. Unable to resist, she turned for a final glimpse of the golden knight. Though she promised herself to make the effort, Diana knew she would never forget their brief encounter.

Chapter Two

April, 1488

Their heads bowed into the wind, Thorn and his band of horsemen rode hard, bracing themselves against the cold wind, pushing their animals to the limit. Beneath their warm plaids, he and his men wore coats of mail and carried claymores and maces.

At last approaching their destination, Thorn slowed his pace, caution now replacing the need for haste. He reined in his horse and stared grimly. They were too late.

Smoke blended with the gray mist until only the odor separated the two components. The blaze itself had died down; but so fierce had the fire been, the charred ruins still smoldered in defiance of the dampness.

"Christ's blood," Thorn swore softly as he viewed the devastation. "There's nothing left but a pile of ashes!" He dug his heels into the sides of his golden stallion, and the animal leapt forward.

The small village situated at the foot of the castle of Dunmoor was indeed a pile of ashes, thatched huts and byres having been set to the torch.

Cattle had been slaughtered, and the villagers and crofters had met the same fate.

As Thorn rode toward the stone keep, his eyes flicked over the bodies. Most were men; some were old women. The absence of young women and girls did not surprise him. When a band of Highland warriors attacked, they usually carted off the females for their own use.

Pausing again, Thorn motioned to one of his men-at-arms. "See if any of them are alive," he said, then he proceeded forward again.

The drawbridge was down and the portcullis was raised. The horses clattered across the wooden structure and into the courtyard.

Thorn frowned deeply as he dismounted. The west wall was damaged, and he surmised that this was where the breach had occurred. Men littered the battlements. None appeared to be alive.

" 'Tis worse than I feared," Angus said, coming to stand at Thorn's side.

His mouth set in a thin line, Thorn turned to his second-in-command. Angus's look of distress came as no surprise. Having neither wife nor child, Angus regarded these people as his family.

"If only we had gotten here sooner," Thorn said.

"The fault is not yours, Thorn!" Angus exclaimed earnestly. "We left as soon as the message reached us."

Lowering his head, Thorn stared at the blood-soaked ground. Though he knew what Angus said was true, the thought nagged: If they had ridden faster, and not rested their mounts, would they have arrived in time?

The message, dispatched as soon as Dunmoor had been threatened, had been woefully lacking in practical information. Thorn had not known who the attackers were; he had not known their number.

"Such a short time might have helped," he whispered, feeling dejected. Pain shot through him, no less acute because it was emotional rather than physical.

Angus grasped his arm. "Thorn, listen."

When Angus fell silent, Thorn looked up to see a figure coming toward them. His hand went to his sword, then came away as he recognized the woman. In her sixties, she was all angles and bones and nearly flat chested. Her hair was braided and pinned on top of her head like a silver coronet. Wisps of those tresses had escaped their confinement to flutter every which way.

Thorn quickly moved forward. "Grizel?"

"Aye. 'Tis me." With a thin hand, she pushed back the unruly tendrils of her hair.

"Was it the English?" Thorn's gruff voice belied his concern. He hoped fervently that it had been the English. A man felt no remorse when he attacked those invaders.

"Nay," Grizel said shortly. " 'Twas the accursed MacLarens. Led by the devil's spawn himself."

Thorn swore again. Things had been bad enough when the old Earl of Sidhean had been alive. In the year since his death, matters had taken a turn for the worse.

The MacLaren clan was now headed by Robert MacLaren, who had assumed the title of earl when his father had died. Hotheaded and vengeful, the 24-year-old MacLaren was proving to be a menace to the Highlands. Hardly a month went by that he did not attack or lay siege to one of his neighbors.

Thorn again viewed Grizel. "My uncle?" he asked, already knowing the answer.

"Dead." Turning slowly, Grizel pointed toward the breached west wall. "He died with honor, as befits a MacKendrick." Then she added, "Lady Catherine killed herself rather than be taken alive."

His mouth tightened. He had not expected that his aunt, too, would be dead. "And my brother, Ian?"

Wearily, she shook her head. "The lad was

taken prisoner. When last I saw him he was alive."

Angus quickly reached out to steady Grizel as she wavered unsteadily on her feet. "Come," he said softly. "Let's get you inside."

Thorn watched a moment as Angus led the old woman to the keep; then he began to inspect the damaged wall.

Heavy rocks had been catapulted against the structure, and beneath the relentless onslaught, the stone blocks at the top had at last given way. The breach was neither wide nor deep; but it was sufficient for a man to scramble up and over the wall.

Thorn motioned to three of his men. "Go into the village. Bring any who are alive inside." He raised his voice. "The rest of you shore up this wall as best you can! Move smartly now! 'Twill be dark soon."

As his orders were being carried out, Thorn headed for the stone steps. Of the two Mac-Kendrick holdings, this one had always been a trouble spot since it bordered MacLaren land, and he cursed himself for having allowed his nine-year-old brother to stay here with his uncle.

Inside the main hall, Thorn saw Angus stoking the blaze in the huge hearth.

The room had been ransacked; chairs and tables were hacked, tapestries slashed. Rushes on the floor had been set afire, leaving behind a pile of blackened rubble.

"Swine are more civilized than the Mac-Larens," Thorn muttered. With a sigh, he righted one of the few benches left intact, then sat on it. "Are you the only one left?" he asked Grizel.

"Nay," she said. "Some of the crofters managed to reach the woods before the first assault. And most of our women and bairns hid in the dungeon. The MacLarens tried to batter down the doors, but they held firm."

"Why wasn't my aunt with them?" Thorn asked sharply.

Grizel shrugged her bony shoulders. "Her ladyship refused to leave her husband."

"And my brother?"

"Och! You can be proud of that lad," Grizel said swiftly with a nod of her head. "Stayed at her ladyship's side, he did. Even when the whoresons broke in."

Despite the calmness of her tone, Thorn knew very well how disturbed she really was. Grizel had been his nurse and nanny during his childhood. She, in fact, had been closer to him than his own mother. His parents had spent months at a time at court for his father had been a favorite of King James.

For his brother, Ian, the ties were even closer, their mother having died while giving birth to him. That was the reason Thorn had allowed Grizel to accompany Ian when he had come to Dunmoor.

Thorn clenched his fist. "Was Ian harmed?" he asked at last.

Grizel shook her head. "Not that I saw." She paused a moment as if to collect her thoughts. "As I think on it now," she mused, "they could have easily cut him down. Seems as though they were making an effort not to harm him."

"They wanted him prisoner," Angus said. "Like as not that was the reason for the attack." He looked at Thorn. "A ransom, do you think?"

Thorn shook his head. "I'd pay that in a minute. And they know it. Nay, not ransom." He got up, agitated and feeling the need to move. "What they want is what they've always wanted. They want the land." One fist slammed into the other. "And, by God, that they'll not have! They'll not get their greedy hands on so much as an inch of MacKendrick land. They'll pay. If it takes every drop of blood I possess, they will pay for this day's deed."

"They find favor with the king," Angus said, practical as ever.

Thorn gave his cousin a sidelong glance. "And which king might that be?" he asked softly.

Angus drew a sharp breath. "You cannot be thinking of siding with Jamie!"

"Why not? The king himself has set his bonnet toward civil war. 'Twill come soon. When it does, we fight at the side of the prince."

Angus frowned. "If the outcome is not as you expect, all will be lost. Are you prepared to face the consequences?"

"Aye!" Thorn replied readily. He turned and his gaze fell upon Grizel. "See to the wounded. When we return to Rath na Iolair you will accompany us. I will leave half my men behind to help with repairs here."

"We could attack the MacLarens now," Angus said as he got to his feet.

"Nay!" Thorn waved the suggestion aside. "They will be expecting an impulsive reaction such as that. We will not accommodate them. Is there food, Grizel?"

"Aye, m'lord," she answered. "Cold meat, cheese, and ale." She cackled. " 'Twas no time to bake oatcakes this day!"

He smiled, hiding his jolt of surprise at her term of address. Yet it was so. With the death of his uncle, he was now the Earl of Dunmoor.

" 'Twill be good enough. Summon the women and bairns. We'll eat what is available. Then you will all wait here. When I get back, we leave immediately for Rath na Iolair." As the old woman left, he walked toward Angus. "Select ten men. We ride to Sidhean."

"Ten men?" Angus looked doubtful. "Do you not consider Sidhean's defenses too formidable for so few a number?"

"It is not in my mind to attack the keep. A hostage for a hostage," he declared grimly. "We will wait. Sooner or later an opportunity will present itself."

Angus rubbed his stubbled chin. "From what I have heard, Robert MacLaren has very few soft spots. Yet there is reportedly one: his wife." His eyes lit up. " 'Tis said the MacLaren's most enamored of her."

Thorn nodded. " 'Twould do no good to take anyone else."

Sometime later, having partaken of the meager meal set before them, Thorn and Angus remained at the table after the women and children had taken their leave.

Thorn's men-at-arms, having eaten their fill of bread and cheese, were either standing guard or stretched out on pallets for a well-deserved sleep. Rath na Iolair, Thorn's own keep, was two days' travel to the northwest, and they had ridden hard, stopping only to rest the horses.

His long legs stretched out before him, Thorn stared into space, plagued by troubled thoughts. At first light the sad duty of burying the dead would commence and then he would have to tend to the living, Ian in particular.

Where was the lad? He was just short of his tenth year, and he did not possess the robust good health with which Thorn had been endowed. It was for that very reason that Thorn had allowed his brother to stay at Dunmoor, which was located inland and protected somewhat from the harsh winds that swept in from the sea. Now, Ian was gone, taken captive by their most hated enemy, victim of a feud that had gone on for generations.

In a violent motion, Thorn threw his cup of

ale at the wall; then he helped himself to a generous dram of whiskey.

Angus sighed and got up. Going to the large hearth, he relieved himself, then returned to the table. "When do you want to leave, Thorn?" he asked as he reached for his cup of ale.

"As soon as the burying is done," he answered. " 'Twill take at least a day to reach Sidhean. I would arrive under cover of darkness."

"Someone from Dunmoor should go with us," Angus said.

Thorn shook his head. " 'Tis not necessary. I know the way."

"Aye, but do you know what the countess looks like? It would do us little good if you were to capture one of her maidservants."

Thorn looked at his cousin for a long moment. "You're right," he sighed with a rueful grin. "Now that I think on it, I wasn't invited to the wedding." He got to his feet. "Get some rest. There will not be much of it in the days ahead."

Chapter Three

Standing on the ramparts of Sidhean Castle, which had been built close to the shore, Diana gazed out over the North Sea. Prodded by a strong wind, the waves lunged furiously for the rocky shore before retreating, once again becoming a part of the vast expanse of gray waters that stretched as far as the eye could see.

"Are you chilled, m'lady?" Sibeal asked anxiously.

"Nay." Diana raised her head as her unbound hair lashed her cheek.

"The wind does seem to be getting stronger," Sibeal said in a voice that matched her expression.

"It feels clean and fresh!" Diana reassuringly patted the arm of her young maidservant; though the term servant was no more than a formality. Diana and Sibeal had grown up together, and they were fast friends despite the disparity in their rank.

Turning away from Sibeal, Diana glanced down at the fish pond. A ten-foot stone enclosure only two feet high, it was inundated during high tide when the waters lapped at the eight-foot thick walls of the castle. When the waters receded, fish remained trapped within its confines.

Designed by her father, the pond provided a continuing, if monotonous, source of food, and it was one of two things that made Sidhean virtually immune to siege. The other was an underground burn. The small stream offered an endless supply of fresh water.

Even as Diana looked at the enclosure now, at low tide, teaming with flounder and haddock, as well as a profusion of clams, crabs, and eels, her thoughts were elsewhere.

In the year since her father had died, Diana had been gripped by a loneliness she had never before experienced. Her father had been the main force in her life, her mother having died when Diana was four. David MacLaren had survived the heart attack that had felled him at Inverness more than two years ago, but another this past year had proved fatal.

Diana's brother Robert was now earl, and though they had never been close, their father's death seemed to have widened the gap.

The tide was coming in now, and the water level was rising.

Suddenly, Diana, stared down into the pond as if transfixed. The dark shapes of the fish seemed to melt together, forming a picture. Slowly, it took the shape of a keep situated in a place she had never seen. Set on a rocky ridge, it overlooked a body of water unfamiliar to her. Its crenelated towers rose high, darkly outlined against a gray sky.

The strange keep beckoned to her with such force that Diana placed her hands on the stone wall and bent forward. There is danger there! she thought, still staring fixedly at the gloomy keep.

As she watched, the dark sky was suddenly whitened by a searing flash of lightning that struck one of the round towers. When the sky darkened again, she saw the blackened patch left behind on the gray stone.

Though the image still beckoned to her, Diana drew away, and as slowly as it had appeared, the image finally faded. She blinked at the sight of the fish that darted in the water.

"You've returned, have you?" Reaching out, Sibeal gently drew the folds of Diana's arisaid across her chest. "A person could catch the lung fever in this chill wind."

Sibeal's anxious voice at last penetrated Diana's thoughts, and Diana turned to look at her maidservant.

"Aye. 'Twas nothing," she said, feeling per-

35

plexed and frightened at the same time. Her visions had always been of people and events. But this one had only been of a castle. Nothing had taken place save for a stroke of lightning that had harmed no one.

With a shake of her head, Diana dismissed this latest, unwanted vision. Gift or no, she hated it because there seemed to be no way to alter what she saw—as in the case of her father. Diana had had no inkling of his being taken ill two years ago at Inverness, 20 miles south of Sidhean Castle. Yet when death had finally come to claim him, she had seen it and had been powerless to forestall it.

Drawing her arisaid tightly against the wind, Diana walked from the ramparts, Sibeal close on her heels.

As they entered the keep, Sibeal paused. Her hands went to the woolen shawl that was draped over her shoulders. Carefully, she repositioned it atop her coppery curls, drawing in the left side so that it covered the scar that marred her otherwise smooth skin.

Diana saw the familiar motion and waited patiently, making no comment. Sibeal had been a comely lass, until Robert's wife, Lady Ellen, had used her dirk to carve one side of Sibeal's face during an evening meal shortly after Diana's return from court.

Being a bastard had earned Sibeal the menial position of serving wench, and recoiling from a pinch on her well-rounded bottom delivered by a drunken knight, Sibeal had accidently dumped a bowl of hot broth on Lady Ellen. Enraged, Ellen had risen, grabbed her dirk from her waistband, and savagely slashed at the helpless girl. Only Diana's intervention had saved Sibeal's life, if not her looks, and she prevented Ellen's banishing the 16-year-old lass after much wrangling with her brother to allow Sibeal to act as Diana's personal maid. She had never regretted her actions because Sibeal had proven to be both loyal and attentive.

Arriving in Diana's chambers, they removed only their outer wraps, since the large room was chilly and drafty away from the perimeter of the fire that burned brightly in the hearth.

"Will you be going on your rounds today?" Sibeal asked as she carefully folded Diana's plaid and placed it in a handsomely carved chest in a corner.

"Nay. Mayhap tomorrow—" Diana fell silent as she heard the clatter of horses' hooves.

Going to the diamond-paned window, she threw open the wooden shutters and looked down into the courtyard to see her brother and his men return after a three-day absence.

She had no idea where they had gone, but from the look of the female captives with them it appeared to have been another raid.

Diana was about to turn away when she saw a boy, his hands bound to the pommel of a horse, its reins held in her brother's gauntleted hand. The lad's hair was mahogany, that pecu-

liar shade which she knew marked the Mac-
Kendricks.

Diana motioned Sibeal closer, then pointed
to the small figure. "Find out who that is."

Sibeal hurried from the room. Less than ten
minutes later she returned.

" 'Tis the brother of the MacKendrick," she
said.

Diana frowned. "I did not know he had one."

Sibeal shook her head. "Nay, I do not speak
of Alexander MacKendrick. He and his lady
have died. 'Tis the brother of the new Earl of
Dunmoor, Thornton MacKendrick."

Shaken by this unexpected news, Diana put a
hand to her throat. "Mother of God," she whispered. What was in Robert's mind? Did he not
know the MacKendrick's nature? The fierce-
fighting warrior had been relentless in defend-
ing his ownership of six sheep! What would he
do in defense of his brother!

"What is wrong?" Sibeal cried, alarmed. " 'Tis
not the first time the men have returned from a
raid with a prisoner." She glanced down into
the courtyard. " 'Tis only a MacKendrick."

Diana forced a calmness into her voice that
was at odds with the churning feeling unsettling
her. "You are certain that the lad is his
brother?"

"Aye," Sibeal said with a solemn nod. "So I
was informed."

Turning, Diana ran from the room to find her
brother.

Downstairs, the great hall was filled with men. In the cavernous hearth the spit was barely visible beneath the venison that was being cooked for the evening meal.

The men, exhilarated by their recent battle, were drinking, laughing, and shouting to one another. Several of them hailed her but Diana did not respond. A sweeping glance told her that Robert was not among them.

Racing back up the stairs, Diana at last found him in his bedchamber. On the threshold, she hesitated a moment to catch her breath.

Robert was aware of her entrance, but he offered only an annoyed glance as he proceeded to remove his sword belt.

Diana took a moment to study her brother, not for the first time bemused that they hardly resembled each other. She knew she favored her mother, having inherited her delicate features and black hair. Robert, on the other hand, had inherited their father's red hair and somewhat ruddy complexion. Only their eyes were the same shade of gray, though Diana's, framed with black lashes, were more striking than Robert's, whose brows and lashes matched his hair.

"What are you going to do with that boy?" she demanded at last.

Robert threw his belt on a chair. "Bring the MacKendrick to heel. Once he agrees to my terms, his brother will be released."

Diana watched as a manservant stepped forward to assist Robert in removing his armor.

39

"And if he does not?" she asked when the man withdrew.

Robert shrugged. "The boy will die."

Diana bit her lip, unable to believe that Robert had spoken so callously. "He is only a lad," she protested.

"Who will grow all too soon into a viper!"

"Robert," she pleaded, raising her hand in supplication. "Father would not have done this! He never waged war on women and children—"

"Mayhap he should have!" he exclaimed loudly. "Then this endless conflict could have been resolved long ago."

Diana took a deep breath. It was difficult enough to reason with Robert under the best of circumstances. When he shouted, she knew his ears were closed.

"You've sent word to the MacKendrick?" she asked cautiously. "He knows that the lad is here?"

"Nay." He removed his boots and threw them into a corner. "Let him stew awhile."

Diana made an effort to control her exasperation. "And if the MacKendricks combine forces and come here to fetch him! What then?"

Giving her a quick glance, Robert laughed derisively. "Like most women, you can never see beyond your nose," he said with contempt. "It so happens that Donald has already notified the Clan Campbell. If need be, they will come to our aid soon enough."

At the mention of Donald Campbell, Diana's

lip curled in distaste. Though she was well aware that Robert wanted her to marry his best friend, she had no intention of doing so.

"I doubt such measures will be necessary," Robert said, his voice reflecting the confidence he felt. "The MacKendrick will wait for word from us. He is not that much of a fool that he would attack whilst his brother is in our care."

Diana gazed at Robert for a long moment before she spoke. Neither time nor distance had made her forget the forceful arrogance of the man they were discussing. It annoyed her that occasionally someone or something would remind her of the golden knight: a bay horse that never quite matched the rich color of his mount; a man who was tall and broad, but never quite conveyed his powerful strength; the restless waters of the sea, which at times reflected his crystal-blue eyes.

"He will not give in to you, Robert," she said at last.

Her brother spun around to face her. "And how would you be knowing that?"

"I've met him."

Robert's eyes narrowed. "Did you? And just where did this auspicious meeting take place?"

Diana told him, and Robert visibly relaxed.

"Och!" he exclaimed, waving his hand. "Three years ago the MacKendrick was naught but a knight." He grinned mirthlessly. "Thanks to me, he is now an earl. He should get down on his knees and thank me for the service I've rendered him."

Once again the unwanted memory of the man astride the golden stallion came to her. The picture conjured by her brother's words was ludicrous.

"I doubt the MacKendrick gets down on his knees to anyone," Diana said quietly.

"By the saints, Diana! I am laird here. I will not be questioned by anyone. Not even my own sister." Going to a table, he poured himself a whiskey. "Time and more I see you wed," he muttered, downing the liquid in one swallow.

Diana shuddered, but her chin rose defiantly. "I'll not be wed to suit your purposes nor any other's save my own!"

Anger colored his face. "You are eighteen! How long do you plan to wait?" He laughed derisively. "Though I can't understand why, there are those who consider you beautiful. But your strong will and sharp tongue effectively destroy that image. You've driven away every suitor presented to you. Only Donald Campbell has remained steadfast."

"Let him," Diana said, her anger now matching her brother's. "I'd sooner take the veil!" Her chin rose as Robert took a menacing step toward her. Once, in the year since their father had died, her brother had struck her for her disobedience. In retaliation, she had thrown a pewter bowl at his head. Only a fortuitous duck on his part had prevented an injury.

Apparently he recalled the incident, for as she turned to leave, he made no move to stop her.

Back in her chambers, Diana sank into a chair, feeling drained, as she always did after trying to reason with Robert.

Sibeal bustled about the room, selecting Diana's clothes for the evening meal.

Diana displayed little interest. She almost always allowed Sibeal to choose her attire. The lass was far more meticulous in her efforts than Diana, for there was no one here at Sidhean she wished to impress.

Sibeal at last selected an emerald-green satin gown. Then, rummaging through the carved chest, she drew out a gold girdle. As she laid the attire on the bed, she murmured, "Cook told me that guests have arrived." When Diana directed a questioning look at her, she added, "The Campbells."

Diana sighed and at last rose from her chair.

Listlessly, Diana donned the shimmering gown, then allowed Sibeal to brush her hair. She would have much preferred to stay in her room on this night.

What is wrong with me? Diana wondered, growing irritated with herself. There was a time when the evening meal had been a joyous occasion—a time when laughter came easily, when bards related romantic stories, when musicians played and singers sang.

Now there was nothing.

As she went down the stairs a while later, on her way to the dining hall, Diana was unpleasantly surprised to see Donald Campbell waiting for her.

And how long, she wondered sourly, was he planning to stay this time? There was no way of avoiding him, and she made no attempt to do so.

He was standing in the corridor, a half smile on his fleshy lips. At 26, he was handsome, in a saturnine way, with black hair and black thick brows over dark blue eyes.

But Diana had learned to mistrust the expression in those eyes. It was cunning and secretive, as if his thoughts were too evil to bear the light of candid scrutiny. He was Robert's closest friend, for they were two of a kind.

As she drew near, his gaze swept over her. She had been prepared to walk by him without a word, but Donald grabbed her arm and pulled her toward him.

"Each time I see you, you grow more lovely."

Diana glared at him, hating the sight of his slack mouth and those eyes that never seemed to gaze into her own.

She glanced down at his hand, and her lip curled. Soft! Everything about the man was soft. Though still lean, his body gave the promise of the fat that would accumulate with the years.

Looking at him again, she said, "Let go of me!"

Anger was clearly evident in her voice, but Donald seemed to be unaware of it as his eyes dropped to her breasts, displayed above the square-cut neck of her gown.

"Not until I get a kiss." His hand dug cruelly into the soft flesh of her upper arm.

In a swift motion, Diana jerked free and reached for the dirk sheathed in the gold girdle that encircled her waist. Some months ago, on his last visit, Donald had cornered her in the corridor just outside her room. She still recalled how he had tried to fondle her breasts. "Touch me again, Donald Campbell, and I'll cut your heart out!"

"My heart is already yours, Lady Diana," he murmured smoothly, but despite his words, he stepped back.

At that moment, Robert came down the stairs, his wife at his side. His eyes met Diana's, and he quickly ushered Ellen into the dining hall. When he turned, his face held a forced smile.

"Is my sister causing you problems, Donald?" he asked in a jovial tone.

Though the smile was still in place, his eyes conveyed a warning to Diana. As always, she chose to ignore it.

"None that won't be solved once we're wed." Donald's bantering tone was belied by his hard and threatening expression.

Diana refused to be intimidated by either man. "Whoever you wed, 'twill not be me!"

She swept past them into the dining hall without a backward glance.

Leaving the windowless alcove, which served as her quarters and which adjoined Diana's bedroom, Sibeal paused at the head of the stairs when she saw Robert and Donald Campbell below. She was reluctant to pass by Robert when she was alone.

The men seemed to be in a heated discussion, one that concerned her mistress.

Changing direction, Sibeal walked along the landing until she was directly above them. From this vantage point she could easily hear their voices.

"Do not concern yourself," Robert was saying as he clapped his friend on the shoulder. " 'Tis only maidenly reserve. Diana will come around."

Donald shook off Robert's hand. "And when might that be?" he demanded. " 'Tis almost a year since I have offered for her hand. Women are told who to marry! They are not asked for their opinion."

"I know, I know." Robert sounded uncomfortable. "However, with Diana, 'tis a bit different."

"Different!" Donald scoffed. "The only difference I can see is that you are too lenient with her. And that's something I will change when the time comes!"

Casting an uneasy glance at the open archway that led into the dining hall, Robert took Donald's arm and led him aside.

Sibeal leaned forward, straining to hear the words they spoke.

"Uniting our clans through marriage would be beneficial to us both. I want nothing more than that," Robert said.

"Then why don't you act on it?"

Robert raked a hand through his hair. "I need not tell you how willful my sister is. I cannot simply incarcerate her. The men would never stand for it." His tone grew earnest. "But know this: Diana will marry you. On that, you have my word. Somehow, I will find a means to make her agree to this union."

Donald stood stiffly. "I hope so. I grow weary of waiting."

Without further words for his host, Donald stormed away.

Sibeal waited until she was certain that Robert, too, had departed. Then she slowly made her way down the stairs.

When she entered the dining hall a few moments later, her gaze drifted across the large room. Those men-at-arms not on duty were sitting at long trestle tables at the far side of the room. She noticed that all had their eyes averted from the earl. Having heard Donald's shouting, Sibeal did not doubt that the men had overheard the conversation in the corridor.

At first concerned and worried that the earl

might take it upon himself to force his sister into marriage, Sibeal relaxed as she sat down. She knew that every man present had been devoted to the old Earl of Sidhean. And all of them respected and admired Diana. She was every bit her father's daughter. Through her veins, from her mother's side, ran the blood of the Countess of Dunbar, Black Agnes, the woman who had virtually single-handedly defended her castle against attack more than a hundred years ago. Everyone, including Sibeal herself, knew the story.

No, she thought as she began to eat, under the circumstances, forcing Diana to do anything would be out of the question.

As she reached for her cup of ale, her gaze fell upon the earl, and her uneasiness returned at the contemplative look she saw in his eye.

Chapter Four

The sky was a patchwork of blue and gray the following morning when Diana, accompanied by Sibeal, left the keep.

Even at this early hour the courtyard was crowded and noisy. On the west side, a group of men were throwing spears at a wooden target, practicing their aim amid the shouts and wagering of their comrades. On the east side, other men were engaged in swordplay, sharpening their skill under the watchful eye of Lachlan Gilbride, who was in charge of Sidhean's men-at-arms.

Diana ignored them as she crossed the flagstoned bailey and entered the guardhouse, which housed both the men-at-arms and their prisoners. Almost as large as the main edifice, it soared considerably higher.

At ground level, the vast communal room's stone floor was the ceiling of the dungeons below. The men slept on the second level, and above that, the watchtower loomed over all. From there, the sentries could see for miles across the land. They could also view the sea, should any danger threaten from that quarter.

Inside, Diana motioned to the man on duty and ordered him to take her to where the boy was being held. It greatly disturbed her that Robert had refused to allow the boy to be housed within the keep itself. Though powerless to alter that situation, she could at least make certain that the lad was well fed and reasonably comfortable.

She followed the guard down the stone steps, careful of her footing. Dampness slickened both the stairs and the walls, coating the surfaces with green mold.

From somewhere below, a woman's shrill scream pierced the stillness. Though Diana frowned, her step did not falter. She knew the reason for that outcry. When women were captured, men made use of them, and there was nothing she could do about it.

At last the guard halted, and Diana commanded, "Open the door."

Hearing the sound of footsteps on the stairs, Diana turned to see Lachlan Gilbride hurrying toward her. In his early forties, Lachlan had been devoted to her father, who had made him his second-in-command, a post he retained when Robert became earl.

"M'lady! What are you doing here?" he asked, coming to stand at her side.

Diana arched her brow. "Is this area of the keep restricted to me?"

"Nay! Of course not," he answered hastily. " 'Tis only your safety that concerns me."

"What threat could a lad pose to my safety?" she asked with a short laugh.

"He's a MacKendrick," Lachlan answered darkly.

Diana turned away to the guard, who had opened the door. "Step aside."

When Lachlan started to follow her, she made a curt motion for him to remain where he was. She allowed Sibeal to accompany her.

Stepping into the cell, Diana paused a moment until her eyes adjusted to the dimness. Only a small barred window offered a semblance of light. It was set so high on the wall that its top end was flush with the ceiling.

There was, of course, no heat. Even covered by her warm plaid, Diana shivered.

With her entrance, the boy struggled to his feet, his slim body stiff and rigid with fear. Diana could see how valiantly he was striving to conceal his alarm.

"Do not fret yourself, lad," Diana said quietly. He was younger than she had at first judged him to be. He could be no more eight, perhaps nine years old. "I mean you no harm. What is your name?"

"Ian MacKendrick!"

She nodded, checking a smile at the pride in his voice. "I am Diana MacLaren."

Ian just stared at her. "You are the countess?" he asked.

Diana shook her head. "I am not the wife of the earl," she said. "I am his sister."

The boy seemed to consider her reply, but made no comment.

"Have you had your breakfast?" Diana asked then.

Ian put a hand on the damp wall to steady himself. "If you count the piece of bread thrown to me last night, then I have."

Taken aback, Diana could not for the moment reply. "You were given no supper last night?" she asked finally.

His head rose. "Nay, but I doubt the lack of MacLaren food would cause anyone distress."

Concealing her anger, Diana went to speak to the guard and then returned.

"What were you doing at Dunmoor?" Diana smiled encouragingly. "Visiting?" she prompted when she received no immediate reply.

Stubbornly, Ian said nothing.

In the dim light, Diana studied the boy. Though Ian's face resembled the one she had never forgotten, his thin frame gave no indication of maturing into the muscular body his older brother possessed.

The heavy door swung out, and the guard

admitted a servant carrying a tray of food.

Diana nodded in satisfaction as she saw porridge, oatbread, a small dish of honey, and a large tankard filled with milk. After the servant had put the tray on the floor, Diana motioned him away. Then she returned her attention to the boy. Though his stance was defiant, she saw the uncertainty in his eyes. A shiver caused his thin body to move spasmodically, and her heart went out to him.

Instinctively, Diana knew that her sympathy would be rejected. Without speaking, she removed her arisaid and went to drape it around his shoulders.

Quickly Ian stepped back. "I'll not be wearing that!" he declared sharply.

Diana smiled and merely dropped the garment to the floor. She headed for the door, where she paused. "I'm certain you will be home within a few days," she said consolingly. "As soon as your brother agrees to the terms of your release, you will be returned to your clan."

"My brother's not likely to be agreeing to any terms offered by a MacLaren!"

Diana was of the same mind, but she did not want to think of the consequences that would result from a refusal. "We shall see," she said softly.

Outside, she watched as the guard bolted the door again.

When that had been accomplished, she leveled a stern look at Lachlan. "Make certain that the lad has enough to eat."

Lachlan looked uncomfortable, then he scowled at the guard. "You were remiss! See that it does not happen again."

Leaving the guardhouse, Diana made her way to the stables, where she gave instructions to the groom to have her horse saddled.

Then she addressed Sibeal. "I'll need to fetch another arisaid."

"You really think the lad will use yours?" Sibeal asked.

Diana laughed ruefully. "Probably not. It appears the color of the tartan is not to his liking."

Entering the keep, they began to ascend the stone steps to the second floor. The torchlit corridors appeared deserted, and Diana was lost in thought when she suddenly came abreast of Robert's wife. The two women eyed each other with an animosity neither tried to conceal.

From the Douglas Clan, the present countess possessed a cold beauty. Her hair was more silver than golden, and her large blue eyes were set in an oval face. Her fair skin was smooth and unblemished. Though 23, Ellen was still slim and her waist still narrow, for she had never birthed a child.

Disliking Ellen, Diana would have placed the blame for this lack of productivity on her shoulders. But the fact was that not one of

Robert's many mistresses had ever conceived, including Sibeal.

Drawing herself up, the countess glared at Sibeal, then at Diana.

"Can't you keep that slut out of my sight!" she demanded of Diana. "She offends my eyes!"

"You would not have the problem, Ellen, had you not caused it!" Diana retorted scathingly.

She knew very well that it had not been an impulsive act of anger that had prompted Ellen's attack on Sibeal. Robert, though he loved his wife in his fashion, had bedded almost every female servant at Sidhean. His attentions were usually short-lived once his lust had been sated. However, Sibeal had caught his fancy, and he had been dallying with her for months. Ellen, knowing this, had used the first opportunity presented to her to do the girl harm.

"All know she's a witch!" Ellen said. She cast a malevolent look at Sibeal. "Else how could she have snared the earl's attention as she did? My maid swears that she saw Sibeal mixing a potion in the kitchen!"

"I'm not a witch!" Sibeal cried out, then fell silent when Diana touched her arm in a warning gesture.

"You speak with a fool's tongue, Ellen!" Diana's tone was sharp. "There are no witches at

Sidhean, save perhaps for the one who stands before me now."

Ellen's eyes narrowed, and her breath quickened. " 'Twould do you well to remember that I am Countess of Sidhean!"

"As was my mother before you!" Diana said. "And 'tis difficult for anyone not to make a comparison between the two of you. I fear, Countess, you fall far short of your predecessor."

"You will regret your words, lass!"

Ellen's low, threatening voice had no impact on Diana as she said, "Not in this lifetime, Countess."

Taking Sibeal by the arm, Diana moved forward without another word.

Sibeal was shaking when they reached Diana's chambers, and Diana said kindly, "Calm yourself, Sibeal. The countess has a sharp tongue. But 'tis not always in accord with her brain."

" 'Tis not her sharp tongue I fear," Sibeal murmured. "I know that as long as you are here, she will do me no further harm. But when you leave—"

"Leave?" Diana looked at Sibeal in surprise.

"I mean, when you marry—"

Diana took hold of Sibeal's shoulders. "I will never leave here without you! I promise you that." She released her hold and gave a short laugh. "And we must remember, there is always the possibility that you will marry before I do."

Sibeal lowered her head. "No possibility of that, m'lady. There's no man who would look twice at me now, much less want me for his wife."

"Och!" Diana waved her hand. "It upsets me when I hear you speak nonsense like that." With a sigh, she sat down, then glanced at Sibeal, a glint of amusement in her eye. "Just what were you brewing in the kitchen?"

Deep crimson stained her face, and the young woman turned away. " 'Twas a potion. Of sorts," she added quickly at Diana's wide-eyed surprise. "Cook told me that if I brewed boar's fat and the bark of the alder and mixed it with lichen and rosemary, 'twould—"

Diana leaned forward. " 'Twould what?" She knew most herbal concoctions, but had not heard of this one.

Sibeal's hand went to her cheek. " 'Twould remove this," she whispered, then bit her lip. "Didn't do much good, though."

"Och!" Diana got up and put her arms around Sibeal. After a moment, she held the girl at a distance. "I believe it did do some good," she declared solemnly. " 'Tis no longer red. Soon 'twill be no more than a thin line."

Sibeal averted her face. "One that will never go away."

"And you never expected it would!" Diana said, releasing her.

Going to the chest in a corner of the room, Diana took out an arisaid and hastily donned it over her riding habit of tan chamois.

"I'll come with you," Sibeal offered.

Recognizing her reluctance, Diana said quickly, " 'Twill not be necessary." She strapped on her sword belt. "I'll not need you."

In the stables, a while later, Diana mounted her favorite mare, Banrigh.

At her approach, the portcullis was raised, and once across it, she set off to make her weekly rounds of the crofters.

This was a practice begun at her father's side, and she had continued it alone since her father's death. Robert had no patience with the crofters and only grudgingly conceded to sit in judgment as arbiter whenever a serious dispute such as murder or thievery occurred.

Happily, these occasions were few and far between. Most disagreements were of a minor nature: a borrowed tool not returned; insults leading to drunken brawls and ruffled feelings; squabbles between women when a husband's eye strayed.

At times, Sibeal would join Diana on these expeditions. But Diana, aware of Sibeal's uneasiness during these sojourns, more often than not left her behind on one pretense or another.

The crofters, even more than most Highlanders, were superstitious and made the sign of the cross when confronted with Sibeal's scarred face.

Diana also did something that not even her father had done. She tried to make it a point to attend every birth at Sidhean. Her youth notwithstanding, Diana was an expert midwife, and it was a mark of honor among the women of Sidhean to have Lady Diana in the room when an infant was born.

She rode slowly, acknowledging the greetings, offering advice when it was needed or requested. Two hours later, her rounds completed, she halted Banrigh on a rise.

She knew that she should return to Sidhean, but the day beckoned to her with its brilliance. Raising her head, Diana took a deep breath of the cold, clean air.

Beneath her, the mare danced a few steps to the side and the horse's enthusiasm was all the encouragement Diana needed.

Leaning forward, she patted the satiny neck. "You would enjoy a run across the glens, wouldn't you, Banrigh? All right, then. You will get your wish!"

She spurred the mare forward, letting the animal find its own pace. As they raced along, Diana felt only exhilaration. She had no compunction about being alone. She was on MacLaren land.

Chapter Five

Hidden by the stand of trees, Thorn and his men saw a rider. The green-and-black plaid draped across her shoulders marked her as a member of Clan MacLaren.

Hugh Montgomery stepped closer to Thorn. "Christ's blood!" he exclaimed softly, sounding disappointed. " 'Tis only Lady Diana, the sister of the MacLaren."

Hugh had served as a groom at Dunmoor, and he was one of the few inhabitants who had survived the attack without injury. Acting on Angus's advice, Thorn had chosen Hugh to accompany him.

"Are you certain?" Thorn asked.

"Aye."

Thorn's eyes returned to the woman on the horse. "She rides alone."

"She's a fearless wench, stubborn and proud like the rest of the lot. 'Tis said even her brother cannot handle her."

Thorn did not make the connection between the rider and the young girl he had seen at court more than two years earlier until she came closer and he saw her ebony tresses.

"She must be at least eighteen," he said, more to himself than to Hugh. "Why is she still at Sidhean? Is she not married?" Most of the young women he knew were married at 16; some younger than that.

"She refuses to marry save on her own terms," Hugh said. "Claims her father gave his word on that before he died."

Thorn smiled, recalling the scathing insult she had delivered to him when he had approached her. He still had that little tartan bow somewhere. Why he hadn't thrown the frivolous ornament away was a question he could not answer. In any event, he had long since forgotten the incident—until now.

"Well, then," he said quietly, "mayhap we should relieve the MacLaren of his problem. A sister for a brother. 'Tis a fair exchange."

Hugh frowned, but spoke respectfully. "If you're meaning to take the lass captive, I'm not sure that's such a good idea, m'lord. Her brother's not too fond of her from what I've heard. His wife, now. Lady Ellen. The MacLaren is quite taken with her even though she's not yet presented him with bairns in all the years they've been wed."

Thorn shook his head. " 'Tis too much to hope for that the countess would venture out alone and unattended. Nay, I am not one to ignore what fate has put in my path. The MacLaren may not be fond of his sister, but he would never ignore her capture. To do so would make him the laughingstock of every clan in the Highlands."

Turning to Angus, Thorn said, "Take four men and ride to the left. The rest of us will circle around to the right."

"She will run as soon as we leave the cover of the trees," Angus said.

"Aye. But from the way she has been racing, I'll wager that her horse is no longer fresh."

"Hold!" Hugh said, pointing. "She's heading in this direction.

Angus turned to look at the stream not far from where they were standing. "Like as not she's taking her horse to the burn for a drink."

Taking cover, they all fell silent as the rider drew closer.

Entering the wooded area a few minutes later, Diana let the mare find her own way. The animal knew where the icy burn was, and her trotting steps brought them to the edge of the stream.

While the horse quenched her thirst, Diana dismounted and stretched. She had not meant to ride this far, but it felt good. The exercise, the solitude, and the beauty of her surroundings were always welcomed.

Banrigh suddenly stopped drinking and raised her head, her ears twitching. Frowning slightly, Diana placed a hand on the silky mane.

"What troubles you, girl?" Her eyes scanned the far bank. She saw nothing amiss. The blue-and-emerald water shimmered, casting darting rays of gold and amber at the chattering birds that swooped along the banks.

Then the snap of a dry twig behind her immediately caught her attention, and she froze. Fear gathered the muscles of her shoulders into a tight knot.

Diana emitted a scream that barely got past her throat as a large, callused hand was placed over her mouth and a powerfully muscled arm encircled her just below her breasts.

"There'll be no crying out now, lass!"

Defiantly, Diana began to struggle, but the arm that was wrapped around her felt like a band of iron.

"Be still!"

The words were spoken quietly, but nonetheless they were a command, and realizing the futility of her efforts, Diana ceased her struggles to escape.

When she was released, she spun around to face her captor. Then she gasped. It was the golden knight whom she had never forgotten.

The moment hung suspended in time as Thorn gazed into those Gypsy eyes, which were as gray as the Highland mist. He felt as if he were perched on an abyss about to plunge headlong into their silver depths.

Though he remembered the bewitching lass who had verbally consigned him to the rushes of the king's dining hall, he was totally unprepared for the stunning beauty who stood before him.

With difficulty, Thorn shook himself free of the seductive feeling and grinned sardonically at the expression of recognition on her face. " 'Tis pleased I am to see that you remember me."

"What do you think you are doing!" she demanded.

"Are you telling me that you are unaware that my brother is at Sidhean?" he asked icily.

Her eyes lowered. "Aye, he is."

Her gaze again met his. Once more Thorn felt the force of those incredible gray eyes, which he had never quite banished from his mind. The hostility he saw reflected there was something he ignored.

"You will come with me," he ordered gruffly.

Diana stared at him. "You know my brother will kill you for this?"

"Will he?" Thorn asked with marked uninterest.

She stepped back. "I'll not be going anywhere with you."

He shrugged. "You will do as you are told."

Gesturing to one of his men, Thorn waited while the golden stallion was brought to him. He swung himself into the saddle, then motioned to Diana, who obediently mounted her own horse.

They rode swiftly across glens and fells and frigid burns. Although Diana kept alert, seeking an opportunity to escape, she was surrounded on all sides by the MacKendricks.

Bred and raised in the Highlands, Diana's mount was no less surefooted than those ridden by the men; nor was her hand less experienced on the reins than were theirs.

It was late afternoon when they at last paused to rest the animals. Someone handed her a piece of cold meat and as she ate, she thoughtfully reviewed her situation.

A small stand of trees surrounded them. Though they had left MacLaren land, they were still many hours from Dunmoor, which was where she surmised they were headed. Each mile made escape less feasible. Yet escape she must.

Having finished the slim repast, Diana glanced at her captor. He was at that moment checking the trappings on his horse and not paying any attention to her. Neither were the other men.

Banrigh was tethered with the rest of the

horses and was too far away for her to reach without being stopped. Diana could make a run for it, but she knew that she would be caught before she even made it to the glen beyond the trees.

If she could not run, mayhap she could stand and fight, Diana thought. Her sword was still strapped to her side. Either her captor had not noticed it beneath her heavy arisaid, or he considered it to be a mere affectation.

At that moment, Diana saw the earl striding in her direction. Since there was no time for further assessment, she made a quick decision. Removing her arisaid, she let it fall to the ground. Then she drew her sword.

Startled by his captive's actions, Thorn came to an abrupt halt, making no move to draw his own weapon.

"If I best you," Diana said, "then you will let me go." Her gray eyes never wavered as she delivered the challenge.

"You brazen wench!" Anger came first; but the scene was so ludicrous he could not prevent the laugh that followed his exclamation. "You would do battle with me?" He put his hands on his hips and glared at her.

His men stood about, grinning. Not one of them would dare try to rescue him from a mere slip of a lass. To do so would have been a raw insult he would have never tolerated.

"Are you then such an expert with a sword that you deem yourself unbeatable?" Her voice shimmered with a mockery that served to increase his exasperation.

"Enough of this foolishness!" he thundered. He stepped forward and felt the tip of her sword at the base of his throat.

A collective murmur came from his men, none of whom were smiling.

Nor was Thorn as he moved back. He had faced men on the battlefield and elsewhere; but never in his life had he crossed swords with a woman. 'Twould be like taking a sweet from a child!

"Very well." Pushing his plaid back over his right shoulder, he drew his own sword. "If you best me, you will be allowed to return home. If not," he added pointedly, "then you will cause me no further trouble. Agreed?"

She nodded. "Agreed."

After only a few tentative thrusts and parries, Thorn realized that, woman or no, he was not facing a novice. There was no hesitation. Her movements were quick and sure. Her sword was lighter than his own, but finely honed and every bit as deadly.

As the minutes passed, she showed no sign of tiring. Nor did he, but he was finding it increasingly difficult to keep from noticing her lush breasts straining against her soft chamois tunic.

Annoyed, Thorn forced himself to concentrate. He was paying more attention to the girl than to her sword!

"Is this a duel to the death?" he gritted at one point.

"If it were, you would be long since gone," she said.

In a lithe motion that was obviously deliberate, she thrust her sword at his shoulder, renting his leather tunic, but stopping short of inflicting injury.

Then Thorn saw his chance. Just behind her was a dead tree stump. Using both hands, he began to wield his sword from side to side in a broad swath as he came toward her.

Taken off guard by his sudden aggressiveness, Diana retreated. The third step brought her heel in contact with the stump, and with a sharp cry she fell backward. Before she could recover, Thorn bent forward and took the sword from her grasp.

"Get up!" he said gruffly. "We've wasted enough time." He threw the weapon to one of his men. Glancing down, he saw that she had not moved. Grabbing her arm, he unceremoniously jerked her to her feet. "When I give an order, I expect to be obeyed!"

"You tricked me!" she sputtered.

"Did I indeed? Had it been a real contest, you would be the one long since gone."

Taking her by the wrist, he began to walk toward the horses. "Mount up!" he called to his men. "We've still a long ride ahead of us."

He glanced down at his captive. Her wrist was so delicate and fine boned that his thumb overlapped his fingers. Startled by her fragility, he immediately lessened the pressure of his hold.

After assisting Diana onto her mare, Thorn swung himself up on the golden stallion.

Chapter Six

Dusk was already on the land by the time they finally reached Dunmoor. Though she refused to let it show, Diana was appalled at the sight of the devastated village. Those crofters who had survived her brother's raid were in the process of repairing and, in some cases, rebuilding their small houses.

Looks of welcome for their earl quickly darkened to hostile stares when they saw Diana. Behind the men, women gathered, their expressions even more hostile. They all recognized the colors interwoven into her plaid arisaid. The angry murmurs that erupted were quickly silenced by only a censuring look from the Earl of Dunmoor.

As they proceeded, Diana fancied she could feel the crofters' eyes boring into her; and in truth, she could not blame them, she thought sadly. The crofters' lives were difficult enough without the added penalty of raids that destroyed both their families and their property.

" 'Tis a harsh life for them," she whispered, feeling the tears sting behind her eyelids.

"Made no easier by the unexpected visit of your kinsmen," Thorn muttered.

Her tears vanished as Diana bristled at the criticism of her clansmen. "Are you going to tell me that you have never made a raid!" she demanded. Turning her head, she glared at Thorn.

He hesitated, then said, "Nay. I'll not be telling you that." He did not add that he had never struck down a man without a weapon—nor a woman, weapon or no.

"Then you are no different, are you?" Diana said scornfully as the horses clattered across the drawbridge.

Despite the hour, a woman was waiting in the courtyard. Her black eyes settled on Diana; confused by the woman's intense scrutiny, Diana hastily averted her eyes. She did not understanding the tense feeling that suddenly came over her.

The earl halted his horse before the woman, who looked up at him.

"There's food," she said without preamble.

Thorn grinned at her. "How did you know when we would return?"

"I knew," she murmured as they all made their way into the keep.

The MacKendrick dismounted and handed the reins to a waiting groom. As he came toward her, Diana braced her left foot in the stirrup and swung her right leg over the back of her saddle, prepared to dismount without any assistance from her captor.

Thorn reached Diana before her action was complete. Putting his hands around her waist, he easily lifted her, then stood her on her feet.

" 'Tis customary for a lady to thank a gentleman when he assists her from her horse," Thorn said as he directed her toward the stone steps.

Diana's gaze traveled the length of him. "If one had, I would." Turning, she sauntered away.

Scowling, Thorn followed her. He was annoyed with himself for expecting civility from a MacLaren. He knew better. From the time he had been a boy, he had been taught that the MacLarens were without the rudimentary courtesy one could expect from a Highlander.

In the dining hall a while later, the men sat down wearily and began to eat. Thorn was pleased to see that, in his absence, the floor had been swept clean of rubble, and it had been strewn with fresh rushes.

While the walls were bare, the slashed tapestries having been removed, the room was furnished with tables and benches brought from other parts of the keep.

Pleased also with the meal set before him,

Thorn offered Diana a plate of oatcakes, but she shook her head.

"I insist you eat something!" he said. "You have barely touched your mutton."

Diana leaned back in her chair, and her smile was sardonic. "You may force me to do many things, my lord. But eating isn't one of them!"

His eyes narrowed, and he slammed the plate back on the table. Leaning on his elbow, he bent toward her. "If you wish to go hungry, you may do so! But don't come crawling to me when your belly aches!"

Her nostrils flared with indignation, and she made no attempt to disguise her revulsion. "You will not live long enough to see me crawl to you for anything!"

With that remark said, the remainder of the meal passed in silence. At last, Thorn got to his feet and nodded to his men. "We will rest here and set out at first light."

Diana looked at him with a mixture of dismay and surprise. Her hands gripped the arms of her chair. "Where are you taking me?" she asked sharply.

"To Rath na Iolair," he said, then offered a wry smile. "You may have noticed that our accommodations here are somewhat lacking, thanks to your kinsmen."

Her mouth tightened. "They should have razed it to the ground!"

"They almost did," he said, not trying to hide his anger. " 'Tis unfortunate that the MacLarens cannot display such energy on the battlefield as they do when ransacking another man's keep!"

Leaping to her feet, Diana glared at him. She reached for her dining knife and went to sheath it, but Thorn quickly took it from her grasp.

"You will not be needing this for a while." He grinned and addressed the room at large. "Lady Diana is the most skilled swordsman Sidhean has to offer!" He rubbed his chin while he contemplated her flushed face. The lass was indeed a lovely piece of femininity.

"I am certainly better than any MacKendrick! You bested me with trickery!" She straightened up, and her expression was haughty. "Had you allowed our contest to run its normal course and not resorted to tricks that would shame a crofter, you would have been beaten!"

Taking a step back, Diana placed her hands on her hips. "Not even a female MacLaren would have felt the need to do what you did. Mayhap you did your training with your nurse!" she further taunted. "For a certainty, it could not have been with a knight!"

Her slender finger poked Thorn in his chest as she added, "If you are the best the MacKendricks have to offer, the rest must be a sorry lot indeed!"

Thorn took a deep breath. Never in his life had he met a woman who so irked him. A trait of the MacLarens, he decided, feeling expansive. He must make allowances—though, in truth, it would be difficult to achieve.

"You try my patience, lass," he muttered at last, narrowing his eyes to slits.

Diana smiled wickedly at him. "I'll be losing sleep over that for many a night to come!"

Rage seemed to gather in a lump in Thorn's throat, and he swallowed in an effort to steady himself. His men were watching him in silence, and he noted their surprise at the tolerance he was displaying.

He ignored them. A verbal gauntlet had been thrown to the ground. Physical supremacy would not decide the winner. He saw the challenge in her silver eyes, in the tilt of her chin that all but invited a blow to bruise its softness.

Diana looked down at his clenched fists and smiled. "You might best me with your hand, m'lord," she said, "but never with your sword."

They stared at each other, neither wavering. Enmity crackled between them.

Thorn knew the lass had stated a truth. His hand could easily best her. Yet in the back of his mind, he knew the victory would be hers.

"You make more of this situation than is necessary, lass. I'll not spar with you." He motioned to Grizel. "Take her to Lady Catherine's room. But, Grizel, do not lower your guard whilst in her company."

Without further words for his captive, Thorn returned to his chair and picked up his tankard of ale.

Her head high, Diana followed the old woman from the hall and up the stairs.

Damn his arrogant hide! she fumed as she placed one foot in front of the other. Somehow, she had to get out of there, and she had to do it soon!

On the landing, Grizel opened a door and motioned to her. After the other woman left, locking the door behind her, Diana glanced around the room. Seeing another door, she quickly went toward it. It was locked from the other side.

Going to one of the windows, Diana pushed aside the shutter and peered outside. Not so much as a ledge broke the smooth expanse of the stone walls. It was a sheer drop of more than 40 feet to the moat below.

Once more she turned and viewed the room. In spite of her predicament, Diana could not repress a stab of guilt. Her surroundings were luxurious compared to what Ian MacKendrick was being forced to endure.

Sitting down, she put her elbows on her knees and her head in her hands. Poor lad. She sincerely hoped that he was not afraid of the dark, as so many children were.

Hearing a noise from the adjoining room, Diana raised her head, and she glanced fearfully at the door. She sat thus for many moments, unaware that she had been holding her breath until it was at last expelled in a long drawn-out sigh of relief when the door remained closed.

Feeling incredibly weary, she finally disrobed and crawled into bed. Sleep came to her almost immediately. But she slept restlessly, caught in the grip of a nightmare in which she and Banrigh raced across the moors in an effort to escape unknown pursuers.

She whimpered and, at one point, gave a sharp cry of terror before the dream at last dissolved and she slept peacefully once more.

In the adjoining room, Thorn had immediately wakened at the sound of her cry. Like most warriors, he slept lightly, alert to any unusual noise that might portend danger.

Quickly, he got up, heedless of the fact that he was clad only in his underbreeches. Unlocking the door, he entered the adjoining room, the uncarpeted floor cold beneath his feet.

Treading quietly, he approached the four-poster and stared down at the slumbering figure. Diana's coal-black hair fanned out across the pillow. Her soft lips were slightly parted. The fur robe that covered her had been partially kicked aside. Her chemise had worked itself up to reveal one long, beautifully shaped leg. Faint as it was, the still glowing embers gave a rosy tint to her ivory skin.

Fascinated, Thorn stood there and gazed down at the face of the woman he had abducted with no more thought in mind than to effect his brother's release. Since she was in repose, he was able to study her features at leisure, without being distracted by her incredible Gypsy eyes.

Her nose was straight, with delicately flared nostrils. Above deeply lashed eyes her brows arched in a graceful curve that was at once provocative and questioning. A slow smile crept onto Thorn's face as he noticed that even in sleep there was a determined set to her jaw. Her neck was long and slender, and he could see the pulse throbbing at the hollow of her throat. An almost irresistible urge came over him to place his lips on that soft spot.

Instead, he drew the fur robe up and tucked it gently around her shoulders. With one final look at her pale oval face, he returned to his own chambers.

Chapter Seven

Diana was sound asleep when she felt a hand shaking her shoulder.

"Best get yourself up, lass," Grizel said in a brusque tone. "The men will be leaving soon."

Diana came immediately awake, but she made no move to get up. She yawned and glanced about her. Though it was morning, the room was still dark and cold. She shivered and wanted nothing more than to snuggle beneath the fur robes and return to sleep. She watched as Grizel went to the hearth and threw peat on the dying embers; soon the fire was burning brightly.

Straightening, Grizel stood motionless and stared at Diana with an expression she could not fathom. Diana bit her lip as she studied the gray-haired old woman before her. In spite of her age, there remained a hint of the beauty she must have been in her youth.

Although Diana had thought to enlist the aid of the old woman, she discarded the idea. While not hostile, Grizel was certainly not friendly.

Absently, Diana wiggled her toes, still making no move to get out of bed. Regardless of her attitude, the old woman was still a source of information.

"Where is Rath na Iolair?" Diana asked casually as she at last sat up.

"Two days' travel to the northwest. 'Tis sparsely inhabited there."

Diana shuddered. "It sounds like a lonely place."

Grizel gave a short laugh. "You'll not be lonely. You'll be surrounded by people."

"Aye," Diana murmured, "MacKendricks." Her hands plucked nervously at the fur robe.

Grizel's eyes narrowed. "What do you fear?" she muttered, annoyed. "You are being held only in exchange for the earl's brother. Once that happens, you will be free."

Turning, Grizel crossed the room to a chest that rested in its shadowy corners. Opening it, she nodded. "You're of a size with the late Lady Catherine," she said without looking at Diana. "There's enough here to keep you clothed for a time." Her tone became brisk. "Get dressed! The earl does not like to be kept waiting."

After Diana had donned her riding habit, Grizel summoned a servant and instructed him to fetch the chest and place it on the waiting cart in the courtyard.

Downstairs, even as Diana ate her breakfast, she was aware of a rising panic. Dunmoor was only a day's ride from Sidhean. There was always the chance that she might escape and make her way home. Once at the earl's keep, however, she might never get away!

When the MacKendrick at last gave the order to leave, Diana stubbornly refused to move.

"I'll not go!" she exclaimed defiantly. "The exchange can be made here more conveniently than at your godless keep! And you well know it!"

He did not argue. He simply picked her up and slung her over his broad shoulder.

As Thorn walked from the room, Diana pummeled his back with her fists, but it was like hitting stone.

"I hate you!" she shouted.

"And I'll be losing sleep over that for many a night to come," he said dryly, repeating the stinging rejoinder she had thrown at him only the night before.

Outside, he placed her on the golden stallion and instructed Grizel to ride her mare. When the earl climbed up behind her, Diana held herself stiffly, leaning forward as far as she could without losing her balance.

"Are you going to sit like a bent twig for the whole trip?" he asked congenially as he prodded the stallion to a walk.

She sensed rather than saw his grin, and she was enraged. "I see nothing amusing! The very least you could do is allow me to ride my own horse! She is not used to an unfamiliar hand."

"Do not underestimate Grizel," he murmured.

Feeling his warm breath on her neck, Diana quickly turned to face him. "What are you doing?"

He drew back. "I wanted to make certain you heard my words," he answered quickly. "She has an affinity with animals."

Only an inch separated her lips from his. "Who?" Diana murmured absently, staring at his mouth as he spoke. His teeth were white and even.

"Grizel. You needn't be concerned about your horse."

"I wasn't." Diana faced forward again.

They rode in a northwesterly direction, and Diana noticed that the terrain was becoming rougher with each passing mile. Though calm, the April day was cold, and presently light snowflakes began to fall.

Twice throughout the long day, they stopped to rest the animals, and at last, shortly after nightfall, the earl led them into a wooded glade, where they would spend the night. It had stopped snowing but the air remained damp and cold.

Sitting on a fallen log, Diana brooded. The more distance they covered, the fewer were her chances to escape. She hadn't been left alone for a moment. Grizel even accompanied her into the wood when necessity demanded a few minutes of privacy.

Oddly, Diana could not find it in her heart to resent the old woman, who puzzled her. She was still uncertain of Grizel's status in the clan. Certainly she was more than a servant. Even the earl fell silent when Grizel spoke.

Diana watched the men as they started a fire. They talked easily and laughed good-naturedly. Diana was beginning to know them by name, especially Angus MacKendrick, who was in charge of the men-at-arms. Though not as tall as the earl, he was even more powerfully built. His thighs and upper arms could have been hewn from solid oak. While some of the men had exchanged a few pleasantries with her during the noon break, Angus viewed her with no more than a watchful eye.

Some time later, Diana looked up to see her captor coming toward her. *How he swaggers!* she thought in annoyance.

He paused in front of her. "You look chilled." Bending forward, he offered her a flask. "Drink some of this. 'Twill warm the blood."

Diana accepted the flask and took a draft. She had expected wine or ale; instead the flask contained usquebaugh, a fiery whiskey popular in the Highlands. With a gasp, she returned the container, blinking the tears from her eyes.

Thorn grinned at her. "The food is ready. You

can eat now." He held out his hand to assist her to her feet.

In the soft glow from the fire, she saw the golden hairs on his wrist. Since Thorn had square palms and blunt-tipped fingers, his hands gave the appearance of great strength. If they ever touched her in an intimate way—

Diana turned her thoughts from that. This was no ordinary man. This was her enemy!

"And what if I do not want to eat right now?" she said, ignoring the burning sensation in the pit of her stomach. She never drank whiskey.

Thorn shrugged. "Then I would guess you go hungry this night."

She inhaled deeply. His cheerful attitude was more difficult to deal with than his irascibility!

A thought struck Diana, and she slanted her eyes upward to catch his gaze. "Do you expect me to tear the meat apart with my hands or my teeth?" she asked sweetly, gratified by his suddenly blank look. "You took my knife."

More swiftly than she could have imagined or hoped for, he produced the silver dirk. "Certainly we would not want the Lady Diana to eat with her hands!"

The words were infused with a mock solemnity that caused a surge of hope within her breast. She forced a demure smile to her lips. "That is kind of you." With a graceful movement, she rose. "I confess that the food smells most appetizing."

He took her arm. "As does everything Grizel

cooks! You've never tasted the likes of the apple tarts she concocts. 'Tis magic!"

"I'm certain no one can duplicate them," Diana said quietly, not caring a fig about Grizel's apple tarts. She had her knife. All she had to do was employ her feminine wiles to keep it.

Sitting on the ground beside her captor, Diana neatly sliced off a piece of the meat and began to eat. Realizing that she was indeed hungry, she spent the next several minutes assuaging her appetite. When she was through, she became aware that the earl was staring at her.

As she turned to look at him, he smiled warmly. It was the first time she had seen him do that, and she found herself bemused by the way the simple expression transformed his face, softening his hard-angled jaw and producing tiny crinkles around his eyes. The color of those blue eyes was vivid and penetrating even in the amber glow of the firelight. Her gaze lowered to his lips. They were still curved in a smile, one that was both sweet and gentle.

The moment lengthened as they both seemed to be seeing each other for the first time. What might her answer have been, Diana suddenly wondered, if it had been someone like Thornton MacKendrick instead of Donald Campbell who wanted to wed her?

"You have lovely eyes, lass," Thorn said softly.

"So do you," Diana murmured without thinking. She caught her lower lip between her teeth as she realized what she had just said, and she hoped he would think that the flush on her cheeks was a result of the heat from the fire.

Hastily, she rose and went back to sit on the fallen log. She watched as the MacKendrick helped Angus douse the fire and as Grizel wrapped the leftover meat in linen.

Soon after, the entire company settled down on the ground. Their warm plaids, having served as cloaks during the day, were used as blankets.

It was then, as Diana lay staring up at the canopy of trees that hid the sky, that she realized she still had her silver dirk. She had planned to use her feminine wiles to keep it and instead had become trapped in the moment.

Turning to a more comfortable position, she saw Grizel's obsidian eyes staring at her. She wondered if the old woman planned to keep watch on her all night. Her thought, however, could not be sustained because sleep beckoned her into its blessed oblivion.

Chapter Eight

Reluctant to leave the sweet unawareness of sleep, Diana came awake slowly. Her first move produced an ache that caused a groan. Though she was used to riding almost every day, she had never ridden all day long in the uncomfortable position of second rider! Nor had she ever slept on the ground.

Her muscles protested as she sat up. No welcome warmth of a fire greeted her—only cold meat and even colder water. With a sigh, Diana accepted both.

Then, going to the bank of the small stream that ambled through the glade, she sank to her knees and splashed the icy water on her face. Whatever drowsiness lingered was quickly washed away.

"Och!" she exclaimed, staring at her reflection. Plucking a twig from her hair, she threw it into the stream and watched as the eddies twirled it in a circle before sending it downstream.

Using her fingers, Diana tried to comb the unruly mass of tangled curls, wincing when she met an unresisting knot. She looked up to see Grizel standing beside her.

" 'Tis a grim way to live," she complained.

Grizel made no answer. Diana was uncertain as to whether her silence indicated agreement or disagreement.

Irked by the woman's silence, Diana got to her feet. "Are you so used to living in the woods like an animal that you feel no discomfort?"

At that question, Grizel's black eyes seemed to sparkle. "Is the life of an animal less than yours?"

Diana made a face as she walked away. There was no reasoning with a MacKendrick, she decided as she returned to the fallen log.

"I hope you spent a restful night," the earl said, coming to stand before her.

The glint of amusement in his eye was not lost on Diana. "Somehow I doubt that my comfort is of any concern to you!"

He bent forward, took her hand, and raised her to her feet. "On the contrary, it means a great deal to me."

His thumb gently moved across her palm, and she snatched her hand away, annoyed by the sudden tremor in her stomach.

"You may find it restful to sleep on the ground," she said to him. "But I do not!" She clasped her hands at her waist in an effort to keep them from his reach.

"I assure you," Thorn said quietly, "that when we reach Rath na Iolair your bed will be much softer."

Diana eyed him warily, wondering what he meant. "If my father were alive, you would not have dared to take me captive!"

His expression hardened. "If your father were alive, Dunmoor would not have been ransacked! Come along. 'Tis time we leave."

He turned on his heel and walked away, issuing orders to his men as he headed for the golden stallion, and Diana swallowed her impotent rage as she reluctantly followed.

A while later, Diana once again riding in front of her captor, they resumed their tedious journey. Under different circumstances, Diana would have enjoyed the early morning ride, for the scenery was magnificent. The mist-laden air seemed to have been painted in pastels. Glens and fells alike were silvered with frost. Undaunted, trees and bushes were responding enthusiastically to the seductive call of spring.

They traveled at an easy pace for most of the morning, stopping once to rest and water the animals, as well as themselves.

Shortly after noon they came to a burn that was wider than most, and the earl slowed the golden stallion. The animal moved cautiously, as if testing its footing.

With the respite, Diana turned to look at the huge man behind her. "Are we almost there?" she asked, not certain that her question would be answered.

"Aye," he said, looking down into the water.

She hesitated, then asked, "And will you let me go when your brother is returned?"

"I know we are a long way from your home, lass. But as soon as Ian is returned I promise that you will be released. You must understand that he is most important to me."

"He is a brave lad," she murmured, facing forward again. She felt his arm tighten about her with a sudden tension.

"You've seen him?"

"Aye."

"Was he well?"

"He was not harmed."

Diana hoped that he would not ask where the lad was being held. In her mind, she could see the small boy, frightened, in the dark and dank dungeon of Sidhean. His arm relaxed, and Diana knew he would pursue the subject no further.

As the hours passed, Diana's back began to ache from the strain of holding herself rigid, trying to keep a scant inch of space between herself and her captor. The comforting warmth of his huge body greatly disturbed her. Why wasn't she repulsed by his nearness?

Time and again she was tempted to give in to the exhaustion that engulfed her and simply rest her head back against his broad chest and sleep. Somehow she knew he would not mind. Perversely, she refused to give in to her feelings, and she continued to sit erect, hour after endless hour.

The sun was low on the horizon and the air was infused with the tang of the sea.

Wearily, Diana studied the landscape. Nothing looked familiar. If she did escape, would she be able to find her way back home?

Of course she would! she told herself sternly. She need only travel east and south; sooner or later she would reach Sidhean.

The golden stallion hastened his steps along a stony path lined with trees sporting pale green leaves.

Diana raised her head to view the stronghold perched on the summit. Rath na Iolair: Fort of the Eagle.

It was appropriate, Diana thought. Set on a high windswept ridge that overlooked the waters of the North Minch, it appeared grim and forbidding.

As they drew near the top of the hill and Diana got a closer look at the gray-stoned keep, she inhaled sharply. It was the edifice she had seen in the fish pond! Danger was here. She did not know what form it would take, and the very uncertainty caused her to shudder with apprehension.

They passed through the square opening guarded by the iron prongs of the portcullis to be greeted by hounds, who came bounding forward, yelping.

Armed men materialized from shadowed corners and crannies as if they had been waiting there only for the return of their chief. All wore broad smiles and called out words of greeting that the earl acknowledged with a wave of his hand.

In the courtyard, Thorn dismounted, then assisted Diana from the stallion. Grizel needed no assistance, and she had her feet on the ground before anyone could reach her.

Diana stood very still, staring fixedly at the darkened patch of stone on the west tower.

" 'Twas struck by lightning," the earl said, standing by her side.

"I know," Diana whispered. Seeing her captor's suddenly perplexed look, she hastily added, "I mean, that's what I had assumed happened."

Thorn nodded, then put his hand on her elbow as he guided her up the stone steps. Inside, her nerves taut, Diana followed Grizel up the stairs.

"You may rest," the old woman said as she opened a door to a bedchamber. " 'Twill be an hour or so until food is served."

Diana made no retort. Heading for the bed,

she stretched out on the fur robes that served as coverings and watched as Grizel quietly left.

Diana knew she would not sleep, and she was still awake when Grizel came to inform her that the earl had summoned her to the great hall. Diana did not move. She suddenly felt as though her nerves would snap if she had to confront that handsome, smirking face yet one more time.

"His lordship said to tell you that he wants you downstairs now!" Grizel repeated, seeing Diana's hesitation.

Diana bristled. Captive though she might be, she would not allow herself to be addressed as if she were a servant!

"Did he? Well, I'll not go!" She waved an imperious hand as she got up from the bed. "You may have my food sent up here. Tell his lordship I have no desire to share a meal with him. Indeed, you may tell him he takes my appetite away—"

Diana broke off with a gasp as she saw the earl standing in the doorway, his broad shoulders almost filling the space between the wooden frames. Spacious as the room was, his presence seemed to diminish it. He was wearing a most forbidding scowl.

"I fear that Grizel did not present my instructions clearly, my lady," he said in a low voice. " 'Twas not a request. 'Twas an order!"

"I take orders from no living man. Only my

father had that privilege."

Two long strides brought him quickly to her side. "You can walk or be carried."

Diana hesitated a fraction too long, and her captor scooped her up in his arms. Rather than protest, she remained rigid in his arms, seething with a fury that made her grit her teeth.

The insufferable clod! she fumed in helpless anger as he made his way down the stairs. Obviously, it was beyond him to win a fight fairly—a distressing trait of the Mac-Kendricks, one that she would do well to remember.

A few minutes later, the earl entered the great hall. Conversation ceased as everyone gaped.

"Lady Diana has deigned to join us for supper!" he called out cheerfully.

His announcement drew loud guffaws from the assemblage that only added fuel to the simmering rage that roiled within Diana.

Halfway across the room, the earl paused and glanced down at her. His smile was one she was learning to mistrust.

"Put me down, you arrogant lout!" she said, seething.

"As you wish." Without warning, he loosened his grip.

Diana screamed as she felt herself falling. She landed on her rump, the soft rushes cushioning the impact. Her legs spread wide in a most undignified manner, she glared up at him. "You're despicable!"

He grinned at her. "So I've been told." Making no effort to assist her to her feet, he ambled toward the carved chair on the dais.

It seemed to Diana that she was surrounded by laughter. For a moment, tears of frustration stung behind her eyes. Sternly, she repressed them. There would be snow in July before she would let a MacKendrick see her in tears.

Slowly, Diana rose to her feet. She would not allow so much as a quiver in her chin. To her, the MacKendricks were like predators. If they sensed weakness, they would attack.

Standing very still, Diana let her measured gaze sweep the room. One by one, each person with whom she made eye contact ceased to laugh. The men began to converse with each other in an embarrassed way. Her head high, she began to walk slowly toward the raised dais.

Seated, Thorn watched as Lady Diana came closer. Amazed, he noted how she walked toward the table, moving with an easy dignity that was more suited to a guest than a captive.

Thorn was forced to admire her bravado, assumed or not. Women had been brought before to Rath na Iolair as captives—for such was the way of life in the Highlands—and it was not unusual for them to cringe, scream, and beg for mercy.

Idly, Thorn wondered what state of affairs would prompt this woman to act in such manner.

His musings were interrupted when Angus put a hand on his arm. Thorn turned to look at him.

"What troubles you, laddie?" he asked, seeing the expression of consternation on his cousin's face.

Angus shifted uneasily. "You're still staring, Thorn," he murmured, releasing his hold. "And in a way that seems more than warranted. If you want her, take her and be done with it! There's none who would believe you hadn't anyway. 'Tis your right."

Thorn gave a short laugh. "You are mistaken if you think I'm attracted to the wench! In fact, I have never met one who so irritates me. And if I stare at her," he said, sounding annoyed with Angus's observation, " 'tis not because I want to bed her! 'Tis because"—he faltered and Angus leaned closer with an air of exaggerated attention—" 'tis because I don't know what she's going to do next. A woman who draws a sword on me is a woman to be watched!"

Though Angus did not comment, Thorn was irritated by the solemn expression on his face; it seemed to convey total disbelief.

Diana had seated herself in the only vacant chair available—the one beside him. Without so much as a glance in his direction, she began to eat in the dainty way he was beginning to recognize.

Her manners and bearing came as a surprise to him. On those few occasions he had been forced to break bread with the Mac-Larens, he had likened them to pigs at a trough.

Of course, he told himself, the wench had spent the obligatory two years at court, acting as lady-in-waiting to the queen. It was only to be expected that she had adopted some of the manners of the court.

Chapter Nine

This meal, Diana thought wearily some two hours later, will never end.

The earl was watching her, but she refused to give him the satisfaction of showing her discomfort. Instead, she proceeded to scan the great hall with assumed interest.

It was larger than the one at Sidhean, being fully 40 feet long, and a huge hearth dominated the center wall. The dais where she sat accommodated a long trestle table that had room for eight or nine people sitting side by side. The earl's chair at the center of the table was high backed and richly carved.

A serving wench hurried forward to fill his tankard with ale. That done, she curtsied and smiled charmingly.

"Welcome home, m'lord," she said breathlessly. " 'Tis a dreary place indeed when you're away."

The MacKendrick laughed and gave the girl a playful pinch on her rosy cheek and a most familiar, Diana thought, pat on her buttocks. "Ailis, you do like to spoil me."

A glance at the girl's flushed face and glowing eyes told Diana that the maidservant adored her master.

That particular scene, with only slight variations was repeated throughout the evening as the wenches vied for the pleasure of serving their lord. Diana's mouth tightened in contempt as she viewed the fawning females. It was apparent to her that the Earl of Dunmoor was no different from her brother. Doubtless, he took advantage of his maidservants every chance he got!

Yet there was one difference, she mused as she took a sip of her wine and placed the goblet back on the table. The girls here not only came into Thorn's presence willingly, they went out of their way to capture his eye and, once receiving it, basked in the brief attention he bestowed upon them. By contrast, female servants at Sidhean avoided Robert whenever they could.

Yet one more maid approached and went through the familiar routine. When the lass withdrew, Diana turned to her captor and remarked sarcastically, "They certainly seem happy to see you back in residency."

He looked surprised. "Why would they not?

The maidservants, standing in a group by the arched doorway, suddenly erupted in a paroxysm of giggles.

The display of merriment caused Diana to view them with a certain degree of curiosity. She tried to recall an occasion at Sidhean when she had seen maidservants standing about in idle chatter and laughter. But she could remember no such incident.

Having eaten her fill, Diana washed her hands in the bowl of water provided for that use, wiped her knife clean, and returned it to its sheath. Tired as she was, Diana sat with her back straight and her head high. Even under these extraordinary circumstances, she was acutely aware that she was representing the Clan MacLaren.

The hour was approaching midnight when, to her dismay, it was not Grizel but the earl who came to escort her from the hall. The room he led her to was not the same one that Grizel had taken her to some hours before. Once inside, Diana could not repress a sigh of relief.

It was large, apparently a corner room, with two windows, both shuttered. In the hearth, a fire burned brightly, and the bed was piled high with fur robes.

Thorn's gaze swept the room, then focused on her. "I do hope your accommodations please you."

Annoyed by his condescending manner, Diana said, "There is only one thing you can do to please me!"

His mouth twitched with a devilish grin. "I would go to great lengths to please you, my lady."

Refusing to respond to his teasing banter Diana gave him a steely look. "Then allow me to return to Sidhean."

"In due time."

Feeling uncertain, Diana turned away. In due time, she thought miserably. The MacKendrick was unaware that her brother was, most likely, glad to be rid of her.

"You have made a terrible mistake," she said. "If you seek your brother's return, you should have selected another means of barter."

Thorn stared at her a moment before he spoke. "Are you suggesting that the MacLarens care naught for their kinsmen?"

She stiffened. "I am suggesting no such thing!"

"Then what are you suggesting?" he asked softly.

Diana bit her lip. "Nothing! Leave me be!"

He stepped closer. Raising his hand, he went to place it on her shoulder. But she backed away. "If you put so much as a hand on me, I'll kill you!" she spat, quickly producing the silver dirk.

Coming to an abrupt halt, Thorn dropped his eyes to the small, lethal dining knife she held.

Watching him closely, Diana could see both

astonishment and anger in his face. Even though she had been using the knife during the evening meal, she knew he had not noticed. If he had, he would have again taken it from her possession.

She was filled with grim satisfaction at this small victory. Apparently, among other things, the MacKendricks were too ignorant to realize that one never took one's attention from a prisoner.

"You flatter yourself, lass," he said at last. "One would think you deem yourself irresistible! Let me assure you that I do not find you in the least attractive." She blinked and he smiled slightly. "You have trouble believing that?"

Rubbing his strong jaw, he walked slowly around her. She did not move, but her eyes followed him until he was lost. Then she found him with her peripheral vision.

"Too tall," he said gravely. Without warning, his large hand gripped her upper arm. Before she could react, he released her. "As I thought," he mused in a casual tone, "a man could be proud of that forearm."

As his hand went to her thigh, Diana slapped it away. "I told you not to touch me!"

"Oh." He looked surprised. "I thought you meant in an intimate way. I did not realize that you had an aversion to a gesture of camaraderie."

"Cam—" she said and choked.

On his face was a look of assumed innocence.

"My apologies, if you misunderstood my intent. Now"—his manner grew brusque—"I suggest that you retire." He turned away, then gave her a last glance. "Keep your knife if it makes you rest easy, Diana. I'll not be battering down the door to avail myself of your charms."

Turning on his heel, the Earl of Dunmoor walked from the room and slammed the door behind him.

Tears of rage stung Diana's eyes, though she was at a loss for a reason. The man was infuriating! Arrogant! Authoritative! All the things she despised in a man.

Without thinking, she raised her hand to her upper arm. Indeed it was firm. But then she had not spent her time embroidering as did so many noblewomen she knew. Since she had been nine years old she had spent several hours of each day training with the men-at-arms who guarded Sidhean. By her fourteenth year, her expertise had rivaled that of Lachlan Gilbride, who was recognized as the best swordsman in their clan.

She murmured with annoyance. It was of no concern to her what the Earl of Dunmoor thought of her appearance. She decided she was grateful that he did not find her attractive.

Feeling a bit more secure, she disrobed and got into bed. With only a glance at the closed door, she put her head on the pillow and promptly fell asleep.

Chapter Ten

Diana's eyes fluttered open, then closed quickly against the glare of a bright morning sun that cut across the room like a golden sword. She burrowed her head in the softness of the pillow and snuggled deeper into the warmth of the fur robes. For a minute or so, she drifted between sleep and wakefulness until a sound caught her attention. Muted footsteps. Someone was in the room!

Diana's eyes flew open again, and she sat up, prepared to do battle. She relaxed when she recognized the maidservant. It was Ailis, the one who had gushed over the earl the night before. No more than 16, and petite but in no way delicate, she had the robust, glowing look of a young serf. Her blond hair was fashioned into two thick braids that fell over her ample bosom.

Beyond Ailis stood a tub, a scant inch of steam hovering on the surface of the water.

"You're certainly not a light sleeper, are you?" Ailis observed dryly. She nodded toward the tub. "I thought you'd be needing a bath."

Diana sighed gratefully. She hadn't had a bath since she had left Sidhean.

Before she could offer her thanks, Ailis bent toward her. "You do bathe, don't you?"

Diana's mouth tightened. "I've been known to do so on occasion."

Ailis straightened up and gave a derisive laugh. "That's pleasant news! The stench of a MacLaren is not to my liking. I'd sooner be in the company of sheep than an unwashed MacLaren."

Diana bit back an angry retort as she got out of bed. She had slept in her chemise and now dropped it to the floor. Without waiting for assistance, she climbed into the tub. Another sigh erupted as the warmth enveloped her. She rested her head back on the rim of the tub and closed her eyes.

"Och!" Diana exclaimed a moment later as steaming water was poured into the tub. Only the cooling water already in the tub prevented serious injury. In an agile movement, she leapt out of the tub. "You stupid wench! You about burnt me alive!" Picking up her chemise, she hastily donned it against the chill that assaulted her warm skin.

Ailis's face was innocent. "I was told that all

MacLarens were thick-skinned."

Diana stared in disbelief. "You blathering idiot! Are you daft? You knew the water was too hot!"

"Aye." Her hands on her hips, Ailis gave a nasty laugh.

Overcome by the frustration of the past days, Diana raised her hand and smartly struck the maidservant's rosy cheek. Startled and outraged, Ailis let out a shriek that Diana was certain could be heard outside the keep.

In the adjoining room, Thorn paused as he was leaving to go down to the great hall.

God almighty, he thought. What was happening?

A few quick strides brought him to the door, which he flung open. For the moment, he was speechless as he stared at Diana. Her bare feet planted wide, her hands on her waist, and her eyes ablaze with fury, Diana was glaring at Ailis. Her dark tresses were in complete disarray and wet at the ends. They tumbled in a shimmery mass that fell almost to her hips. Her chemise was damp and clung to her body, outlining every curve, swell, and hollow of her lush form.

Still staring at the vision she presented, Thorn's mouth went dry. Then Ailis made a lunge for the lady. Roused from his bemused state, he at last reacted.

"Christ's blood!" He rushed into the room and grabbed the girl, who was about to attack

Diana. "What the devil's going on here?"

"She complained that the water was too hot!" Ailis screamed. Raising her head, she added, "Look what she did to me!"

Seeing the reddening flesh, Thorn scowled at his captive. "You did this?" he demanded.

Diana raised her chin. "Aye."

Thorn wondered why he had expected lady-like behavior from this woman. It seemed that he was continually forgetting who she was.

"You are a MacLaren," he growled.

"Aye." Her silver eyes challenged him. "Do you think to change that?"

"No one could," he said in the same tone.

"No one would dare!" Diana countered with a toss of her head.

"You must have shamed your father with your temper!" he bit out.

"On the contrary," she replied evenly. "My father never appreciated a woman without spirit—or a man without sense!"

Exasperation overwhelmed Thorn. "Upon my honor, wench! 'Tis glad I'll be to return you to your clan at the first opportunity!"

Diana sniffed scornfully. "Honor, is it? An Englishman has more honor than a MacKendrick."

"And a MacKendrick has more honor than a MacLaren," Thorn said. "Where, then, does that leave your clansmen?"

He expected the predictable spurt of her anger. To his surprise, her response was a smile as frigid as the burns in midwinter.

"I never ceased to be amazed by your ignorance," she mused. "For a man to make such a judgment, he must first know the meaning of the word. Obviously, you do not."

Roughly, Thorn grabbed Diana by her upper arms, almost lifting her from her feet, and scowled down at her. He heard her sharp breath of fear.

"You deserve a good thrashing to curb your ways!" he yelled, his own temper fraying. He was unused to being contradicted, much less insulted! It took little thought on his part to decide that he didn't like it! "And if you continue to speak to me in such a manner, I will be glad to take the task upon myself!"

When the earl released Diana, she quickly stepped back. Her chin jutted out, and she raised her head. "If you think the force of your hand would change my ways, you are mistaken!"

He drove his fingers through his hair. Christ, he thought. Men had fallen to their knees at the slightest sign of his displeasure. And this woman only glared at him defiantly!

" 'Tis no surprise to me that you're not wed," Thorn muttered. "A man would indeed be without sense to bid for a temper-ridden shrew such as yourself!" Despite his forceful words, he made certain that he did not gaze into the silver depths of those compelling eyes. Turning, he addressed Ailis: "From now on, Grizel will see to Lady Diana's needs."

You fool! Diana thought as her captor stormed away and the servant followed, looking smug.

Walking to the hearth, she chafed her arms, not understanding the heavy depression that overshadowed the tingling feeling produced by the hot water.

Minutes later, after dressing, she sat in a chair and did not look up when the door opened.

You're too hotheaded, lass. Best learn to control your temper if you hope to survive.

As the words ran through Diana's mind, her head swung toward the door and her eyes widened in shock.

"You understood me," Grizel said flatly.

Diana blinked, realizing that the older woman had not voiced her thoughts. "Aye," she whispered in a breathless wonder tinged with fear.

Grizel nodded slowly. "I knew you had the sight when first I laid eyes on you. We recognize our own." She motioned to Diana as she headed for the door. "Come. They'll be eating soon."

As Diana followed Grizel, she was distinctly uneasy with what had just taken place. Were even her own inner thoughts to be held captive while she was in this gloomy keep? The idea was not a comforting one.

By the time they reached the great hall, Diana's equilibrium had returned. Grizel had the sight, though in a different form than she herself possessed it. Grizel was no threat to her, she decided.

As for her captor—well, she'd not let him get the better of her. Grizel had been right: She must learn to control her temper. Though, Lord knew, it would be difficult when that man was around.

Seating herself, Diana began to eat the hearty breakfast put before her. For a time, the earl did not speak to her, but when the servants began to clear the table, he at last addressed her.

"I have spoken to Ailis," he said.

Diana raised her brow. "Have you? And no doubt she confirmed your opinion of me as a temper-ridden shrew." She turned away and affected uninterest.

Thorn cleared his throat. "I apologize for my harsh words," he said at last. "The fact of the matter is that Ailis explained everything. She confessed that the water was indeed too hot."

Diana turned to him again and asked skeptically, "You chastised her?"

He rubbed his chin. "Let us say that I reprimanded her."

Diana sniffed. "Servants like that would not be tolerated at Sidhean."

"I don't doubt it," he murmured. "It is not my intention to make your stay with us unpleasant."

Diana raised her eyes to the ceiling, but made no comment. His next words, however, caught her undivided attention.

"Would you care to take a ride about the grounds?" he asked.

Excitement rose inside her, though not with the anticipation of a day's outing. Once outside this gray-stoned fortress, she might be able to escape.

"I would indeed!" Diana made certain that her smile was bright with pleasure.

He nodded. " 'Tis settled then. We can leave now, if you like."

With a quick step, Diana followed the earl as he led her to the stables.

Banrigh was brought forward from her stall by a young groom Diana judged to be no more than 13.

"At least you appear to have been well fed," Diana whispered, rubbing her cheek against the satiny nose.

"I've seen to it myself, m'lady," the lad said as he assisted her into the saddle. When she was settled, he grinned up at her with an admiration that was beyond his years to conceal. "I've even brushed her this morning."

Diana's smile was warm as she viewed the young groom. "My thanks to you—"

He quickly doffed his cap. "Richard, m'lady."

"Your kindness will not be forgotten, Richard," Diana murmured, amused to see the blush that stained his smooth cheeks.

"If you are done extolling your virtues, Richard," the earl remarked dryly, "mayhap you could hand the lady the reins."

The boy's blush deepened. "Sorry, m'lord." Hastily, he did as he was told.

" 'Twas unkind of you to make fun of the lad," Diana said when they spurred their mounts forward. Though her voice was low, it nevertheless conveyed her annoyance.

The earl looked at her with a twinkle in his eye. "I've no doubt that you do not want for suitors, my lady. But the lad is too young for you."

He chuckled as she expressed her outrage. But she quickly dismissed his insult from her thoughts as they rode from the keep. With a bit of luck, she might soon be on her way home.

Chapter Eleven

Once clear of the steep path that led to Rath na Iolair, Diana and the Earl of Dunmoor set their horses to a canter. Even with spring barely greening the land, Diana could see that the Highlands retained their fierce beauty. To the north, the mountains rose majestically and were host to countless burns whose crystal waters gave the appearance of silver ribbons in cragged settings. Deep, cold lochs were set like jewels in hidden glens nestled within gently rolling fells.

At last, the MacKendrick drew rein. Bending forward, he affectionately patted his stallion's neck.

Once more, Diana was forced to admire the magnificent beast. "What is his name?" she asked in a quiet voice.

"Sian," came the reply.

She quirked her brow. "Sian? He does not look like a storm to me."

"Oh?" he asked, sounding a bit defensive. "And what does he look like?"

Like a meadowland in autumn, Diana thought. But she said, "He does not seem to have the temperament for such a name."

"You've not seen him in battle!" Thorn declared, still stroking the horse's neck.

Diana shifted her weight in the saddle to better view her captor. "But I have," she replied and, at his surprised look, added, "I was there in the glen outside Edinburgh when you fought for six sheep."

He frowned. "And did not your kinsmen participate?"

"Only because you would not grant them what was rightfully theirs! The animals belonged to one of our crofters."

"Did they?" He pursed his lips as he turned to look at her. "I was informed they belonged to one of ours."

"Then you were misinformed," she remarked tartly.

"Mayhap we should discontinue our ride and return to your chambers, where we can settle this dispute once and for all!"

She swallowed, checking an angry retort. That was the last thing she wanted to do. "I think we can lay this matter to rest," she said hastily, "once and for all."

They moved forward again, the earl leading the way through a stand of trees to the clearing beyond. On a slight rise, he motioned to the body of water before them. "Loch Maree," he said.

Dismounting, he helped her off her horse, and they walked to the water's edge. The breeze had a sudden chill to it, and Diana became aware that the clear morning was rapidly giving way to gray skies. A fine mist hovered at the edge of the water, giving it an ethereal look.

"Och," she exclaimed softly. " 'Tis the most beautiful loch I have ever seen."

"Aye." He seemed pleased with her reaction. "There's none finer in all of Scotland."

Toward the center of the loch was a tiny, shrub-covered island. Diana pointed to it. "Have you ever gone to the little isle?"

Thorn laughed and shook his head. "Nay. 'Tis said 'tis inhabited by the kelpies. We wouldn't want to be disturbing them, would we?"

Diana shivered. During her youth, she had heard many stories about the small, ghostly water horses. They were said to be able to entice a person into mounting them; then they would carry that person to the bottom of the loch.

"Have you ever seen one?" she whispered.

"At times," Thorn answered seriously.

She believed him, for no one took lightly the tales of the fey creatures, any more than one would be foolish enough to discount the existence of the monster that dwelled within the

119

deep waters of Loch Ness.

"Mostly in the gloaming," he added. "They allow themselves to be seen only when they want to." He touched her arm. "Come along. We'd best be getting back."

Without seeming to, Diana eyed the two horses. If she could manage to mount her own horse and cause the earl's to bolt, she might have a chance to get away.

Casually, she took a few steps toward the horses, raising her head to view the sky. " 'Twill rain soon," she mused, noting the gray clouds that were scudding by.

He followed her glance. "Aye."

While he contemplated the worsening weather, Diana quickly undid the brooch that secured her plaid to her tunic and concealed it within the palm of her hand.

"Och!" she exclaimed in dismay, fumbling with the plaid as he turned to her. "My brooch." She began to look around. "Please help me find it. There!" she pointed toward the shore. "See the glitter of it?"

The earl took a few steps toward the water. It was all the diversion Diana needed. With light steps, she bolted toward Banrigh and in an instant was in the saddle. Raising her hand, she slapped the rump of the golden stallion as sharply as she could. To her utter dismay, the animal merely snorted and took a step to the side. Her captor was upon Diana before she could recover. He yanked her from the mare with such force she fell to the ground.

His feet planted wide, he towered over her. "Had you caused Sian harm, your life would be forfeit."

"And of what use would I be to you then?" she spat as she got to her feet. With agitated motions, she brushed clinging twigs and dried leaves from her habit.

Thorn eyed her coldly. "You are of no use to me now, save as a means of exchange." His hand gripped her wrist, and he twisted it cruelly. "Give me your word that you will not try to leave until the exchange is made!"

"I'll not give you my word!" Diana said, trying without success to free herself.

"Mayhap you'd like to spend your time with us in the mens' quarters, where you can be constantly supervised?" he said in a low voice.

Diana froze, wondering if he was really capable of turning her over to his men. But why should it be otherwise? she wondered bitterly. She had seen her own brother do the same thing with a woman when he was done with her.

"The choice is yours!" he said sharply when she did not answer. "I cannot watch you every minute of every day." He grinned, though without humor. "But I'll wager that my men would be more than willing to assume that responsibility."

When she only stared at him, he growled, "I await your answer!"

Diana's shoulders slumped. "Very well. You have my word." He released her, and she refused to rub her wrist.

"I hope the word of a MacLaren is equal to that of a MacKendrick," he mused.

Her anger returned to wash away her moment of submission. "You filthy swine!"

Grabbing her by her shoulders, he roughly pulled her toward him. "You will learn to curb your tongue, lass!" he said. "When you speak to me, you will do so with civility!"

His tone and manner frightened Diana, but this was not revealed in her face as she looked up at him. "You have my word, my lord. But you will have nothing more from me that you do not earn!"

His mouth flattened in anger, and he drew her so close to him that her body seemed molded to his. Thorn took a deep breath, and Diana grew restive beneath his silent scrutiny, noting how his suddenly lustful glance dropped to her breasts.

She shivered in apprehension even as she met his eyes boldly. She was no stranger to a man's lustful ways. When the warriors of Sidhean returned from their bloody forays, they always brought back women captives, who were then passed from man to man.

However, she very much recognized that hers was no ordinary capture. Her safety—up to a point—lay in the fact that she was being held in exchange for the earl's brother. Nay, he would not give her to his men unless things went horribly awry. That, of course, did not preclude his taking her for himself.

Turning away, Diana bit her lip. Once her virginity was taken from her, no man would want her for his wife. And if she were unlucky enough to have the seed of life planted in her belly, she would like as not be turned out of her clan—a virtual death sentence unless she could find a household that would offer her refuge.

Angrily, Diana swung back to her captor. He knew all of this, for such were the ways of their people. A bastard was considered broken, no longer part of any clan. The life of a mercenary was usually his lot. As for a woman—She took a deep breath, not wanting to think about that!

Diana recoiled from the smoldering look she saw in Thorn's eyes and she recoiled, too, from the provocative feelings that stirred within her beneath that hot gaze. It was almost as if she wanted him to kiss her, wanted to feel those strong, callused hands on her own soft flesh, wanted him to—

Insanity! she told herself sternly. Regardless of how she felt, yielding to this man would be yielding to her enemy.

As if in a trance, Diana stood there, her eyes locked with his. Her breath caught in her throat as he bent his head, his mouth finding hers in a persuasive kiss. She stood as still as a statue in his arms. When he at last drew back, she gazed up at him. She was shocked at the reaction she felt in response to his touch.

"You should not have done that," she whispered breathlessly.

"You're right," he agreed solemnly. "I should not have." His arms tightened as he drew her even closer. "And I should not be doing it again," he murmured as his lips once again found hers.

Heat flowed between them, threatening to burst into a flame of desire that took both of them by surprise. The mist turned to rain, but neither of them seemed to notice.

Chapter Twelve

That night Thorn tossed and turned on the fur robes that covered his bed. He did not have to look far to find the cause of his sleepless state. Merely by turning his head he could see beneath the door the flickering light from the hearth fire in the adjoining room.

Was she still awake? Had their moment of intimacy earlier in the day affected her as it had him? He ran his tongue over his lips. Imagination or no, the taste of her as cool as mist-touched heather was still with him.

With a muttered curse, Thorn got up and stood glaring at the door as if it had offended him. He never had trouble falling asleep. Many had been the times when he had been involved in a siege that had lasted months! When night came, he slept. Yet here he was, wide awake after almost an hour in his bed!

Irritation rippled along his nerves. What the devil was the matter with him? He was acting like an inexperienced squire! There was no reason to torment himself so. Angus had been correct: He wanted the wench. And it was his right as her captor to bed her. As Angus had noted, it was expected to the point where no one would believe he had not taken her.

Few and far between were the women Thorn had taken against their will. The experience had always left him dissatisfied. Since his fourteenth year, women had been his for the taking, and in most cases it had not been necessary for him to do the asking. And it would do no good to ask the MacLaren lass; that much he knew. Yet she had kissed him. There was no denying it.

His jaw set, Thorn moved forward and opened the door. Diana was not in bed. Wearing a woolen robe over one of Catherine's nightshifts, she was seated before the fire, brushing her hair. A true black, there was no hint of red in the luxurious tresses. At his entrance, the brush fell from Diana's hands, and Diana got to her feet.

Thorn was clad only in his breeks. The warm amber glow of the fire highlighted his sun-streaked hair and bronzed his chest. One look at the desire that glowed in his blue eyes told her why he was there. She searched his face for the gentle smile she had seen only once. But all she saw was cold determination.

"Must you sneak around, scaring the wits out of a body!" she demanded, hoping to turn his lust to anger.

"I do not sneak around the rooms of my own keep." he said, moving toward her.

Her limbs felt suddenly weak, and she placed a hand on the back of the chair for support. "What are you doing here?"

"I think you know." His tone was flat and as determined as his expression.

It had to come, Diana realized, fighting a dizziness that threatened to send her sprawling to the floor. It had been foolish of her to think that this man was any different from her brother or, for that matter, Donald Campbell. All men were indeed alike, she thought resentfully. And the MacKendricks were the worst of the lot.

Turning her head slightly, Diana darted a quick glance at the dressing table. Her silver dirk was where she had placed it when she had come into the room. Its blade glinted temptingly.

"Don't try it, lass," Thorn said quietly, seeing the direction of her gaze and easily interpreting her intent. " 'Twill do you no good."

She moistened her lips and decided to try reason. "I admit I kissed you this afternoon," she said, annoyed to hear the quaver in her voice. "But it meant nothing! I do not love you."

His brow shot up, and he laughed. Diana shivered. Somehow his deep laughter rumbled like the sounds of merriment that the devil himself might produce.

"Love? 'Tis not your love I want, lass."

Anger at his brusque manner shot through her and warmed her cheeks. " 'Tis a good thing! For you will never have it!"

Thorn took another step forward. "Keep your emotions to yourself, lass. I'll not ask for what cannot be given. But I will have what is within my power to take, if I so desire it. And I do," he added quietly.

Her chin rose defiantly. "Do you?" she asked in a deceptively mild tone. "Take me if you will, my lord," she taunted, pleased that her voice no longer gave indication of her inner turmoil. "But know that, even as you possess my body, you will never possess me!"

"So be it," he remarked as he came toward her.

Panic shot through Diana. She stepped back and raised her hand as if it alone could halt him. "No!"

Striding forward, he picked her up in his arms. Her struggles were futile.

"Put me down!" she demanded, pummeling his chest.

"Not until you're in my bed, lass," he shot back. "Then we will know who is master here."

Inside his room, Thorn deposited her none too gently on the pile of fur robes, where she lay, glaring up at him.

"Take off your clothes," he ordered, "or I will do it for you."

In response to that command, Diana scrambled to the other side of the bed. Before she could get up, he was beside her.

"As you wish," he said.

Ignoring her struggles, he roughly tore off her robe and nightshift. A moment later, his breeks were on the floor beside them.

Diana drew back. Clutching at the furs, she tried vainly to cover her nakedness. As she looked up at him, Thorn was startled to see a tear fall from her eye, trailing down her cheek like a ribbon of silver. His hand went to her cheek. With his thumb, he gently brushed away the moisture.

"You've never known a man?" The thought came as a surprise. Diana was 18, no longer a youthful maiden by any standards. She made no reply, but in her eyes he saw the answer. "Well, then," he murmured, "that does put a different light on it."

Drawing her close to him, he pulled the robes up to cover them both. For a long time, denying his need, he held her in his arms, brushing soft kisses across her cheek and neck, pausing to linger over that delectable hollow in her throat. She put her hands on his chest in a gesture that suggested she might push him away; but she did not. Feeling her body relax, Thorn's hands began to gently stroke her back.

Beneath her palms, Diana could feel his heartbeat quicken, and she knew that her own had joined that tempo. A languid feeling crept over her as his powerful hand encircled her breast. At last, her arms went around his neck, and she found herself returning his kisses with an ardor that left them both breathless.

A gleam of triumph sparked in his vivid blue eyes. Though Diana disliked the thought that he had sensed her weakness, she was powerless against the unaccustomed stirrings that rippled through her body.

Thorn's mouth moved to her ear, and he gently bit it. She felt his warm breath and shuddered. Slowly, his hand went from her breast to her stomach, then moved on, leaving little fiery darts of pleasure in its wake.

Her skin seemed to be suddenly infused with heat wherever he touched her. His hand moved in ever lowering circles against her abdomen. She shivered with pleasure as his fingers began a more intimate exploration. She knew she should resist, yet even a token effort was beyond her.

Minutes went by with only her whimpers to mark the passing time. When he at last entered her, Diana raised her body to meet his, writhing shamelessly and without restraint. Her breath came in no more than short spurts. She cried out to him, but he put his mouth over hers, reducing her voice to a sobbing sound in her throat. She had been prepared for pain, expected it, then accepted it. It was fleeting.

Feeling the pulsing length of him inside her, she moaned, and her hands clutched at his muscled back. Without conscious thought, her body began to match the seductive rhythm of his increasingly rapid thrusts. In spite of her initial resolve to resist, she responded in ways she'd never thought possible. Her nails raked his skin heedlessly as her hips arched to meet his demanding thrust.

Part of her mind deplored her wanton behavior, but the other part urged her on and on as she instinctively strove for the unknown plateau that beckoned to her. Her senses reeled, then fused into the very core of her being. At last, as if he sensed her overwhelming urgency, Thorn quickened his thrusts until she quivered beneath him in a violent spasm of passion. A moment later his body stiffened and a groan escaped him.

Somewhere, in the back of her mind, Diana was aware that she had always dreaded this assault on her body to which she knew one day she would have to submit. At the very best she had imagined it would be humiliating, something merely to be endured. Instead, she had responded as might a lute beneath the practiced strumming of a master musician. There had been none of the humiliation she had anticipated, only a sharing, a glorious culmination, a fulfillment that left her feeling complete.

In the midst of her rapturous mental wanderings, Thorn's voice rudely jarred her. "You please me greatly, lass," he murmured contentedly, stretching his long body. "From now on, you will be spending every night in my bed."

Diana drew a sharp breath of outrage. His tone was so casual, he could have been speaking to one of his maidservants! When her heartbeat at last slowed to its normal rate, cold fury replaced the hot passion that only moments before had held her in its relentless grip. She had virtually given away that one priceless commodity that should have been saved for the man who became her husband!

Raising herself up on her elbow, she glared down at the man beside her. "I hate you!"

Thorn stifled a yawn. "Aye, we have established that feeling between us."

His handsome face was beginning to grate on her nerves. That grin of his was positively mocking! Casting modesty aside, Diana leapt from the bed and stood there with her hands on her hips. "How can you be so pompous!" she demanded.

Thorn looked up at her, all innocence. "Practice?"

Turning, she began to head for the door.

"Lady Diana." His voice halted her. Her hand on the latch, she turned to look at him again. "You will return to my bed. And you will do it at once!"

Her eyes narrowed. "You've had your way, my lord. Now be done with it!"

He raised himself up on his elbow. "I do not think we will ever be done with it," he murmured in a serious tone.

When she made no move to obey him, he said

quietly, "I suggest you do as you are told."

Ignoring him, Diana opened the door. She was no more than two steps into her room when he caught her arm and spun her around to face him.

"When I give an order, I expect to be obeyed!"

His tone frightened her, but Diana refused to be intimidated. As calmly as she could, she gave the hand on her arm a pointed look, then stared into his eyes. "It does not come as a surprise to me to learn that a MacKendrick cannot get a woman into his bed unless he forces her into it!"

His face flushed with anger, and his jaw tightened at this slur upon his manhood. Though her lower lip trembled at her own audacity, she stood very still, wondering if he was going to strike her. She knew very well that she had delivered an insult few men would take lightly.

The earl released her arm. "Most women enter my bed willingly," he said in a quiet voice that nevertheless held the hint of lingering anger.

"Not this one!" she said. With as much dignity as she could muster, considering the fact that she was still as naked as a newborn bairn, Diana straightened up and spoke haughtily. "Will you please take your leave? I wish to get some sleep this night."

His smile was lazy. "And so you shall sleep, my lady. Eventually."

"You—You—" Words failed her. Balling her fists, she began to strike at him in helpless fury.

Ignoring her loud protests, Thorn picked her

up. In his room, he kicked the door closed with his foot. Diana was still struggling when he threw her back on the bed.

With a low grumble, he reached for her, and the gentleness that had marked their first union was gone. In its place was the frenzied coupling of a man and woman who wanted more than satisfaction: They wanted to possess each other!

When their joining was over and his breath at last calmed, Thorn turned to view the woman at his side. He couldn't recall a time when he had lain with a woman whose passion had matched his own. She was asleep, her firm breasts slowly rising and falling with each measured breath.

As he drew up the fur robes, he gave into the temptation to place his lips in the soft hollow of her throat. She murmured, but did not awaken. Then he put his head down on the pillow beside her, his cheek resting on the silken strands of her hair. His arm around her waist, Thorn closed his eyes. In only moments he, too, fell asleep.

Chapter Thirteen

Just before dawn, Diana awoke. When she tried to move she found herself pinned beneath the powerful arm of the Earl of Dunmoor. Only a glance told her that he was still asleep.

For a time, she lay very still, fearful of awakening him—and his desires! Finally, moving with the greatest care, she slid away from his grasp and out of bed. Tiptoeing, she headed for the door, hoping that he would not awaken and summon her back to his bed.

As silently as she could, she opened the door and retreated to her own room, praying that no one would know where she had spent the night, praying that no one would learn of her shame!

Inside, Diana grabbed a soft woolen robe from Catherine's chest and hastily covered her nakedness. Then she wearily sat down in a chair. As tired as Diana was, she knew she would be unable to go back to sleep. Morosely, she stared ahead of her, seeing nothing. Remorse and shame lay in the pit of her stomach like pieces of undigested mutton.

The first rays of the sun sent a shaft of light into the room, but she did not stir. The dancing sunbeams seemed to mock her with their purity and innocence, neither one of which she possessed any longer. Both attributes had been stolen from her by her captor. She should have fought harder, she thought in anguish. She had brought dishonor upon her clan, and she was acutely aware of that fact.

The door opened, and Grizel entered the room. Though aware of her approach, Diana could not rouse herself sufficiently to bid the woman good morning.

Pausing before Diana's chair, Grizel handed her a cup of hot mulled wine. "Drink," she said. "I will have your bath readied."

Diana accepted the wine, but made no immediate move to drink it. Instead, she held the cup in both hands, feeling the warmth on her palms.

"Not even a bath will cleanse me on this morn," she murmured, more to herself than to Grizel.

"You could not have done otherwise than you did," the woman said quietly.

"Couldn't I?" Diana asked bitterly. It did not surprise her that Grizel was aware of what had happened the night before. Grizel, it seemed, knew everything worth knowing. "I could have killed myself!"

Grizel seemed to consider that. "Aye," she said at last, "you could have."

"You think I should have?" Diana asked in a voice that was no more than a whisper.

"Nay." Grizel shook her head. " 'Twas not your destiny to do so. Fate has other things in store for you."

Diana made a sound of annoyance as she took a sip of the wine. "You mean the earl has other things in store for me."

"Perhaps they are one and the same."

Maidservants arrived with pails of hot water, and in a short while, Diana was comfortably ensconced in the perfumed water. But it was as she thought it would be. When she at last emerged from her bath she felt no cleaner than when she had entered it.

When Diana was dressed, Diana said to Grizel, "I am disinclined to break my fast in the company of others."

To Diana's surprise, Grizel offered no argument. " 'Tis not necessary for you to make an appearance. I will have the food sent to you."

When the woman had left, Diana ambled about the room, glancing from time to time at the door that led to the earl's chambers. She fully expected him to make an appearance. But he did not.

At first relieved, she found herself becoming

irritated. Surely he had awakened and discovered her absence. A while later, finding herself at the window, she paused abruptly at the sight of the MacKendrick and Angus in the courtyard below. When she opened the window the sound of their voices came clearly to her. The men were enthusiastically discussing where they would spend the day hunting!

Diana's mouth tightened in resentment. Not once did he so much as glance up at the window where she stood in plain view. His attention seemed to be centered solely on his companion. At that moment, Diana saw a young lad come running at top speed toward Thorn.

"M'lord!" he called out breathlessly. "Today's the day! I have reached my twelfth year. And you promised—"

Thorn rubbed his chin as he observed the slight figure before him. "Has it arrived so soon then?"

"Aye!" The boy's face was flushed with excitement as he gazed up at the earl.

Thorn's hand rested on the lad's shoulder, and he spoke solemnly. "It shall be as I said. This day marks your entrance into manhood. To honor the occasion, you may join the hunt."

"Thank you, m'lord!"

Thorn tousled the boy's hair. "Run along. Tell the groom to get you a suitable mount. We will be leaving in a few minutes."

Diana smiled. From the look of the boy, one would have thought that he had just received a priceless gem for his birthday. Hearing the servants bustling about the room, she turned to see them bringing in food. Going to the table, she sat down.

Diana was pensive as she ate. The lad in the courtyard had not been a member of the Clan MacKendrick. His homespun attire marked him as a crofter's son. She wondered whether what she had just witnessed was an isolated incident or the policy of the MacKendrick. If the latter, it was most unusual. Diana could not help but compare the earl's actions to those of her brother, who habitually distanced himself from his crofters and who judged them harshly when the occasion presented itself.

The clatter of hooves told her that the men were leaving. At the sound, her miffed state returned. One would have thought that last night hadn't happened! Then her expression brightened. Perhaps, she thought, since Thorn had had his way with her, he would not bother her again.

After the servants had cleared the table, Diana began to prowl the room in nervous agitation. She didn't want to think about what had happened; and right now, she could think of nothing else.

If her father were alive, what would he have thought of her actions? It was small consolation that she would not, at least, have to face him.

A groan escaped her lips. Did her father, from his rightful place in heaven, look down upon her shame? That thought really was too much to bear!

"What ails you, lass! One would think you were the first woman to have been forced into a man's bed! You be neither the first nor the last!"

Startled, Diana spun around. Often, when Grizel was in the room, she was so silent and unobtrusive that Diana forgot she was there. The need to speak to another woman overcame her reticence.

"Have you ever been taken against your will?"

"Once."

The answer made Diana feel easier in her mind. If someone as formidable as Grizel had been ravished and survived the degradation, then Diana felt there was hope for her.

"Well," Diana noted, " 'tis obvious that you did not kill yourself."

Grizel's thin lips twitched in what could have been a smile. "Nay, I killed him."

Defeated, Diana sank into a chair. She felt so miserable she never noticed when Grizel left the room. It was late morning before Diana sufficiently roused herself from her melancholy state enough to get up out of the chair. Inactivity was beginning to grate on her nerves. Briefly, she considered altering another of Catherine's dresses. But she knew that would only occupy her hands, not her mind.

Aimlessly, she walked about the room, at last pausing in front of a wooden cabinet. Curiously, she opened it, blinking in surprise at the books. She had assumed the Clan MacKendrick to be illiterate. The books were a bit dusty; no doubt they were there for show.

Selecting a volume, Diana settled herself comfortably, oblivious to the passing of time. The sun had set by the time Grizel once again entered Diana's chambers.

"His lordship's come back," the old woman said in her usual blunt manner. "He said to tell you that he will join you here for supper."

Diana put down the book. "Will he indeed?" she said in a tight voice.

Grizel allowed herself one of her rare smiles. "So he said. But if you wish, I'll send word that you are indisposed and will be eating alone."

Diana took a deep breath. One part of her wanted to do exactly that. However, the quiet solitude of her room seemed to be growing by the hour.

"I'll receive him," she said at last.

Refusing to acknowledge her breathless state, Diana quickly walked to the chest that contained the late Lady Catherine's clothes and selected a blue silk gown. While she dressed, servants brought in food.

Chapter Fourteen

The table before the hearth was set with steaming bowls of barley broth, a dish of capons, and a plate of fried trout. Dressed and coiffed, Diana stood by the window as the servants withdrew. A short while later, the earl entered her room without knocking.

And why should the master of the keep bother with such amenities? Diana thought resentfully, her hands clasped at her waist. What did one say to a man with whom one had slept the night before?

Though Diana was very much aware of Thorn's presence, she did not immediately turn in his direction. After a long moment of silence, during which time she sought to control herself, she finally faced him. Her gaze slid over him, barely noting his maroon surcoat and frothy white shirt.

Diana offered no greeting, but Thorn smiled at her. "And what did you do today?" he asked pleasantly.

"Do? What would you have expected me to do?" she exclaimed with a short laugh. "Go off on a day's hunt, mayhap?"

He raised his brow. "Ah, I see now. You are miffed because I was gone all day." He leaned toward her. "You would have preferred that I spent the time with you?"

"Certainly not!" Lord, she thought, he wasn't back but a few minutes and already he was exasperating her. " 'Tis of no concern to me how you spend your day!"

"Umm," he said, straightening up, "then I'm sure you will be pleased to know that the hunt was most successful."

"That pleases me greatly," she said dryly.

Noticing the volume on the mantel, he picked it up, then gave her an indulgent smile. "Did you enjoy the illustrations?"

She bristled. "No more than the text!"

Irked by his frankly disbelieving look, Diana took the book from him, opened it to a random page, and read a few lines.

"I confess that I did not know you could read," he said when she was through.

Despite his efforts, his surprise was not hidden from Diana, and she took satisfaction in his reaction.

"Most MacLarens can," she said with some exaggeration as she again placed the volume atop the mantel.

A thoughtful look on his face, Thorn moved to the table and poured them both a goblet of wine. "It appears that we have much to learn about each other," he remarked quietly.

"I see no need for that," Diana countered loftily. "We will not be spending that much time together." She was suddenly very much aware that they were alone in the room. "Where are the servants?" she asked, feeling a tug of nervousness.

"We will be dining alone."

With a shrug she hoped conveyed indifference, Diana sat down and began to slice a portion of the game. When she was finished, Thorn helped himself. For a time, they both applied themselves to the food.

He at last leaned back in his chair and observed her. The intensity of his gaze caused her to move restlessly in her chair.

"What are you staring at!" she demanded.

"Aside from the fact that I am dining with a beautiful woman, I confess that the gown you are wearing caught my eye. Unless I'm mistaken, it belonged to Lady Catherine."

She stiffened, not certain of the source of her anger. "You are not mistaken! I assure you 'tis only out of necessity and not choice that I am wearing clothes that belonged to your aunt!" She sniffed. "If you prefer, I can ask Grizel to fetch me the garb of one of your scullery maids!"

Thorn raised a placating hand. "My remark was not meant as a censure," he said, then grinned. "On the other hand, I think you would make a fetching scullery maid."

Diana gave him an annoyed glance and continued eating. They were silent for a few moments.

"Have you received word from my brother?" Diana asked at last in a calmer voice.

Thorn shook his head. "Not yet." He gave a short laugh. " 'Twould seem as though the Earl of Sidhean is not too upset by your absence."

Diana flushed. Having appeased her hunger, she washed her hands in the bowl of water, then dried them with the soft linen cloth that had been folded beside the bowl.

"Robert will answer in his own good time." Confident though her words sounded, her heart sank. Robert cared little for her welfare. Only pride would prompt him to action.

"No doubt," the earl responded noncommittally. He, too, washed his hands. "Though I'll wager your father would not have hesitated this long."

Diana looked at him with surprise that bordered on astonishment. "You knew my father?"

Slowly, Thorn nodded. "I was only a squire when I first met him. I spent two years at the keep of the Clan MacAlpine. A dispute arose between your father and the MacAlpine himself, and 'twas decided that the two of them would settle it on the field of battle.

"They were both fierce warriors, and the engagement went on for almost twenty minutes before one of them was unhorsed. 'Twas the MacAlpine who fell to the ground. His sword landed a distance away, and he was defenseless. I rushed forward to assist him to his feet, for he was in full armor. Your father had dismounted and was standing there, sword in hand. He could have easily cut us both down."

Thorn paused to sip his wine, and Diana waited impatiently for him to continue. She had never seen her father in battle.

Putting the goblet down on the table, Thorn continued. "Instead, your father waited until the MacAlpine was once again on his feet. I retrieved the sword, handed it to the MacAlpine, then stood there, uncertain as to what I should do next. Your father said, 'Best get yourself back, lad, lest you suffer unnecessary injury.' Only when I did so did the Earl of Sidhean once again raise his sword."

Diana leaned forward. "And who won?"

"Your father did. He fought bravely and won with honor. Though the times were few and far between, I did see the earl in battle again." Thorn laughed shortly. "We always seemed to be on opposite sides. Yet each time I was forced to admire his skill and to respect his conduct." He smiled at her. "Does it surprise you that a man can respect his enemy?"

" 'Tis a thought that bears contemplation," she replied cautiously. She did not yet know whether she even liked her enemy, much less respected him. Her tone softened. "I thank you for telling me that story. I was very close to my father."

"But not to your brother."

Her head shot up. "Why do you say that?"

" 'Twas no more than a guess on my part." He shrugged his shoulders. Then, getting to his feet, he extended his hand to her.

She made no move to take it. Instead, she clasped her hands in her lap and stared at him. "The hour grows late, my lord. I think you should leave and allow me to retire."

"Do you?" Amusement laced his voice.

From beneath her lashes, her gaze swept over him. Her anger flared at the arrogance she saw in his stance and expression. She clenched her hands tighter to prevent them from clawing it off that damnably attractive face.

In a slow movement, she rose to her feet. "Have you not humiliated me enough?" she demanded in a low voice. "How much shame must you heap upon me before you are satisfied?"

The arrogance slipped from his face as perplexity crossed his brow. "Humiliate you?" He sounded truly mystified.

"Do not think to beguile me, my lord. I see you very clearly for what you are."

He clasped his hands behind him. "And what am I?" he asked in a stony voice.

"A MacKendrick!" She spat the word as if it were an obscenity.

"And proud I am to be!" he retorted, glowering at her.

She tilted her head and glanced at him sideways. "Then you have little to be proud of," she said sweetly.

"And what would you be knowing of what a MacKendrick takes pride in?" he asked.

"Humiliating a MacLaren?" she said with an arched brow.

"If you are any indication, 'twould not take much of an effort. There is little challenge in such an endeavor."

She could sense his waning patience and was growing desperate. "We at least know how to conduct ourselves with honor."

"Hah! As if your brother understood the meaning of that word!"

Her eyes widened in outrage. "I will thank you to speak of my brother with the respect to which he is entitled as chief of our clan!"

"I give that which is deserved."

Diana took a breath. "And I deserve that which you give?"

His manner seemed to soften. "You seek merely to delay the inevitable." Once more he extended his hand. "Come along now. We've wasted enough time."

Heat flushed her cheeks and tears smarted her eyes in response to her impotent rage. "Why is it so difficult for you to understand that I do not wish to share your bed!"

A smile tugged at the corner of his mouth. "You seem to feel differently when you are in it."

She was getting nowhere; that much was obvious. She also knew that she had nothing with which to fight him—except, of course, her wits.

"Your modesty astounds me, my lord." Diana forced a smile to her lips, one that matched his mocking one. "I have an idea that you are giving too much credence to the words of your fawning maidservants. All of whom no doubt praise your capabilities as a lover," she added sarcastically.

"I confess that I have had no complaints."

Imitating what he had done to her, Diana circled her captor. Finger to her lips, she viewed him critically, as if assessing his merits.

In front of him again, she studied him coolly. "If I were to speak the truth, I would admit that, for a MacKendrick, you are a fine specimen. But, as to your capabilities as a lover, I fear I must reserve judgment."

His eyes narrowed. "Explain yourself."

Diana walked slowly back to the table. A trace of wine remained in her goblet, and she drank it before she answered him.

"A man does not judge a banquet by the first course he is served." She turned to look at him. "And I will wager that I am not your first course, my lord. However, you will have to accept the fact that you are mine. Therefore, you may or may not have something of which to be proud. You see, I have no basis for comparison."

"Very well," he said in a mild tone. "I shall see to it that you not only sample the second course, but the entire banquet as well."

Her poise slipped. "What do you mean?"

Moving toward her, he grabbed her arm and all but dragged her from the room. Stumbling and tripping, she increased her pace until she was almost running in an effort to stay on her feet. He was not taking her to his chambers, she realized once they were in the corridor.

"Where are you taking me?" she gasped.

"How many courses would you have to sample, my lady," he asked in a tight voice, "in order to make a knowledgeable assessment of the banquet? Five? Six? Fifteen?"

"What are you talking about!" She tried to break free, but was unsuccessful.

He paused at the head of the stairs, and his smile sent a shiver of dread through her. "The men of Rath na Iolair would be happy to provide you with as many courses as you need to allay your appetite."

Her eyes widened and she felt numb. "You wouldn't dare."

"I will, of course, expect a full accounting from you in the morning," he said, as if she had not spoken.

"You wouldn't dare," she said again, less strongly than before. They had shared the same bed, their passion. Not even a MacKendrick could be so unfeeling to do what he was proposing.

"Dare?" His brow rose in disbelief that she could even think such a foolish thing. "For a person to dare anything presupposes the threat of retribution. Do you honestly believe any awaits me here at Rath na Iolair?"

"Of course not," she said bitterly. "Your word is law, is it not? You could throw me to the hounds and no one would lift a hand to stop you."

"No one. But since I prize my hounds and would not wish to cause them indigestion, you need not concern yourself with such a possibility."

Thorn went to grab her arm again. With all her strength, Diana slapped his hand away. She then raised her hand to strike in him the face, but he caught her wrist.

"You could be put to death for what you have just done," he said in a controlled voice that belied his anger.

"Aye! And 'twould be preferable to spending another minute in your company!" As soon as she'd spoken, she was sorry she had. But, damnation, the man pushed her to the limits of what civility she possessed.

" 'Tis not death I offer you, my lady," he said in a voice colder than she had ever heard him use. " 'Tis an opportunity to satisfy your own curiosity. Come along!"

He began to descend the steps. In desperation, she sat down and wrapped her free arm around the balustrade.

"I'll not go!"

He released her arm, and she wrapped that, too, around the stone post.

"I fear, my lady, you have no choice."

"I do. I do have a choice."

He bent toward her. "Would you care to tell me what it is?"

She glared. "Damn you! Damn your soul to hell! You know perfectly well what it is!"

He straightened up. "I would hear it from your own lips, my lady. And it had better please me," he added in a hard voice.

Still shaken, Diana rose to her feet. Smoothing her skirt, she glanced at him, trying to gauge his mood. He was not smiling. "I"—she swallowed and he cocked his head—"I—"

"You said that. And if that is all you have to say, we had best be on our way. Come along."

Diana drew back. "I would rather spend the night in your bed," she said in a rush.

Thorn pursed his lips. "A good choice, Lady Diana," he responded curtly. "And before you enter my bed, you will assist me in my bath."

Without looking at her, he strode toward his chambers. Behind him, Diana clenched her fists as she followed him. Once inside his room, she retained enough audacity to slam the door. He did not seem to notice.

The tub was waiting. With a wave of his hand, he dismissed the servants, then began to undress. Her arms folded beneath her breasts, she watched him for a moment. Then her gaze rested on the tub. It appeared to have been made especially for him, for it was oversize. At the moment, it was filled almost to the brim with warm water. Her eyes returned to him.

"I agreed to share your bed," she said coldly. "I did not, and will not, agree to assist you in your bath!"

The last of his clothes fell to the floor. "You will agree to whatever I tell you to do," he said. "And right now, I am telling you to assist me in my bath!"

Diana could see he was once again growing annoyed. He was standing next to the tub, glaring at her.

"Before I assist you in it, I will drown you in it!" Stubbornly, she stood there, refusing to move.

He turned away slightly. "I take it then that you prefer me in your bed unwashed?"

"I do not prefer you in my bed at all!"

Moving toward her, Thorn came to a halt at the foot of the tub. His hands on his hips, he scowled at her. "I have been lenient with you! But I am in no mood for any more of your foolishness! You will assist me in my bath or receive that thrashing I have been so long promising you!"

Unfolding her arms, Diana smiled. So it was a bath he wanted, was it?

"Very well, my lord," she said in a sweet tone

154

that matched her smile. "You have me at a disadvantage. If 'tis a bath you wish, then 'tis a bath you will get."

Putting her hands on his chest, Diana pushed him. Taken off guard by her sudden action, he fell backward, landing in the tub with a great splash. Water spilled over the sides to the floor.

Sputtering and gasping for breath, Thorn brought his head up from beneath the water and attempted to brush the liquid from his eyes.

"Let me assist you, my lord," she said through clenched teeth. Grabbing a cloth, she thrust it into his face, rubbing as a hard as she could.

"Damnation! Let me be!" he howled, waving his arms. His legs hanging over the rim of the tub, he couldn't straighten up.

"Nay! You insisted on a bath, my lord. And that is what you shall get!"

Grabbing a handful of his thick hair, she jerked his head forward. Then, putting the cloth to his back, she proceeded to rub it with as much vigor as she had his face. At last she released him and threw the cloth to the floor.

"There, my lord," she said in grim satisfaction, "you've had your bath."

Slowly, Thorn righted himself and stepped out of the tub. Standing there, he looked at her from beneath flattened brows.

A thrill of fear spiraled down her spine. Now, she thought to herself, she would receive that thrashing. Her chin rose. So be it. It had been worth it. Henceforth, the MacKendrick would think twice before he again attempted to use her in the capacity of a servant.

Taking a step forward, he towered over her. She swallowed. Her bravado was fading with his nearness. He could indeed throw her to the hounds if he had a mind to do so.

"Did you enjoy your bath, my lord?" she asked in a small voice.

A long moment of silence followed. Then suddenly, Thorn threw back his head and began to laugh with a vigor that brought tears to his eyes. Reaching for her, he pulled her into his arms.

Feeling weak, Diana rested against his still wet body.

"I confess I've never had the likes of it before. And isn't it time you called me Thorn?" he said huskily as his lips found hers.

Chapter Fifteen

Outside, on that late April evening, Angus was conducting his nightly tour around the bailey to make certain that everything was secure for the evening. His men hailed him with a mixture of respect and rough affection. Though stern, he was known to be both fair and fearless.

The drawbridge that spanned the moat had not yet been raised, although the portcullis was down, barring entry to the courtyard. This was not an unusual state of affairs. The bridge was seldom raised before dark; and now, with spring well on its way, the twilight, or gloaming, extended for more than an hour after the sun had set.

About to give the order for the drawbridge to be raised, Angus came to an abrupt halt. His brows rose in astonishment at the sight of a solitary figure on the far side of the wooden structure. It was a woman; that much he could make out in the dimming light. What caused his astonishment was that the woman was alone and on foot! Rath na Iolair was miles from the nearest keep.

Angus immediately discounted the idea that this might be a messenger from Sidhean. No clan used a woman in that capacity. A trick, then?

His hand on his sword, Angus peered toward the wooded area beyond the bridge. As far as he could see, nothing moved. Still and all, he wasn't about to raise the portcullis just yet.

Patiently, he waited. The woman was walking very slowly, almost hesitantly, as if she were either exhausted or uncertain as to her whereabouts. Finally, she reached the iron gate, where she paused.

"Who are you? What do you want here?" Angus demanded.

"You would not know my name," the woman answered wearily. "I am here to see the earl."

Angus stared at her a moment. Her shawl put her face in shadows, but he could see that she was young. 17, perhaps 18, he judged. Instinct alone told Angus that the woman was there with a purpose. Motioning to the guard on duty, he instructed that she be admitted. Nevertheless, he kept a sharp eye on the bridge and the area beyond until she was at last in the courtyard and all was secure again.

Still not taking any chances, Angus took the woman's arm in a firm grip as he led her inside to the great hall. Even when they entered, he did not release her as he guided her across the room to Thorn's table. To his surprise, it was Lady Diana who reacted to their unexpected guest. With a startled gasp, she leapt to her feet, her mouth gaping open in shock and surprise.

"Sibeal!" she cried out. "What are you doing here?"

Angus viewed his chief, feeling as much surprise as he displayed.

"You know this woman?" Thorn asked Diana.

She nodded. "She is my maidservant—and my friend."

Angus, still having a firm grip on the arm of woman beside him, released her at the instruction of his chief.

Thorn's tone softened as he addressed Sibeal. "Come here, lass. Do not be afraid."

"I'm not," Sibeal said staunchly.

Angus checked a smile, knowing the answer to be untrue. He had felt her trembling when he was holding her arm only a moment ago.

"How did you get here?" Diana asked, her expression one of disbelief.

"I walked," Sibeal replied simply. Her shoulders squared as she faced the earl. "With your permission, m'lord, I have come to serve my lady."

Thorn got to his feet. "You are most welcome, Sibeal. And I can only hope that those who serve me do so with a devotion such as yours."

"Thank you, m'lord." Sibeal visibly relaxed.

"Can you give me news of my brother?" the earl asked as he again sat down.

"Not as to his welfare, m'lord. I can tell you that he is alive," she added quickly, taking note of his darkening countenance. "But I've not seen him since that first day he came to Sidhean."

Thorn's frown deepened, and he sighed. Then he looked at Sibeal curiously. "Why do you keep your face covered, lass?"

The girl flinched. After a brief pause, she slowly removed the shawl. Standing behind her, Angus watched as Sibeal divested herself of the woolen mantle and held it in her hands. The first thing he saw was an abundance of red hair. At the sight of it, his breath caught in his throat. Infused with the shifting shades of firelight, it fell to her waist. Only once before had he seen the likes of it.

And were her eyes the color of emeralds? he wondered. With an air of expectation, he waited for her to turn in his direction. When she did, he saw her dark green eyes. He saw nothing else, for nothing else mattered to him.

For once, the earl seemed to be at a loss for words. Angus heard him clear his throat before he again spoke.

"You may do as you wish, lass," he said, "but there's no need to cover yourself here. There'll be none who will make comments on your appearance." Slowly, his eye traveled the room. "And if such an unfortunate incident occurs, you will tell me. Do you understand?"

With dignity, Sibeal inclined her head. "Aye, m'lord." Despite her words, the shawl went back on again.

The earl snapped his fingers at a maidservant. "Take Sibeal to Lady Diana's chambers. Then have food sent to her."

Making no move to return to his duties, Angus watched as Sibeal left the hall.

Chapter Sixteen

As soon as Sibeal left the hall, Diana rose to her feet. "I would go with her," she said to Thorn.

About to move forward, she found herself detained by his hand on her wrist. "A reasonable request," he murmured. "And you have my permission to do so." He gave her a meaningful look. "But when your visit is concluded, you will come to my room."

She flushed hotly. "And If I do not wish to?"

He ignored her answer, as if her wishes were of no concern to him. "No later than midnight," Thorn said.

She was fast becoming annoyed at how casually he was beginning to demand her presence in his bed. At the snap of his fingers, she was expected to do his bidding!

"You can expect whatever you like, my lord! But do not think to order me about as if I were your lackey!" He still held her hand, and she wrenched it from his grasp.

Displaying no haste, Thorn got to his feet and towered over her. "You are right, my lady," he said, taking her by surprise. " 'Tis unnecessary for me to order you to come to my room. Far easier for me simply to pick you up and take you there now. Would that be preferable to you?"

Though his voice was low, and the tone even, Diana easily understood that he would, without a second thought, do exactly as he said. Uneasily, she glanced around the hall. No one was paying attention to them. That, she knew, would change soon enough if the earl picked her up and carted her from the room.

Diana swallowed. She tried to avoid his direct gaze, but it held her with its intensity. "I will think about it," she said, striving to maintain a modicum of control in this impossible situation.

Though Thorn smiled languidly, his eyes informed her that he was displeased with her resistance. "Do not think too long. As you have discovered by now, patience is not one of my more endearing traits."

"I have yet to find one that is," Diana muttered under her breath.

He leaned forward. "I beg your pardon?"

She cleared her throat. "Nothing, my lord."

"Midnight," he said, straightening up.

Diana barely managed a nod as she ran to follow Sibeal. Upstairs, she gave Sibeal a quick hug, then held her at arm's length.

"How did you know where to find me?" she demanded. She still couldn't believe that Sibeal was here.

"The message to your brother states that Ian MacKendrick must be brought here and that here is where the exchange will be made."

Diana's brow creased in puzzlement. She knew that Sibeal could not read. "Robert told you what was in the message?"

"Nay, the conditions of the exchange do not sit well with his lordship," Sibeal said. "He's been complaining about it every chance he gets. 'Tis no secret that you are being held at Rath na Iolair."

After servants brought food, Diana seated herself and watched as Sibeal began to eat heartily. Only when the girl had filled her plate for the third time did Diana again speak.

"How did you manage?" she asked wonderingly. "Surely you did not walk the whole distance!"

Sibeal raised a foot, and Diana saw that the sole of her boot was worn through.

"I did get a ride once," Sibeal said as she resumed eating, "on a peddler's wagon." She gave a short laugh. "But he paid more attention to me than to his wares. I left at the first village we came to."

Diana was pained. "He could have done you harm!"

Sibeal only laughed. "He was a dwarf of a man. No threat to anyone but himself. However, his fumblings did annoy me."

"What did you do for food?" Diana asked then.

Sibeal shrugged. "There were a few days when I did without. I brought as much as I could carry. When it was gone, I either begged for food or stole it," she added matter-of-factly.

Diana paused a moment before her next question. "And why?" She leaned forward. "Why did you make such an arduous and dangerous trip? You could have been injured—or worse." She shuddered at the thought.

Sibeal pushed her plate aside, and her smile was shy as she gazed at Diana. "I thought you needed me. So I came."

Diana's laugh verged suspiciously on a sob. "Och, lass. There's no truer friend in the world I have than you."

Sibeal's smile turned into a grin that conveyed some relief. " 'Tis glad I am that you are not annoyed with me for what I've done."

Diana blinked back her tears as she grasped Sibeal's hand. For the moment, words were beyond her.

Sibeal's green eyes glinted with mischief as she said, "Besides, you did promise to take me with you when you left."

"So I did." Diana laughed. Then she got to her

feet. "And here I am, chattering away when you must be weary to the bone!"

"Aye," Sibeal said as she stood.

A comfortable-looking pallet had been placed near the hearth, and Sibeal moved toward it.

Diana shook her head, still overcome with wonder. Having traveled to Rath na Iolair herself, she was well aware of how hilly the terrain was between Sidhean and there. It must have been an arduous journey for Sibeal.

"I confess I had fears that I might have to bed down with you in a dungeon," Sibeal said as she began to remove her clothes. "But your lodgings seem comfortable enough—and private."

Sibeal gave Diana a sharp, questioning look and her mention of dungeons was a painful reminder of Ian's plight. "The lad," Diana said quietly. "Did you speak true when you said you had no knowledge of him?"

"Aye," Sibeal said. "I've not set eyes on him since that first day."

Diana sighed and consoled herself that, if nothing else, the boy was at least being fed well. After extinguishing the tapers, she disrobed and stretched out on the bed. Sibeal, she knew, would fall asleep quickly. How could she do otherwise after having walked all those miles?

Having satisfied her immediate curiosity as to Sibeal's sudden and extraordinary appearance, Diana allowed her thoughts to focus on Thornton MacKendrick. She had been all but commanded to his bed! The arrogant lout was beginning to think that she was his personal property! The idea made her mouth tighten. Damn him! she fumed in indignation. She would not go!

When a few minutes had passed, Diana could hear Sibeal's even breathing, and she knew the lass was asleep. She raised herself up on her elbow and glanced at the door that led to Thorn's chambers. In her mind, she could picture him strolling about his room, perhaps sipping from a cup of wine, confidently awaiting her arrival—with bated breath, no doubt!

Well, let him wait! Diana thought. She would not go crawling into his bed at the snap of his fingers! She was a MacLaren, after all. Feeling righteous, she lay down again.

As tired as she was, Sibeal slept lightly, a part of her mind always alert to any summons that might be received from her mistress. When she heard the door open, Sibeal came instantly awake.

Light framed the doorway, silhouetting the massive figure standing on the threshold. Without moving her head, her eyes sought her mistress. She saw Diana draw the fur robe up under her chin. She lay very still and seemed to be feigning sleep. A minute passed. It seemed an hour before the figure finally spoke.

"Your decision, my lady?" The man's voice was quiet, without emotion.

"Go away!" Diana hissed.

He began to move forward. Sibeal tensed, wondering if she should get up to aid her mistress.

Diana raised hand. "Please," she said in a whisper, "I will come to you. Leave now!"

He hesitated a moment, then turned and was gone from view. The door remained opened. Diana got out of bed. Disdaining shoes or even a robe, she crossed the room barefoot.

Sibeal could remain silent no longer. "M'lady?" she called out softly as she sat up. "Is anything wrong?"

With a sigh, Diana turned. "Nay, Sibeal. Go back to sleep."

With Diana's departure, Sibeal lay back on her pallet and stared up at the darkened ceiling.

As soon as the servant who had brought her there had left, Sibeal had immediately surveyed her surroundings. In this room, one door led to the corridor. One led to the chambers of the earl. That was the one Diana had used.

Of her own accord? Aye. Sibeal could not believe otherwise. Diana had this night walked out of this room of her own free will into the adjoining room. Sibeal had no need to ask herself why. She knew.

No man captured a woman and did not make use of her. Sibeal was not naive. Her naivete had been snatched from her at the same time as had her virginity. A woman could resist, but in the end she had to submit.

Settling herself comfortably, Sibeal sighed.

An unaccustomed feeling of peace came over her. For the moment, she was uncertain as to the cause. Then she realized that, odd as it sounded, she felt safer here than she did at Sidhean, where she had been born and raised.

Her mother had been a stepsister to Diana's father. Who her own father had been was something Sibeal had never discovered. She had been only four years old when the same plague that had killed Diana's mother took the life of her own mother. And all good things had come to an end with the death of her mother. While her mother had lived, Sibeal had been loved and protected. Afterward, she had become painfully aware of the stigma of her bastardy. Taunts and jeers had been her lot until she had been befriended by Diana. The following years had been reasonably happy. Then Diana went to court. Soon after, Robert had taken a fancy to her and the nightmare had begun.

Cocking her head, Sibeal listened. She could hear nothing of what was taking place in the adjoining room. Yet the absence of any outcry was comforting. Whatever was happening, her mistress did not appear to be in distress. With that in mind, Sibeal rested her head on the pillow and fell asleep.

Chapter Seventeen

Once inside Thorn's chambers, Diana closed the door firmly. Standing by the hearth, he turned, but offered no greeting. Instead, he glanced pointedly at the clock.

"You are late," he said. "The hour approaches one o'clock."

For a moment, Diana stood there, her rage smoldering. "Don't you ever do that to me again!" she said at last in clipped tones. She was livid with anger, trembling with the force of it.

Thorn gaped. Before he could recover, she continued in the same tone. "A captive of yours I might be. But never think to treat me as a servant! I will not be ordered to your bed as if I were one of your fawning maidservants!"

His chin drew in. "Whether it pleases you or

not, as long as you are in this keep, you will do as I command!"

As far down as his chin went, hers rose. "I would sooner spend my stay in your dungeon!" So angry was she that the thought actually appealed to her.

" 'Tis something that can be arranged."

Thorn took a step forward, but Diana stood her ground, knowing the closed door was at her back. Her gaze never wavered in the face of his threatening approach. A MacLaren neither cringed nor begged for mercy during a battle. She would not so dishonor her clan by displaying either weakness.

"You are beginning to sorely try my patience, wench!" he muttered, pausing in front of her.

She raised her head, so as to keep eye contact. "I hope so, for your term of address sorely tries mine." Her demeanor had not softened.

"Do you not realize you have no say in this matter!" he said.

Then he calmed down as a slow smile came to his lips. Seeing it, Diana grew wary. His anger was something she could deal with and return in kind. But that innocent smile of his was something to be treated with caution.

"You once offered me a challenge," he mused softly. Diana's wariness increased as he went on. "If you bested me with a sword, you would be allowed to return home."

"You tricked me!" she said, her face flushing

with humiliation at the memory of that incident.

"So you say." He sounded unconcerned, but she noted that he did not contradict her. "Now, I pose you a challenge, my lady."

"Which is?" she asked in a quieter voice than she had been using. Had he attempted to overpower her, she would have fought, as befit a MacLaren. But a challenge was not so easily dismissed.

Crossing the room, Thorn poured himself a cup of wine. Turning, he cast a questioning look in her direction.

"Nay," she said firmly. She had had enough wine this night. One more cup would leave her befuddled; and if that was his plan, he was about to be sadly disappointed.

Diana was beginning to feel chilled. She rubbed her arms. "Are you going to tell me what it is you have in mind? Or am I to guess?" she added with no little sarcasm. "I believe you mentioned something about a challenge."

He nodded. "If after five minutes in my bed you wish to leave, I will make no move to stop you."

At first, she stared in amazement. She could not believe she would be allowed to leave that easily! From his face, she discerned he was serious.

Relaxing then, Diana smiled. If nothing else, the lout was confident, she thought smugly.

This would not be at all difficult. "Five minutes?"

"By the clock," he said solemnly.

She took a breath. "Agreed." She began to head for the bed.

"But"—his voice halted her—"you must be unclothed once you are in it."

She spun around, suddenly suspicious. "Why?"

He raised a brow. "If you took five minutes to disrobe, 'twouldn't be fair, would it? Of course, if a MacLaren cannot meet a fair challenge, then 'tis best we claim a victory for the Mac-Kendricks."

"You'll have no victory from me!" she declared emphatically. She removed her clothes more quickly than she had ever done before.

Thorn refused to look at her, knowing that, if he did, she would easily win. "Get into bed," he said. "I will join you there. Then the time will begin."

Diana did as she was told. Sitting quietly, her spine straight, she stared at him and watched as he divested himself of his clothing. Before the fireplace, he stretched, seeming to revel in the warmth that highlighted the golden hairs on his body. And, God knew, there were enough of them! Diana thought. His arms, his chest, and his long, muscular legs were covered with golden down.

Coming toward the bed then, he stood, his legs astride, his hands on his hips. One look told

Diana he needed no arousing. She shifted uneasily, envisioning those hands, those lips upon her vulnerable flesh.

"Are you ready, then?" he asked with a smile.

She cleared her throat, feeling a disturbing sensation in the pit of her stomach. "Five minutes!"

"Agreed. By the clock."

Thorn was beside Diana. She felt the warmth of his skin before his body touched hers.

"Is the time to begin now?" Her voice sounded, to her, like a squeak.

"You pick the time."

Taking a deep breath, she glanced at the clock. Three minutes to one. She steeled herself. "Very well. You may begin now."

Thorn chuckled, taking note of how her breasts rose and fell as her breathing quickened.

"You have already begun, my lady," he murmured as his lips found hers.

Chapter Eighteen

Opening her eyes, Diana pulled the fur robes closer against the chill of the early morning, and turning her head, she glanced at Thorn. He was sleeping soundly. She smiled. He looked younger when he was asleep—and less arrogant.

Resisting the urge to touch him, she slipped from beneath the warm blankets and eased out of bed. Picking up her nightgown from the floor, where she had thrown it the night before, she hastily donned it. Then she returned to her own room. As early as it was, Sibeal was awake, waiting to serve her.

Diana bit her lip. She had hoped that she would be able to slip into her bed unnoticed. "You needn't have gotten up so early," she chided softly.

" 'Tis no earlier than I usually get up," Sibeal said.

Diana nodded. "I hope you spent a restful night," she said lamely.

"Aye, I did."

Without further words, Sibeal went to the hearth and began to stoke the fire. Watching Sibeal, Diana expelled a long breath. She knew perfectly well that there was no chance of keeping a secret from a good servant; and Sibeal was one of the best.

"You think less of me for what I did?" she asked at last.

Sibeal shook her head and spoke truthfully. "Nay, m'lady." She put the poker aside and folded her hands in front of her. "You can do nothing that would make me think less of you."

"Ah, Sibeal." Diana passed a hand across her brow. "You deserve so much better than you have."

"And so do you, m'lady," Sibeal murmured softly.

Crossing the room, Sibeal was about to knock loudly on the door to summon the servants. To her surprise she found it unlocked. Turning to Diana, she said, "The earl allows you a great deal of freedom."

Diana averted her eyes. "I have given my word that I will not leave until the exchange is made."

Sibeal inclined her head in acceptance. There was nothing more to be said.

Stepping into the corridor, Sibeal collared

the nearest servant and instructed him to have water sent up for Diana's bath. In a short while, the tub was ready. Sibeal ushered the servants from the room, then assisted Diana into the warm water.

Diana paid no attention as Sibeal fussed over her. She was trying hard, without much success, to forget the night before. The arrogant lout had won his wager! She could not imagine what magic the man possessed to evoke such passionate responses from her! With a groan, Diana put a hand over her eyes, as if in so doing she could also blot out her memories.

Sooner or later she would have to face him. She would have to look into those knowing eyes and endure that mocking grin. The idea was galling, overshadowing for just a moment the shame she felt.

How could she have ever agreed to such a stupid challenge? She gritted her teeth. She had agreed because she had been confident that she could remain passive beneath those searing lips, that hot mouth of his that had traveled the length and breadth of her before the clock had even struck one!

Mother of God, she lamented silently as hot mortification swept color into her cheeks. Before the allotted time had gone by, she had indeed been the captive of the MacKendrick, in every sense of the word.

Sibeal approached and put a towel around Diana's shoulders as she at last emerged from the tub. After Sibeal toweled her dry, she dressed and went no farther than the nearest chair, where she sat, her back to the hearth to allow the heat to dry her hair. Then she heard Sibeal get into the tub to bathe.

By the time Sibeal got out of the tub and dressed again the temperature of the room had dropped noticeably. Outside, rain had begun to fall in a gentle drizzle that nonetheless gave a chill to the air. Sibeal closed the shutters and again stoked the fire, adding more peat until the room was comfortably warm.

"Och! 'Tis more like winter than spring on this day!" she exclaimed, brushing her hands.

Diana made no response as she sat thinking of Thorn. Even after Diana had left court, she had never forgotten the golden knight. One day, one brief encounter, had been seared into her mind, the image never fading, never diminishing.

Yet he was her enemy. And by God, she wished she could think of him as such! Ever since she had been a small girl she had been told that the MacKendricks were her enemies. Loyalty to her clan should have prompted her to plunge her dirk into the heart of her abductor at the first opportunity.

Her father, she knew, would have expected a vastly different mode of behavior from her under these trying circumstances. At the very least he would have expected her to resist. Instead, she was sleeping with her abductor of her own free will.

Had she resisted in a more aggressive manner, would he have taken her by force? Diana really could not answer that. Her resistance had been only token, at least in her own mind. Somehow, she sincerely doubted that Thorn would have forced her into their intimate relationship. Certainly he would have refrained from doing so last night. If she were correct in her assumption, then she knew she had betrayed her clan.

With her fingertips, Diana rubbed her forehead in an effort to banish her unwelcome musings. She had known that danger awaited her here in the stronghold of the golden knight. But never in her wildest dreams had she realized the form it would take. Harm to her body was a thing for which she had been prepared. Harm to her heart, to her very soul, was something she had not counted on. Agitated, she got to her feet and began to pace the room.

"I curse the day I went to that wood!" Diana cried out to Sibeal, who appeared startled by the sudden outburst after such a lengthy silence.

" 'Tis not pleasant, being a captive," Sibeal said cautiously.

Her hands clasped at her waist, Diana spun around to stare at Sibeal. " 'Tis not!" she exclaimed so vehemently it appeared that she was trying to convince herself.

"There's no argument you'll be getting from me," Sibeal murmured. She bit her lip. "Did he mistreat you, m'lady?"

Lost in her thoughts, Diana made no answer.

Her cheeks pink with anger, Sibeal got to her feet. "I will kill him when next I see him." Her calm voice was at odds with the proposed violence contained in her statement. "He will not be paying any attention to me, so 'twill be easy—"

Taken aback, Diana gaped at her maidservant. "What are you saying?"

Sibeal blinked. " 'Tis obvious to me that the earl has treated you badly."

"Och!" Diana sank back into her chair, fighting laughter that threatened to very soon turn into hysteria.

In an instant, Sibeal was at her side. Puzzled, she was nevertheless adamant. "You need only say the word, m'lady, and 'twill be done."

Diana clutched Sibeal's hand and brought it to her cheek. "You misunderstood me, lass," she said in a quiet voice. " 'Tis not the MacKendrick who is at fault."

Sibeal's green eyes widened in indignation. She was prepared to slay anyone Diana named. "Who then?"

Diana released Sibeal's hand. "Speak no more of killing," she admonished sternly. "There has been enough of that. I have not been mistreated. My agitation stems from the fact that the exchange is taking so long."

Sibeal nodded. "Aye. If it had been Lady Ellen who had been taken, the exchange would already have been made." Then her expression clouded with worry. "Your brother will hold you at fault, you know. He wanted the land, and he counted on the lad's capture in getting it for him. Instead—" She made a vague gesture.

"Instead, Robert is to get me! Don't you think I know that? Och!" Diana leaned back as if she were exhausted. "None of this would have happened if it hadn't been for that miserable pile of dirt!"

As the morning progressed, the light rain ceased. Gradually, the skies cleared. The sun was slanting to the west when the earl finally made an appearance.

Over plaid trews, his saffron tunic was belted at the waist. He strode into the room in his usual authoritative manner, nodding pleasantly to Sibeal, who quickly got up and dipped in a curtsy. He paused in front of the chair in which Diana was seated. Reaching out, he tenderly cupped her chin with his hand and tilted her face upward. For an instant, he stared at her with a devilish grin.

"You must have a wee bit of the sorceress in you, lass," he whispered.

"Why do you say that?" she asked breathlessly. Earlier misgivings faded away. Even as she deplored his touch, she was powerless against it.

"Because each time I gaze into your eyes I

183

find myself bewitched, caught in a spell I cannot seem to break."

With a slight smile, Diana deliberately closed her eyes. "There. Now you are released from the spell, my lord."

When his lips brushed Diana's chin, her eyes flew open. Staring at him, she searched her heart for the hate it should contain, did, at one time, contain. It was not there, and Diana refused to look at what was there in its stead.

Neither Thorn nor Diana noticed Sibeal; indeed, they both had forgotten her presence.

"You have not been out today," he said, looking at her with a warm smile.

In the soft light from the fire, Diana studied her captor. She liked the clean, sharp line of his jaw, the arrogant tilt of his chin, the uncompromising look in his eye.

Thorn was her enemy, she reminded herself. Why then did she feel this yearning to be held in his arms?

"It rained this morning," she said at last.

He looked puzzled. "Since when is the weather of concern to a Highlander?" When she did not answer, he grinned. "Well, 'tis not raining now," he said. He held out a hand. "Come. We will ride to the loch. If we are fortunate, the kelpies might favor us with their presence."

Chapter Nineteen

When the door closed behind her mistress and the Earl of Dunmoor, Sibeal's brow creased with worry. Kelpies, was it? She had heard of them, but never had she seen one. Then her gaze went uneasily to the window. In this god-forsaken spot, almost anything was possible.

Turning from the window, Sibeal sat down in a chair to await Diana's return. Sibeal had no difficulty in accepting the fact that her mistress was sleeping with the earl. When all was said and done, it was only prudent for a woman who was being held captive to make things as easy as possible for herself. To resist was to invite a beating. Sibeal knew that from experience. However, Diana's manner bespoke something more than acquiescence; and that worried Sibeal.

She put a hand to her breast, her heart suddenly heavy with apprehension. Surely her mistress could not be so foolish as to fall in the love with the one man she could not have! Then her mood lightened. You're the one who is being foolish, she silently chided herself. Of course her mistress was pretending. Pretending until the exchange was made, she decided, feeling easier in her mind.

Getting up, Sibeal busied herself by straightening the room.

Savory cooking odors were pervading the keep when Diana at last returned to her room. She smiled in pleased surprise when she saw Sibeal, who was attired in a woolen gown of forest green. Her hair, as always, was loose and brushed forward so that it fell in waves that effectively concealed the sides of her face.

"You look bonnie!" Diana exclaimed. "I've not seen that dress before."

"Grizel came while you were gone and told me that I could wear anything I found in that chest. But if you think 'tis not suitable—"

"Nay!" Diana said quickly. "It suits you well."

Hoisting her skirt, Sibeal displayed black velvet slippers. "Grizel said you mentioned my boots were worn. She could not find any to fit me, but she said I could wear these until a new pair can be made."

Seeing how pleased Sibeal was, Diana said, "I think I can persuade her to allow you to keep those, as well." Aware that her voice was breathless with the excitement of her day, Diana turned her mind to a more serious question. "When you left Sidhean, did Robert give any indication as to when the exchange would be made?"

Sibeal picked up a brush, and as Diana seated herself, she coaxed the black shining mass into soft curls. "He said the exchange would take place when he is ready and not before."

When Sibeal at last put the brush aside, Diana got up. "I don't suppose that Robert took it upon himself to visit the crofters in my absence?"

Sibeal shook her head. "Not to my knowledge." She reached out to pat a wayward curl on the top of Diana's head. "Nothing seems to be amiss though."

Sibeal selected a dress and assisted Diana into it before the evening meal. Diana viewed herself in the mirror with an unusually critical eye.

"Do you think the rose color makes me look pale?" she asked at last.

" 'Tis most becoming," Sibeal murmured, "if that's what you want to be."

Diana gave her maidservant a sharp look. "Of course I want to look my best! What woman would not?"

Sibeal shrugged. "Only a woman who does not want a man to think her beautiful and desirable."

With a sigh, Diana sat down on the bed. "I did not realize it was so obvious."

"You are not in love with him?"

Diana's head shot up. "Nay! What nonsense you speak, Sibeal."

Before Sibeal could say more, Diana hastily left the room. Watching her go, Sibeal drew a deep breath. So be it, she thought, as she followed Diana down to the great hall. In her mind, her mistress could do no wrong. Sibeal hadn't walked all those miles to contradict the woman who had saved her life.

On her way to the table a few minutes later, Sibeal found her way barred by one of the men-at-arms. From the way in which he was swaying from side to side, she correctly judged him to be drunk. Grinning at her, the man suddenly picked her up by her waist, swung her around, then set her on her feet again.

"Don't worry about your face, wench," he leered. "The rest of you is more than tempting!"

From out of nowhere, it seemed to Sibeal, a large fist landed on the man's jaw, knocking him to the rush-strewn floor.

"You will not be treating the lass like anything other than the lady she is!"

Sibeal gasped as she saw the ferocious countenance of the knight who had admitted her to this keep at the edge of the world. Even though he had defended her, she was unable to quell the fear that rose up in her breast. This was not a man to be crossed!

The fallen man winced as he stumbled to his feet, and he hastily muttered an apology to Sibeal. When the knight turned in her direction, she felt her muscles tighten in apprehension. She was fully prepared for him to blame her for what had just taken place. When his hand grasped her arm, Sibeal thought she might faint. But when he spoke, she detected a protective gentleness in his voice, one she had never before heard from a man.

"That will never happen again," he said in a firm voice. "I can assure you."

" 'Twas nothing to make a fuss over," Sibeal whispered in embarrassment as the man proceeded to escort her to the table.

" 'Twill be more than a fuss I'll be making if any man tries that again," he muttered. He waited until she was seated beside Diana; then he returned to sit with his men.

Diana gave Sibeal a playful poke. "Seems as though you have a champion."

Sibeal's face flamed. "He was only following the earl's orders."

"Rather enthusiastically, I'd say," Diana said, then changed the subject to other matters.

Chapter Twenty

The hour grew late, but no one would leave before the earl. And he seemed disinclined to move. Diana began to fidget. The hard seat was beginning to find every bone in her rump. More than once, she glanced in Thorn's direction. He seemed to be eating so slowly she was certain that minutes passed between each spoonful he put into his mouth!

Though she thought to speak to him, his demeanor prevented it. It was not anger. She knew that look well enough. It was preoccupation that had him in its grip.

Despite her weariness, a small smile etched her lips as she reached for her cup. Seldom had she spent a more enjoyable afternoon than she had this day. She and Thorn had gone to the loch. The kelpies, unpredictable as ever, had not shown themselves. But she and Thorn had sat patiently on the banks of the beautiful lake, waiting, talking, laughing—and making love.

Her smile vanished as she thought of the question she had earlier asked Sibeal as to when the exchange would be made. Diana was beginning to wonder what she wanted the answer to be.

Finally, when sleep was beckoning to her in a seductive invitation, Thorn got to his feet. Offering his arm to her, he escorted her from the hall. He did not lead her to her chambers; instead he took her directly to his own.

After he had closed the door, he smiled at her. "I have something to give to you," he said, sounding a bit mysterious.

Going to the desk, he opened a drawer, impatiently thrusting aside ledger books and spare quills until he found what he had been searching for.

Patiently, Diana waited. At last he walked toward her. At first glance, she saw nothing. Then he held out his hand.

"Once before I offered this to you," he said quietly. "Will you take it from me now?"

Speechless, she stared at the little tartan bow that so long ago had been torn from her skirt. She could not have been more surprised if he had plucked a star from the night sky and offered it to her. It still looked small within his large hand. This time, she picked it up.

"Why have you kept this?" she asked wonderingly.

"It reminded me of a bonnie lass I once met."

She took a breath. " 'Twas foolish of you to keep it!"

"Aye, a man sometimes does foolish things. Do you want it?"

Oh, God, she thought. This was impossible! "I do not want it!" She threw the bow into a corner. She expected to see a hurt look on Thorn's face; instead, she saw an angry one.

"If you do not want it, 'tis best to discard it."

So saying, he walked across the room, picked up the little bow, and threw it into the fire.

With a startled exclamation of dismay, Diana raced forward and plunged her hands into the flames. In an instant, Thorn was upon her. Roughly, he pulled her away from the hearth.

"What are you doing?" he exclaimed, sounding genuinely concerned. "If you wanted the frill, you could have taken it!"

Her eyes brimming with tears for which she could find no cause, Diana looked up at him. "If you wanted it, you would not have returned it!" she said in a small voice.

Thorn groaned and raked a hand through his hair. "Diana," he whispered, reaching for her, "I kept the little bow because it reminded me of you. Now that I can hold you in my arms, I no longer need the token of remembrance." He nuzzled her ear. "Do you understand me, lass?"

She did not answer as her arms went around

his neck. Once again, he held her close to him; once again, she could not draw away; and once again, her body responded to him with a fire she'd never known she possessed before she had met this man.

Chapter Twenty-one

In the courtyard the following morning, Sibeal watched as her mistress rode away with the Earl of Dunmoor. Their laughing faces said more to her than could any words. The feeling of worry that had plagued her the previous day returned in full force.

All during her long and arduous trek from Sidhean, Sibeal had been assailed with tormenting visions of how cruelly her mistress was being treated. There had even been, in the back of her mind, the possibility of assisting her to escape. Yet with her own eyes, she could see that not only was Lady Diana unafraid of the huge man who was her captor, but she seemed to seek out his company.

When the earl and Diana were at last out of

sight, Sibeal sighed and began to head back to the keep.

"Good morning to you, lass!"

Startled, Sibeal turned to see the knight striding toward her. Her cheeks grew warm as she remembered how he had come to her defense the night before. Save for the Lady Diana no one had ever done that before.

In front of her, he paused and gave a courtly bow. When he straightened up, he grinned at her. " 'Tis Angus MacKendrick at your service."

Murmuring a soft greeting, she studied the man who was standing before her. Though not as tall as the master of Rath na Iolair, Angus was an inch over six feet. Where his chief had the lean, long-legged look of elegance, Angus had the broad-shouldered, compact body of the warrior. His auburn hair, though tinged with gray, was thick and wavy. The ruggedness of his face was softened by brown eyes that were flecked with gold.

Recognizing the interest in those eyes, Sibeal was afraid. Unable to help herself, she feared all men, but most especially those who took an interest in her. Robert MacLaren's attentions were still vivid in her mind, and none of her memories were pleasant.

She stepped back, but if Angus noticed her withdrawal, he gave no indication. "Would you care to take a look around?" he asked congenially. " 'Twould be my pleasure to escort you, if you have no objection."

Sibeal darted a glance toward the open portcullis. "Maybe I should wait. When my lady returns, she might need me."

Angus passed a hand across his mouth. "I do not think they'll be back before noon."

Sibeal remained uncertain. It was true that this man had come to her defense; but what did she really know about him? He was a MacKendrick; that much she knew, but nothing else. She had known only one man, and that one against her will. Now, of course, no man would look at her, save to shudder in revulsion.

However, Angus was looking at her directly. And he was smiling as he waited for her answer. Nothing, she decided, awaited her inside the keep at this time except hours of solitude.

"Well, if you think I'll not be needed."

She was still uncertain, and Angus took her arm before she could make a further protest. For the next quarter of an hour, Angus led her around the bailey. Though she tried not to show it, Sibeal was impressed. The bailey here at Rath na Iolair was more pleasant than the one at Sidhean. The entire southeast corner had been given over to a garden with trees, stone benches, and flowers.

Angus explained that the garden had actually been here before the keep and that the stone walls had been built around it. Walking slowly, adjusting his long stride to hers, Angus began to lead her across the bridge.

On the far side, Sibeal paused. "I do not think

I should leave the keep."

"You're not a prisoner, lass," Angus noted quietly. "You came here of your own free will."

Sibeal nodded. "So I did," she said gravely. "Yet it might not be viewed kindly were I to leave without permission."

"You need have no fear," Angus said quickly. "Only one voice carries more weight at Rath na Iolair than mine."

Sibeal hid a smile. "That would be the earl's?" she ventured in mock seriousness.

"Only his," Angus said, and they began to walk down the path toward the Minch.

"You're a brave lass," Angus said to her after a while, "coming this distance all by yourself."

"You are not to think that!" Sibeal protested hastily, embarrassed by his assumptions.

He considered her statement, then shook his head in denial. "I would think twice about traveling that route alone on horseback, much less on foot. And once you got here, you could not have known what your reception would be. For all you knew, you could have been clapped into a dungeon the moment you set foot into the bailey."

"If that's where my lady was, I would have gladly joined her there."

Angus hesitated, then asked, "Will they not question your absence at Sidhean?"

She did not answer, and Angus pursued the matter no further. As they neared the rocky beach, he put his hand beneath her elbow.

" 'Tis slippery at low tide, lass. Watch your footing." He held her until they paused at the water's edge.

The far banks of the Minch, a broad body of water that was an extension of the North Sea, was on this day obscured by a heavy mist that rose and blended with low hanging clouds.

"The waters seem angry today," Angus said.

"Aye."

Turning, he studied her for a moment; then his hand moved to touch the hair revealed beneath her shawl. "My wife had the same color hair as you do."

Startled, Sibeal slapped his hand away. "I'm not your wife," she said sharply, "and don't be touching me as if I were!"

He drew back. "Surely you cannot take offense from an old man such as myself."

Sibeal saw and recognized the pain in his warm brown eyes. "You're not so old," she said in a softer tone, sorry that she had reacted so violently. He made no response, and after a moment, she asked, "Your wife is gone, is she?"

"Aye." His tone was a bit more reserved. "Some ten years now."

She looked at him in surprise. "You have never remarried?"

"I never found a woman I wanted to spend more than a night with," he replied simply.

"Was it an illness that took her?" she asked hesitantly.

He shook his head. "Nay. It happened whilst we were traveling to Edinburgh. Late one afternoon, we were set upon by brigands. Since we were fifty strong, I still cannot to this day understand why they were foolhardy enough to attack us. They were a band of less than twenty. All were slain. Only two of us were killed. Thorn's father and my Adele."

"You loved her?" she whispered.

He nodded. "Very much."

She bit her lip. "And I remind you of her?"

Angus tilted his head to the side. "At first, you did."

As her fingers went to her cheek, Angus reached out and took her hand. Slowly, he brought it to his lips and brushed an exquisitely tender kiss on her fingertip. With a gasp, Sibeal wrenched away.

They began to walk along the beach, the silence between them comfortable. At last, Angus halted and glanced up at the sky.

"We'd best be getting back. I think 'twill rain soon."

Sibeal nodded, but when he went to take her arm, she quickly drew away from him.

He frowned. "You're afraid of me, lass. Why? I mean you no harm."

Her chin rose. "Not till you get me in your bed!"

His frown deepened. "If you were in my

bed, 'twould only be because you wanted to be."

"You wouldn't want me," she said. "I am not a maiden."

Angus was quiet for a time; then he asked cautiously, "Do you want to tell me about it?"

"What do you want to hear?" Her tone was caustic. "That the Earl of Sidhean took me at his whim? Or that his wife used her dirk to leave her mark of displeasure on me?"

"At his whim?"

The intense manner in which the question was posed took Sibeal by surprise. " 'Twas not with my consent, if that's what you thought!"

He relaxed and his smile was broad. "Then you're still a maiden!" he declared emphatically.

Sibeal halted, gaping at him. She had never known a man who did not prize a woman's virginity above all else. His attitude was one that she had never before encountered.

"You're a strange man, Angus Mac-Kendrick," she said at last.

Throwing back his head, he laughed. "Nay, 'tis only the men you have known who are strange, lass."

Sibeal and Angus returned to the courtyard just in time to see Diana and Thorn return. In some bemusement, Sibeal noted the flushed and smiling face of her mistress as the earl assisted her from her horse. She had never seen

Diana so radiant. She looked like a woman in—

Sibeal put her fingertips to her lips. Och, no! she thought in dismay. The fates would not be so cruel.

Chapter Twenty-two

From her window on this late cloudy afternoon Diana viewed the activity in the courtyard below. Grooms and stableboys were diligently tending to a group of horses, providing them with food and water, and she saw Angus walking about, issuing orders that were instantly obeyed.

The morning before, unexpected guests had descended upon Rath na Iolair in the form of the Clan Carmichael, long friends and allies of the MacKendricks. With them, they brought minstrels and bards from Inverness. Greeting his visitors with genuine affection, Thorn had declared their stay to be a time of festivity.

Diana turned from the window when Sibeal entered the room. The servant's face was flushed with excitement.

"Och! And you should see the preparations going on this day!" she exclaimed. " 'Twill be a feast the likes of which I've never seen! Capons and fish. Venison and boar! There's no room on the spits, either in the kitchen or the great hall."

Diana smiled at Sibeal's show of enthusiasm. "I should have known that you would be visiting the kitchen sooner or later."

"They have three kilns!" Sibeal said in a breathless state of wonder. "The bread alone would feed an army. And the tapers—" She paused to catch her breath.

Diana raised her brow and laughed. "Now what could possibly be so unusual about tapers?"

"Cook told me they're of the finest beeswax in all of Scotland," Sibeal confided. "Not even the king has any finer!"

"Well, now," Diana commented when Sibeal was through, "if I am to witness these wonders, I'd best be getting dressed."

With a quick step, Sibeal went to fetch Diana's gown, and as she assisted her mistress, Sibeal murmured, "M'lady, I'll not be required to assist the men in their baths, will I?"

Diana glanced at Sibeal in surprise. "Whatever gave you that idea?"

Her maidservant moistened her lips. "Well, it seems that every room in the keep is occupied, what with the Carmichaels and all. And I heard one of the maidservants saying they were short-handed. There's not enough of them to go around."

Dressed now, Diana patted Sibeal's shoulder. "You'll not be assisting anyone in the bath but me!" she said firmly. She gave the lass a gentle push. "Get dressed now. We do not want to be late."

While Sibeal was thus engaged, Diana went to the looking glass and fussed with her hair. Though the evening meal had not yet begun, she could hear music and laughter from below stairs. Satisfied, she at last stepped back to look at herself.

Her gown, one of Lady Catherine's, was of heavy satin. The color of apricots, it had wide, elbow-length sleeves trimmed with a band of sable. The full skirt was gathered up on one side to reveal a black lace underskirt. A girdle of silver mesh encircled her narrow waist. In honor of the occasion, Sibeal was also to wear one of Catherine's dresses, which Diana had helped her alter.

Diana turned away from the mirror casually glancing at Sibeal. Having finished dressing in the modest pale green silk the lass was warming her hands at the hearth. Diana smiled, thinking how pretty Sibeal looked in her finery, her slim body silhouetted by the glow of the fire.

Suddenly, Diana's smile vanished. The blood drained from her face, and she felt as though her legs would no longer support her. Sibeal was speaking; Diana knew that because she could see her lips moving. Diana stiffened, hearing nothing over the drumming in her ears.

The fire seemed to leap out to encircle Sibeal. Round and round the flames went, burning ribbons that seemed to engulf her from head to toe. With a cry of terror, Diana reached for her.

"What is it?" Sibeal's voice sounded alarmed.

Making no response, Diana stared as the flames seemed to uncoil and recede back into the hearth.

"M'lady?" Sibeal's voice was shrill.

Diana's hand shot out to grab Sibeal's arm. "Step back from the fire!" she admonished sharply. In answer to Sibeal's bewildered expression, she added in a sheepish tone, "You were too close, lass. Your skirt—"

Diana was still shaken when they entered the great hall a few minutes later. She made a conscious effort to shut out the image she had seen. It could not be true. She would not allow it to be true.

Foolish, anyway, she told herself. What she had seen had not been a building or even a room ablaze. And there could be no other way in which flames could consume Sibeal. Most likely what Diana had seen had been symbolic, she thought, at last relaxing.

Feeling reassured by her own reasoning, Diana leaned back in her chair and listened with enjoyment as the minstrels played. Some time after that, a veritable parade of servants trooped into the hall, each carrying huge platters of food. While the guests availed themselves of the magnificent repast, bards related tales of true love.

Diana listened with only half an ear. Why, she wondered as she nibbled on a piece of venison, was love so elusive? She thought of the suitors who had approached first her father, then her brother—the latest and most persistent of whom was Donald Campbell.

Not one of them had provoked so much as a feeling of affection within her. The touch of their lips on her hand as they greeted her had produced, at best, no feeling at all or, in the case of Donald, ripples of revulsion that actually made her flesh crawl.

Washing her hands, Diana reached for her wine goblet, her eyes straying to Thorn. On this night, he was dressed as elegantly as any lord she had ever seen. Over a tartan kilt he wore a fitted dark green velvet jacket. A silver brooch emblazoned with the MacKendrick crest was affixed to the baldric that was positioned diagonally across his broad chest. The leather sporran he wore around his lean waist was encrusted with gems, as was the hilt of his dress sword.

But it was not the finery of his clothes that projected the image he conveyed of the authority and strength of a born leader. Her gaze lowered to view one of his powerful hands, wrapped around his tankard. A small shiver flared through her as she remembered that hand caressing her. The touch of this man caused no revulsion; nor could she say that it left her unmoved. Desire awakened within her each time he came close enough to her that she could feel the warmth of his huge body.

But love? No, she thought as she averted her eyes from the man she found so difficult to eject from her thoughts. She must never confuse desire with love, she told herself sternly. The examples set by her brother and even by her own father had clearly demonstrated that lust was a transitory emotion.

Of course, Diana thought wryly, accepting a sweet tart from a passing servant, no one had ever told her that a woman could also be subject to such fiery emotions. If she were to be honest with herself—and she was seldom otherwise—she had to confess that this man had captured her imagination from the first time she had laid eyes upon him.

Under different circumstances, Diana had to further confess to herself, she would have had little problem falling in love with him. He appealed to her as did no other man. Alas, circumstances were not different. In fact, right then, they seemed insurmountable.

When the lavish meal at last came to an end, the party began in earnest. Pipes skirled, and men from both clans now vied with each other in displaying their skill at the many colorful dances native to the area. Even Thorn took the floor, and Diana watched in amusement and admiration as he effortlessly executed the intricate steps to a spirited Highland fling. The skirling of the pipes grew particularly enthusiastic as the dance concluded. A moment later Thorn came to sit at her side.

"I had no idea you were so talented, my lord," Diana said with a smile.

Despite the exertion, he was not even out of breath. Only a tousled curl on his forehead suggested that he had been doing anything more strenuous than lifting his tankard.

"Och, lass!" He winked at her. "There's more to me than meets the eye."

At that moment, a white-haired man approached Thorn. Reluctantly, he turned from Diana to speak to the chief of Carmichaels.

She took the moment to let her gaze travel the room. The smile faded from her lips as she spied Angus heading in Sibeal's direction. She noted how casually—and how carefully—the knight positioned himself beside Sibeal at the table. While she could not hear the words he spoke, she could easily see the flush that crept up Sibeal's cheeks as she eagerly turned toward him.

Noting the unusually animated expression in the green eyes of her maidservant, Diana sighed. She was not unaware of the knight's interest. And it was just as obvious that Sibeal, whether she would admit to it or not, was beginning to return that interest. Not that anything could come of it, Diana reflected gloomily. Any more than could come of her own affair with the Earl of Dunmoor.

Diana turned away. Ah, Sibeal, she thought as she drank her wine, do not make the mistakes that I have made. She knew that Sibeal's heart, even more than her own, was vulnerable. Lost in her thoughts, Diana gave a start at the sound of Thorn's voice.

"Is something wrong?" he asked, reaching for her hand. "A moment ago you were smiling. And now you appear pensive. Unless," he teased, " 'twas my absence that caused your smile to go away?"

"I'm sorry," she said, trying without success to summon back the smile. "I did not mean to appear grim."

He chuckled and, taking advantage of the growing noise level, put his lips close to her ear. " 'Tis my opinion," he whispered huskily, "that on your face even grim looks lovely. 'Twould be a lie upon my tongue if I said I had ever seen a woman I desire more than the one who sits before me now."

Feeling his warm breath, Diana shuddered. Matters were taking a turn for the worse, she realized in some dismay. Not only was his touch affecting her, even the husky timber of his voice was setting off tremors deep inside her.

Thorn's voice fell to a whisper. "Tonight, I would request your company, my lady."

A slow smile came to her lips, but her eyes smarted with unshed tears. "You request, my lord?" Her voice held disbelief. With his nod, her voice turned teasing. "And if I refuse?" He could not know that she was fast approaching the point where there was nothing she could refuse him.

He assumed a crestfallen look. " 'Twould be a sad ending to a most happy day." He squeezed her hand. "What say you, my lady? Will you favor me with your company?"

Diana took a sip of her wine and made a show of considering the invitation. "And if I decline, will you come storming into my room to claim what you seem to think is rightfully yours?"

He grew serious. "Nay, not on this night. On this night, I would have you come to me only because it is your wish to do so."

She pursed her lips. "I will think on it, my lord," she said softly.

To Diana's surprise, he got up and left the hall without so much as a backward glance in her direction. Feeling a bit foolish, she continued to sit at the table. No one was paying any attention to her, not even, she noted with some amusement, Sibeal.

Most of the guests were by then in their cups; noise and confusion were pronounced. Diana felt certain that Thorn's departure had not even been noticed. A small smile played about her lips. Probably hers would not be noticed either. Getting up, she made her way from the great hall. No one gave her a second glance. Moments later, she knocked softly on Thorn's door. It opened immediately.

He was still dressed, and sweeping her a courtly bow, he said, "I am the most favored of men, my lady. 'Tis most pleased I am that you have accepted my invitation."

" 'Twould have been churlish of me to ignore such a nicely put invitation, my lord," she answered in the same light tone that he had used.

As she came into the room, her step faltered when she saw the cast-iron tub filled with warm water.

A maidservant, in the process of draping a linen cloth over the rim, hastily withdrew when Thorn made a gesture of dismissal.

A mixture of anger and disappointment prompted her to cast an accusing look at him. Was he expecting her to once again act in the capacity of a servant? To scrub his back? Mayhap he had not learned his lesson the last time.

Thorn stepped closer, and his arms encircled her. As if mesmerized, Diana made no move to pull away. His kiss sent her spiraling into an abyss of emotion that recalled the exquisite pleasure he always seemed to arouse within her. His tongue, tasting of sweet wine, began to explore the softness of her mouth, teasing and tantalizing her with its seductive movements. When he at last drew back, Diana took a deep breath in an effort to calm the rapid pounding of her heart.

Looking down at her, Thorn spoke in a husky

voice. "On that first night we were together, I disrobed you."

"And none too gently!" she said with a nervous laugh, wondering why he was reminding her of that.

"Tonight," he said in the same tone, "I would like to see you disrobe yourself—slowly."

Feeling a stab of shock, Diana allowed her eyes to widen. What was he about now? "I have never—"

"Disrobed?" He smiled, and his thumb gently caressed her cheek. "You are more lovely than any woman I have ever seen," he whispered. "Every inch of your body is perfection." He released her. Removing everything but his breeks he sat down in a chair.

Diana's nervousness grew more pronounced as he stared at her. What exactly did he expect her to do? she wondered. Her instinct was to turn her back to him. But somehow she knew he would object to that show of modesty. Yet, undressing in front of a man whose eyes were already devouring her was positively unnerving!

"You may begin now."

His tone held an authority that, for once, Diana dared not question. Her fingers were clumsy as she began to fumble with ribbons and laces. She knew her cheeks were flushed, though whether from embarrassment or excitement, she couldn't tell.

"Slowly!" he commanded. "Perfection should not be viewed in haste."

Caught up in the novelty of the moment, she divested herself of the apricot gown, her movements deliberate and unhurried. In the same measured way, she stepped out of the black lace underskirt. Then, with one hand resting on the back of a chair, she took off one of her slippers. Hesitating a moment, she playfully threw it at Thorn, who caught it in one hand. The other slipper followed.

The smile on his face faded as she now slowly pulled her chemise up over her head, then carelessly dropped it to the floor. He sat very quietly as his eyes traveled the length of her. Getting up, he went toward her, his eyes still devouring her. His hands cupped her buttocks, and he pulled her close against his hard body.

Diana whimpered as her arms went around his neck. She raised her lips to meet his, but instead of kissing her, Thorn picked her up in his arms. Crossing the room, he deposited her in the tub. Soaping his hands while she watched him in bewilderment, he placed them on her shoulders, then moved down her arms to her fingers.

"Relax, my lady," he whispered. "Tonight, I am your servant."

His hands cupped her breasts, sliding easily over their surface before encircling her rib cage and working down to her waist. Her eyes closed as her thighs were molded by those strong hands. But she did not believe what he said. Thornton MacKendrick was servant to no man! Her eyes flew open as he lifted her out of the tub, and once again she felt herself pressed against his muscular body.

His hands buried themselves in her tresses, and the kiss he bestowed upon her made her head swim. When it ended, his lips began to travel the path his hands had previously explored in the tub. On his knees before her, his mouth tasted deeply of her womanhood, causing her to cry out as a delicious heat suffused her body.

Just when she thought her legs would no longer support her, he again picked her up. This time her resting place was on the fur robe before the hearth. She felt the heat on her body, but was uncertain as to whether it came from the fire in the hearth or the fire that inflamed her blood. Her nails sank into his broad shoulders as she drew him to her. When he entered her, Diana moaned in delicious anticipation of what lie ahead.

"Hurry!" she cried out, moving her body at a quicker pace in an effort to force him to quicken his tempo.

"Nay," he whispered in her ear and maintained the same, maddeningly slow thrusts.

As she clung to him, the first wave of pleasure took her by surprise and caused her to stiffen. Thorn's pace began to quicken, causing yet another spasm of ecstasy to engulf her. When

Thorn at last found his own release, he paused, still inside her. Raising himself up on his elbows, he looked down at her.

She gazed back at him. Incongruously, her thoughts settled on something she had said to him on the night they had supper in her room. "Robert will answer in his own good time," she had said.

And how long would that take? she wondered, suddenly uneasy. Her hand went to Thorn's cheek, then slipped down to his powerful shoulder, which was as damp and warm as she knew her own flesh was. Would he answer soon enough? Or would his answer arrive when she would no longer want to leave?

Chapter Twenty-three

On the banks of Loch Maree, Thorn brushed a light kiss across Diana's brow. Both naked, they were lying on her arisaid with his plaid partially draped over them.

The late May day was calm and the sun warm. Diana pushed the plaid aside. Her arms over her head, she stretched like a contented cat, feeling the sun's warmth caress her body.

Raised up on his elbow, Thorn watched her. "Why is it," he murmured, "that I never tire of looking at you?"

His hand moved to her breast, and he kneaded it gently. His thumb brushed her nipple, and it grew taut.

"Umm." She felt too languid even to move.

Bending forward, Thorn suckled the taut nipple. His action elicited a gasp from her, and she entwined her fingers in his thick wavy hair. Then his hand crept between her thighs, and the languor fled as her breath quickened. She parted her legs to receive him, but he stretched out on his back and pulled her on top of him.

" 'Tis not fair that I do all the work," he said huskily.

Startled at first, she grinned down at him. " 'Tis not."

Placing a knee on either side of his lean hips, she grasped his hardened member and guided it inside her. Her movements at first unsteady, she quickly caught the rhythm and reveled in the freedom it gave her. Bending forward slightly, she placed her hands, palms down, on either side of his chest and moved slowly, enjoying the pulsing length within her. She tightened her muscles, and Thorn groaned. He grasped her buttocks, but she would not be hurried.

She looked down at him, and her hair fell forward to caress his cheeks. His hands feverishly played about her breasts, and knowing her climax was near, she increased her pace, grinding her hips in a frenzied motion. Release came to them both at the same time. Exhausted, Diana fell forward, her breasts flattened against his broad chest.

For a time, they rested, until at last Diana rolled off him to lie at his side. In only moments, sleep claimed them both.

Diana awoke to birdsong some 30 minutes

later. Thorn was awake, his arm protectively around her. With a sigh, Diana snuggled closer, her fingertips toying with the soft hair on his chest.

"I have decided that I like this coupling of a man and woman," she announced, planting a feathery kiss on one of his nipples.

His arm tightened about her. "Have you? I hope I had something to do with your decision," he murmured.

"Umm." Raising her head, she gently bit his lower lip, an action she had learned from him. "You had everything to do with it, my lord," she agreed with a soft laugh.

For that, Diana was rewarded with a deep, lingering kiss. When Thorn drew back they both stared into each other's eyes for a long moment. Unspoken, forbidden words suddenly thickened the air like an approaching thunderstorm. For the first time, the silence between them was awkward.

Moistening her lips, Diana sat up. Her hands shook as she threaded her fingers through her hair. In an effort to lighten the sudden tension, she gave a nervous laugh. "Of course, when your brother is released and I return home—"

The rest of her words died in her throat as Thorn sat up abruptly.

"Get dressed! We have been gone too long as it is. Mayhap word has come, and I was not there to receive it," he said brusquely.

Without looking at her, he hurriedly began to

put on his clothes. Hurt by his tone, Diana did as she was told. Her hands were clumsy as they fumbled with ribbons and ties. But in vain, she waited for assistance.

As Thorn and Diana were making their way back to the keep, Sibeal was leaving it. She hummed a little tune as she hurried down the path toward the Minch. She had taken to meeting Angus there several times a week. A warrior by trade, Angus was a fisherman at heart. He had been taking her out in the small wooden boat he used when the weather permitted.

Gradually, Sibeal was finding a peace of mind that she had thought was gone forever. She was so used to skulking about the halls of Sidhean, fearful that she would come upon the earl or his wife, that at first she had found it difficult to move about with the freedom she had found here at Rath na Iolair. The feeling was akin to having been released from prison.

In the grip of this newfound contentment, Sibeal took note of a cluster of delicate crocuses and snapdragons. Pausing, she bent down to touch a fragile petal. Had they been so beautiful before? She thought not. Surely this was an unusual spring.

Straightening, she continued on her way. He was there, at the shore, when she arrived. His back to her, his hands were on his hips as he stared out across the choppy waters. Against the backdrop of a mist-laden sky, a sea gull screeched, swooping gracefully down to the surface of the water in an unsuccessful attempt to snare a fish. Sibeal's heart sank, for she could see at a glance that it was too rough to put the boat in the water.

Coming to his side, she asked plaintively, "We'll not be able to go out today, will we?"

His hand cupped her chin. How warm it felt on her cool skin. She no longer flinched from his touch. Only in Diana's company was she more at ease.

"Not unless you want to see us in the water instead of on it." His hand released her, and he pointed. "Look there. Have you ever seen the likes of it?"

Her glance followed his, and she caught her breath. Arcing across the far shoreline was the hugest rainbow she had ever seen.

"You should make a wish," Angus urged. " 'Tis said the larger the rainbow, the more likely 'twill be granted. And from the size of that one, 'tis certain to come true."

Though he spoke jovially, Sibeal answered in a serious tone. "I've nothing to wish for."

"Och!" he exclaimed with a laugh. "Everyone has something, lass."

"What would you wish for?"

"True love," he answered without hesitation. " 'Tis as rare as white heather, and just as elusive for a man to find."

"I do not believe either exists," Sibeal declared flatly.

He raised his brow, and the corners of his mouth turned up. "Don't you?"

"I've never seen white heather," she remarked in the same toneless voice. Nor true love, she thought with an inner sigh.

"I'll admit 'tis hard to find. But then a man has to be diligent if he hopes to find anything that is rare."

She studied him a moment, curiosity getting the better of her. She had heard of white heather, but she had never seen it. Good luck came to those who found the oddity. "You've found the white heather?"

He nodded. "Aye, once." He stared at her a long moment before adding, "I hope to, once again."

Without warning, his lips brushed her cheek. Before she could react, he straightened, then grinned at her. "I hope that just because I stole a kiss you will not be thinking 'tis my intention to get you in my bed, unless"—he cleared his throat—"you would be willing to give it a try."

Her reply was swift. "Nay!"

He laughed softly. "Ah, lass. Someone's not treated you with the gentleness you deserve."

She made a face, and her tone was prim. "And you will not be the first!"

Reaching out, he placed his hands on her shoulders. Bending his head, he gazed deeply into her eyes. "I'd never do anything against your will, lass. Will you believe me when I say it?"

Sibeal sniffed, but made no move to step away from him. "You could take me here and now," she noted, "and no one would call you to task!"

"Aye." His hands fell away. "But I'll not do it."

It took several seconds before she realized that he meant what he said. In a casual manner that not even Sibeal could find fault with, Angus took her hand as they walked back to the keep.

Chapter Twenty-four

Just before the evening meal, to the surprise of both Diana and Sibeal, Thorn entered their room, looking as somber as either woman had ever seen him.

"Please leave us, Sibeal," he ordered in an unusually curt voice. "You may go downstairs to take your meal now."

When Sibeal quickly left, Diana laughed nervously. "Am I then to be deprived of my supper?" she teased, sitting by the fire.

No answering smile greeted her words. "A messenger has come."

A long moment passed before Diana asked, "What was said?"

"The exchange will be made."

"As it should be," she murmured. Flames

danced within dark corners, and she watched the shadowplay.

"Aye," he agreed quietly. "It could be no other way."

Diana clasped her hands with such force, her knuckles whitened. Oh, but it could! her heart cried out. If you would never let me go, I'd never leave you!

She never said the words; nor did she look at him, afraid that her eyes would betray her thoughts. It was beyond Thorn to allow his young brother to suffer. She could ask, but she did not want to know the answer. There was no answer, after all.

"When will the exchange be made?" Diana was surprised at how calm her voice sounded. Inside, she felt as if her heart had died. It would continue to beat. But no emotion would henceforth propel its lifegiving motion.

"They will arrive sometime tomorrow," he answered without looking at her.

How emotionlessly he said that, she thought. No doubt he had been waiting for this distasteful business to be concluded. Her tone matched his as she said, "I will be ready."

She rose from her chair, her languid movements suggesting she might have been in a trance. In a way, she was, for she could see nothing but his face. Her steps were measured as she drew closer. Slowly, her hand raised to caress his cheek. But he drew away, and she saw his controlled look, his grim mouth, his shuttered eyes. All bespoke withdrawal. Her one gesture of submission had been denied. There would be no other.

The evening meal was subdued, unrelieved by the skirling of pipes or the usual bawdy witticisms exchanged between the men. Thorn noticed that all spoke in hushed tones, taking their cue from his somber demeanor. Side by side, he and Diana ate in silence.

Though he had been resisting it, he at last turned to look at her, seeing her profile, for she was staring straight ahead.

How odd that he had never before noticed that her features were so perfectly sculpted. Nothing was out of line. He was viewing perfection; and the loss was suddenly too much for him to bear.

Feeling helpless, he turned away, fearing that emotion would override logic. He could not let her go! Yet he could not consign Ian to the death that would surely be his if he refused the exchange.

His mind skimmed back over the years. Unlike almost every lad and young man he had known, Thornton MacKendrick had seldom looked twice at a woman. He loved them all and that was the problem. Never was he able to stay with one for more than a few months before his interest waned and his eye strayed. To him, women were like a bouquet of flowers. Lovely, delicate, and precious, they were to be admired and loved during their season.

He stifled the wry laugh that forced its way into his throat. It appeared that he had fallen in love not with a rose, but with the thorn that decorated its fragile structure. A man did not remove an embedded thorn as easily as he threw away a flower.

He groaned, unaware that Diana had turned to look at him. Och, lass, he thought to himself. You've found your way into my heart, and that I will never let you know. 'Tis the only weapon you would need to be my undoing.

When the tedious affair was at last at an end, he retired to his chambers, where he paced the floor like a caged animal; indeed he felt like one.

Tomorrow he would have to send Diana away; and the thought wrenched his heart. How could he release the woman who had become so important to him? And how long would it take to forget?

Pausing, he glanced at the door that separated their rooms. For the first time since she had come to Rath na Iolair, he had bolted his door. There was nothing he wanted more than to hold her in his arms once again, to make love to her, to taste the sweetness of her. And if he did, he knew he would never let her go. What would become of Ian then?

Oh, sweet Christ, he thought as he sat down on the bed. His elbows on his knees, he put his face in his hands. Even though he hated to admit it, he confessed to himself that had Ian been older and sturdier, he might actually have tried to keep Diana here.

The knock on the door caused him to raise his head. At first, he thought it had come from Diana's door. Then he realized it came from the door that led to the hall. He stood up and bid the visitor to enter.

Grizel bustled in, followed by a maidservant carrying a tray. "You hardly touched your supper," she scolded.

He inspected the tray. In addition to cold meat and bread there was a full decanter of whiskey. He looked at Grizel, and in her eyes he saw awareness of his own troubled state of mind. Not for the first time he wondered how this woman always seemed to sense his needs. The maidservant, having deposited food and drink on the table was looking at him with an adoring smile.

"Thank you, lass," he said with a brief nod. "That will be all."

She dipped a curtsy. "You're welcome, m'lord. If there's anything else you want, you need only send for me."

When the girl left, Grizel poured some of the whiskey into a cup and handed it to him. "It can be no other way." Though her tone was brisk, her black eyes offered sympathy. "If you weaken, Ian will die."

Thorn took the proffered cup and stared into the amber liquid for a moment; then he downed it in one long swallow.

*   *   *

In the adjoining room, Diana was too restless even to attempt sleep. She knew the door was barred. She had tried the handle and found it locked. So, she realized dully, Thornton MacKendrick was done with her. Having gotten what he wanted, he no longer had any use for her.

She heard voices and knew that he was not alone. One of the voices she was certain had been that of a young female. One of his adoring maidservants no doubt, she thought bitterly.

Diana moved away from the door. She'd be damned if she would lower her pride and knock on his door!

So be it. From this moment on, she would pluck every thought of Thornton MacKendrick from her mind. If he could so easily shut her out of his life, she would do no less.

"You must get some rest," Sibeal urged. " 'Twill be a long ride tomorrow."

"I am not yet ready," Diana replied as she headed for the door. "I feel the need for fresh air and solitude," she said as Sibeal made ready to join her.

In the bailey a few minutes later, Diana halted uncertainly. She had had no destination in mind when she left her room. She had only felt the need to be alone.

Aimlessly, she walked, at last ascending the stone steps that led to the ramparts. The guard eyed her curiously, but did not bar her way. Her hands resting on the stone wall, she gazed ahead of her. In the valley below, the fog was thick, giving her the illusion that Rath na Iolair had suddenly been set atop the clouds.

Some minutes later, Diana turned to see a figure heading in her direction. Too small for a man, she at first thought it was Sibeal, then realized it was Grizel.

Diana's smile was grim as the woman came to stand at her side. "Are you here to make certain that I do not escape at the last moment?"

Grizel sniffed. "You could have left long ago if you had been of a mind to do so."

"I gave my word!" Diana was upset with the observation. "You know that as well as I do!"

"Aye."

Diana laughed shortly. "Then mayhap you think I am going to jump."

"That time, too, has come and gone."

"Then why are you here?" Diana demanded, growing annoyed. She wanted to be alone with her thoughts. Though, God knew, few of them were pleasant.

" 'Tis it so unusual that I would bid you good-bye and Godspeed?"

Diana was so surprised that for the moment she could not speak. "Aye," she said at last, " 'tis unusual."

"We are not so different, after all. Would you not agree?" the old woman asked.

Diana shifted uncomfortably. When she had first been abducted she had hated every

MacKendrick in Scotland. They were, she had thought, untrustworthy, vengeful, illiterate, unfeeling barbarians. The list went on and on. But one by one, her misconceptions had toppled like little toy soldiers beneath the willful hand of a child.

"You have been kind to me," Diana allowed finally, feeling the need to speak the words. "You could have made my stay most uncomfortable if you had chosen to do so."

"More than you know." Grizel chuckled. Then she sobered. "You will return to Sidhean to be betrothed."

Diana's head spun in Grizel's direction. She could not see her face in the shadows. "Nay!"

The old woman continued as if she had not spoken. "And you will agree to that betrothal."

A chill colder than the fog and dampness that it brought with it wended its way down Diana's spine. Turning away, she looked out upon the shrouded landscape. It appeared to her like her own future.

She did not question Grizel. Who would? she wondered, swallowing against the hysterical laugh that gathered in her throat. And she did not question the woman because she did not want to know the answer. Of course, she told herself, a trifle cynically, it was a safe prediction. Woman did, eventually, marry.

Below them, the fog swirled, as if seeking a hiding place.

At last Diana turned again to Grizel. "Have

you ever been married?" she asked tentatively, realizing how little she knew of this enigmatic woman.

"Nay, I've never been wed," Grizel said. Diana's surprise must have been evident, for Grizel went on to explain. "When I was sixteen, I was in love with a man. Conall was his name. Och, a bonnie lad he was. We were betrothed. Then he was killed in a raid. After that, my eyes never strayed to another man. 'Tis like that for some women." She looked at Diana, who was quick to avert her gaze. "Aye, for some women there is only one man. 'Twas like that for me. I have an idea that you are the same way, lass. 'Twould be a mistake to fight it."

Without waiting for a reply, Grizel walked away and in only seconds seemed to blend with the night. Shaken, Diana continued to stand there for many minutes until, at last, she made her way back to her chambers.

Sibeal had not retired. As always, she was waiting patiently for Diana's return. Feeling contrite, Diana viewed Sibeal's anxious face and realized that the girl herself would not rest until she saw her settled. Obediently, Diana went to bed, divested herself of her clothes and crawled beneath the warm furs.

Long after Sibeal had fallen asleep, Diana remained wide awake, staring without seeing into the shifting flames of the fire that burned in the hearth.

Chapter Twenty-five

Not having slept at all, Thorn was on the ramparts at first light. His eyes searched the mist-shrouded glen for the approaching MacLarens. Word of their imminent arrival had come in the form of an outrider more than an hour ago. Hearing footsteps, he turned to see Angus climbing the steep narrow steps.

"Do you see them?" his cousin inquired, coming to stand beside him.

"Not yet," Thorn answered.

Angus peered as if to justify the observation. Satisfied, he again faced Thorn. "The men are ready."

His nerves frayed, Thorn gestured to his second-in-command. "If one man so much as moves to let loose an arrow, I will slay him with my own hands!"

"Rest easy, Thorn." Angus gripped Thorn's arm. "Nothing will go amiss. There's not a man here who would put Ian's life in jeopardy."

Thorn sighed. "You are right, of course. 'Tis just that—"

He broke off as he saw the group of riders emerging from the cover of trees. A quick glance told him that they numbered no more than fifty. In silence Thorn studied the wooded area for a minute; then he nodded to himself when he saw no signal. He knew Angus had deployed two of his men within the leafy branches of a tree and had instructed them to raise an alarm in the event that the Earl of Sidhean chose to conceal a portion of his men until Rath na Iolair's defenses were lowered.

" 'Tis an acceptable escort," Angus murmured.

Thorn, however, was edgy. "Do not raise the portcullis until I give the signal."

"Aye," Angus responded as he went back down the steps.

Anticipation of seeing Ian battled with deeper emotions Thorn did not now want to face. Deliberately, he cleared his mind of all thoughts and stood there stoically as the men-at-arms led by Robert MacLaren approached the keep. They paused before they reached the drawbridge, but they were within hailing distance.

As Thorn watched, he saw the Earl of Sidhean nudge his mount a few steps forward. Although a coat of mail covered his short-sleeved tunic, Robert wore no other armor. His plaid, secured by the usual brooch, was thrown back from his shoulders and fell in graceful folds across the rump of his horse. He wore no head covering, and his red hair was tousled by the ever present breeze.

Thorn noted that although Robert's men kept their swords sheathed, they were as eager for battle as his own men. He had, however, given strict orders that no man was to let loose an arrow unless he gave the command. And he was not a man who dealt lightly with disobedience.

"I would see my sister, MacKendrick!" Robert shouted, staring up at him. "The lad will not be released until I am assured that she is unharmed."

Thorn's eyes went to the slight figure on the horse just behind Robert. Ian's head was bowed, his shoulders slumped, and Thorn frowned.

Just then, Ian raised his head, and Thorn breathed a sigh of relief. The lad appeared to be all right.

Thorn did not trust himself to do the simple task he delegated to Angus. "Fetch the women!" he called down.

A few minutes later Angus appeared in Diana's chambers.

"Your brother is waiting just across the bridge," Angus said quietly. His eyes went to

Sibeal, but she was standing with her head lowered.

Diana did not have to be told this news. She had observed the approaching men from her window. She had hoped that Thorn would come for her. Instead, he had sent his cousin. From the moment word had been received of the exchange, Thorn had absented himself. She supposed she should be grateful that he had taken the time to inform her in the first place. That, too, could have been easily handled by a lackey.

She looked at Angus. If she needed to be convinced that the Earl of Dunmoor was glad to rid himself of his troublesome captive, she now had proof of it.

"I am ready," Diana said in a low voice.

Without waiting for Angus to respond, she walked quickly past him. Dressed in the tan chamois outfit she had arrived in, she carried nothing. She would leave as she had come: empty-handed. When she emerged into the courtyard, her horse was waiting patiently. Standing beside Banrigh, Richard was viewing her with sorrowful eyes.

"Thank you again, Richard," she whispered.

Taking the reins from the young groom, she began to walk toward the portcullis, which was at this time being raised. Looking up, she saw Thorn standing on the ramparts. For a long moment, they stared at each other, their eyes saying things they dared not speak. When the massive iron contrivance was raised, Diana stepped forward so that she was in plain view. Pausing, she raised her arm to indicate her well-being.

Behind Diana, Angus stepped closer to Sibeal.

"You could stay," he whispered to her.

Sibeal raised her eyes to look at him. "Would you stay if it meant abandoning your lord?"

He bit his lip as he considered. "Nay," he admitted. "I would not."

"Then you expect less of me?" she asked.

He shook his head. "I should not have asked." Impulsively, he took her hand. "If you are ever in need, send word to me. Or come to me if you can."

Mutely, she nodded. With great reluctance, he released his hold on her.

Slowly, leading her horse, Diana began to walk from the courtyard, followed closely by Sibeal.

A distance away, Robert lightly slapped Ian's horse on the rump, and the animal moved forward.

For a moment, Diana was puzzled. Why, she wondered, had Robert permitted the boy to take the horse? The animals were valuable. No man gave away a horse once it was in his possession.

Doubtless, she thought as she stepped onto the wooden bridge, Robert sought to impress the Earl of Dunmoor with his wealth. It was the sort of gesture she knew her brother would make.

Then Diana came abreast of Ian in the middle of the bridge, and she took a sharp breath. The lad was ill, his eyes bright and feverish, his skin flushed crimson. Observing him, she knew why Robert had allowed him the horse. It was obvious that the boy could not walk. She raised her head to look up at Thorn on the ramparts and realized that all he could see was the top of Ian's head. He apparently saw nothing amiss.

With effort, she sternly repressed the urge to assist the lad, whose frail body seemed to be listing to the side of his saddle. If she did, she knew she would spark a battle. Grimly, she set her mouth and continued across the bridge, coming to a halt in front of her brother.

Robert merely glanced at her, a brief, cold look that told her that it was her own fault that she had been captured. Without a word she mounted Banrigh, helping Sibeal up to sit behind her.

Diana was unable to resist one last look at her lover. Aye, for that was what he was. However their affair had begun, she did not fool herself into thinking she had done otherwise than submit to the passion of his strong arms. They would never meet again, she knew. For either of them to accept a clan enemy would be to invite a slow death at the hands of the Clan Council.

240

A thin drizzle began to fall, almost as if the mist itself had begun to weep. Diana raised her hand, uncertain as to whether it was rain or tears she brushed from her cheek. Robert gave the order for the men to move out. Just as Ian's mount stepped into the bailey, Diana turned away and prodded Banrigh forward.

Angus caught Ian as the boy fell from his saddle.

"God's blood!" Thorn exclaimed as he came swiftly down the stone steps. "What's wrong with him?"

"I don't know," Angus replied. "Let's get him into the keep."

A while later, having removed Ian's tattered clothes and laid him gently on the bed, Thorn frowned deeply at his brother's wasted figure.

"He's no more than a pile of bones! Christ, didn't they feed him at all?" He motioned to Angus. "Summon Grizel. Then have food sent up." His hand went to his brother's feverish brow, and Ian's eyes flicked open.

" 'Tis sorry I am, Thorn," the boy whispered.

"Were you ill treated?" Thorn was amazed at how calm his voice sounded. Inside, he was roiling with fury.

Ian shook his head. "Nay, none came near me save the Lady Diana. She gave me food and her plaid. I told her I would not wear it," he added hastily, then bit his lip. "But I did." He averted his face. "I'm ashamed, Thorn."

241

"I'll not have you feeling shame!" Thorn said quickly in a sharper tone than he had intended.

He took a breath, striving for the control that was his only a moment ago. The last thing he wanted was for his brother to feel in any way chastised. Reaching out, he took hold of Ian's small hand.

"I am very proud of you, Ian. You have shown great courage. And there will be no man who will speak otherwise to me." Seeing the boy's doubtful look, Thorn's tone became earnest. "Heed me, Ian! Courage comes in many disguises; at times, it even wears the cloak of cowardice."

Ian appeared shocked. "Never would a knight mistake one for the other!"

Thorn smiled and gently squeezed his brother's hand. "You are confusing the code of honor with bravery, lad. A man's honor can never be in question. But for a knight to unnecessarily jeopardize his life is not courage—'tis foolhardiness in the extreme! Using a warm covering on a cold night is prudent. And the weave of the covering does not bear consideration." He patted Ian's hand before releasing it. "You did the right thing. I would have done the same."

Thorn paused a moment, still not believing Ian's deteriorated condition. "When the Lady Diana left Sidhean, did no one else bring you food?"

"For a while. Then there was only bread and ale." Ian grinned weakly. "And an occasional piece of tough mutton. The MacLaren's cook is not as good as ours."

Thorn's mouth was a flat line as he began to pull the fur blankets up over Ian. In the midst of this action he noticed two red puncture wounds just below the thin calf. "What's this?" He ran his fingertips over the wound, and Ian winced.

" 'Twas a rat that bit me one night. I killed it," the lad said proudly.

Thorn took a breath and spoke carefully. "Where exactly was it that you were kept in the keep?"

In spite of his low opinion of the Clan MacLaren, Thorn could not quite believe that rats abounded through the rooms at whim.

"In the dungeon beneath the guard rooms," Ian replied. " 'Twas not all that bad," he added hastily when Thorn sucked in his breath angrily. "Though I do wish the pallet had been softer."

For a moment, Thorn was speechless. "Dungeon!" he exploded at last. He clenched his fists, wishing they were around the neck of the MacLaren.

Even discounting his youth, Ian had been no ordinary prisoner. It was unconscionable for the Earl of Sidhean to have acted in such manner.

Aware that his furious outburst had frightened Ian, Thorn made an effort to keep his voice even. "So," he said, "you were kept in a dungeon and fed bread and ale during your stay at Sidhean."

"Aye," Ian said with a solemn nod of his head.

Not trusting himself to speak further, Thorn tucked the blankets snugly about the boy. He straightened up as Grizel bustled into the room, followed by a servant carrying a bowl of hot broth and a thick slab of oatbread.

"He needs something more substantial than that!" Thorn protested, viewing the meager fare.

"More than this, and he'll throw up," Grizel said with a look that defied him to take exception to her nursing skills.

Thorn checked an angry retort, something he would not do for any other living soul save this woman. As for Grizel's nursing skills, he had to admit there were none better. Many a warrior of both Dunmoor and Rath na Iolair had survived fierce wounds only because of her expert ministrations.

"Very well," he said at last as he headed for the door. "Oh, there's a wound on the lad's leg. I fear it may be infected."

Grizel's head shot up, and her piercing black eyes seemed to bore right into him. "What sort of wound?"

"A rat bite." Thorn was about to leave, but the look on Grizel's face gave him pause. He followed her back to the bedside and watched while she pulled aside the covers to inspect the wound.

"When did you receive the bite?" Grizel asked Ian.

" 'Twas more than a week past," Ian replied.

Grizel's sigh of relief was so pronounced and so audible that Thorn asked, "What is it? If something's amiss, I insist on knowing about it!"

With a glance at Ian, who had begun to eat, Grizel moved away from the bed. When Thorn was at her side, she lowered her voice. "There are times when a bite from a rodent produces the same horrible, fatal illness as that from a mad dog," she said. "Why it is not always so, I do not know." Noticing the horror that crossed Thorn's face, she quickly added, "But if that terrible illness were to come upon Ian, it would have done so by now. Less than a week passes before it makes its presence known. We need no longer have any concern about it."

"But the wound is infected?" he said, not entirely at ease with her words of comfort.

"Aye, but—" She fell silent when she saw Ian put aside the bowl of broth, and they both returned to the boy's bedside.

"I did think I was more hungry," Ian said apologetically as he placed the bowl on a side table.

" 'Tis rest you need now," Thorn said soothingly.

Gently, he pushed his brother back against the pillow. Before he could draw the covers up, Ian was asleep. Thorn stood there a moment longer; then he left the room.

Chapter Twenty-six

It was dusk on the third day after the exchange when the MacLarens arrived to the outskirts of Sidhean.

"I thought we'd never get here," Sibeal murmured.

Diana turned to her maidservant, who was still seated behind her. " 'Aye," she agreed with a sigh.

"The earl will be questioning you, you know," Sibeal said in the same low tone. "He'll not be keeping his silence as he has been doing these past three days."

Diana only nodded. Captives were always interrogated upon their return. She faced forward again, staring at the keep where she had been born and raised. The sight of it should have produced a feeling of joy; instead, she could not help wondering what she had left behind at Rath na Iolair.

Sibeal gave Diana a gentle poke, and she realized that she had halted Banrigh. Quickly, she pushed her knees into the sides of the mare, and the animal obediently moved forward.

As the horses clattered into the bailey, grooms rushed forward to take the reins. Dismounting, Diana trudged wearily up the steps, Sibeal close on her heels.

Inside, Diana paused uncertainly. Lachlan Gilbride was waiting in the hallway. Robert seldom took Lachlan with him when he left the keep, preferring to leave his second-in-command in charge of matters in his absence.

After greeting Robert, Lachlan glanced briefly at Diana, and she offered a tentative smile. When it was not returned, her heart sank. From Robert she had expected cold anger and had not been disappointed. From the rest of the men, Lachlan in particular, she had expected a welcome upon her return. Feeling drained and tired, she rubbed the back of her neck. She wanted nothing more than to retire to her chambers.

Robert, as he had been doing for the past three days, ignored her. Trailed by his men, he led the way into the great hall. Reluctantly, Diana followed. Despite her hopes, her interrogation was not to be conducted in private.

Much to her annoyance, she saw that Donald Campbell was waiting there. She was further annoyed to see Lady Ellen seated beside Donald. The countess was dressed as if she were about to attend a court fete. Her gown of peach-colored silk was trimmed with fur both at the hem and the ends of the wide, elbow-length sleeves. A gold girdle encircled her waist. Emeralds blazed around her neck and wrists. An elaborate headdress soared eight inches above her hair and was draped with gold mesh that flowed down past her shoulders.

Diana turned to Sibeal and spoke quietly. "You may go upstairs if you wish."

"Nay." Sibeal shook her head. "I will stay with you."

"Ahh! Lady Diana." Ellen's blue eyes glittered as Diana stood in front of the table on the dais. " 'Tis been a long time since we have had the pleasure of your company."

Ellen's smile complemented her perfect features. Something Robert would appreciate. Something that only made Diana suspicious.

" 'Tis been a while," Diana acknowledged cautiously. She did not sit down, nor did Robert, who stood beside her.

"The earl gave you more than ample time to escape," Ellen went on in a deceptively soft tone of voice. She leaned back in her chair, her long fingers toying with the stem of her wine goblet. "Knowing how resourceful you are, we can only assume that you were held under lock and key."

"I was watched," Diana responded warily.

"And, it appears, well treated," her sister-in-law said with that same smile.

"Better than Ian MacKendrick was treated!" she shot back. "The lad was ill when he was returned."

"We are not discussing the spawn of the MacKendrick!" Robert said in an angry tone.

Before Diana could respond, Donald stood up. "I, for one, would find it of great interest to know just how well you were treated!" he said in a tight voice. "Wined, dined, and treated to the renowned shaft of the MacKendrick?"

Diana's head swung in his direction, outraged that he dared to question her on what was, after all, a family matter. " 'Tis no concern of yours!" she snapped.

" 'Tis very much my concern!" Donald countered, viewing her through narrowed eyes. "I would know how my future wife fared at the hands of my sworn enemy."

She glared at him as if he were some vermin skittering across the floor. "Then why are you asking me?"

"Will you come to your wedding bed a virgin?" Donald's fist came down on the table with a force that caused his goblet to teeter precariously.

Diana's smile was cold. "Since you will not be there on my wedding night, that, too, should not concern you." She tilted her head, daring him to take exception.

"Enough!" Robert ordered angrily before Donald could again speak. He faced her. "We

will know what happened to you at Rath na Iolair. And we will know it now!"

"Just what is it that you wish to know?"

Though her voice was calm, Diana clasped
her hands to keep them from trembling. It was
within Robert's power to banish her from Sidhean. Nor could she refuse to answer his questions. She could refuse to answer anyone else
in the room, save himself.

Robert's cheeks reddened as his temper rose.
He moved closer, bending toward her. "He used
you, didn't he? Didn't he!"

"You would not believe otherwise." Her eyes
were level as she stared at him.

Robert tilted his head to the side. "I might,"
he said softly, "if you were to say otherwise and
give me your word on it."

Diana lowered her head. Robert, she realized,
was going to harp on this one subject. Not even
the defenses of Rath na Iolair seemed to be of
any concern to him.

Robert drew in his chin. "In view of the fact
that you offer no denial, we can only assume
that you are no longer a virgin." He waited a
moment, and when she did not answer, he continued. "What man would want you now, Diana
MacLaren?" he taunted. "Whore! You should
have killed yourself rather than have suc-
cumbed to such defilement!"

Diana glanced around the hall. Men who had
all her life treated her with respect and admiration were averting their eyes, as if unwilling

to look upon her shame.

Her gaze swung back to her brother, who was looking smug, as if he had achieved a triumph.

Prudence dictated caution. Weariness overcame it. "Had I been the captive of the likes of you, I would have killed myself!"

The slap on Diana's cheek caught her unaware; it was vicious, delivered with full strength. Though she staggered a step backward, she managed to retain her balance. Sibeal hastened forward, but Diana waved her away.

"Even at the hands of our enemy I was not treated thus!" Diana's words were low and intense.

In a quick motion that took her by surprise, Robert grasped her hand and held it high. "Is there any among you who would bid for this used and defiled woman?"

Again, eyes were averted. In an angry motion, Diana pulled her hand free. Robert's expression reflected only satisfaction. Not one of the men had come to her defense. That would not have happened before she had been abducted. Turning slightly, Robert exchanged a glance with Donald. Both men smiled at each other.

"Have you any further questions for me?" Diana demanded.

Robert again faced her. "Not at the present time. You may retire."

Her head high and her spine rigid, Diana walked proudly from the great hall, Sibeal at her side. As soon as they reached her bedchamber, Sibeal hurriedly fetched a cloth and wet it in the basin of cold water on the dressing table.

"Och!" she exclaimed in dismay, seeing Diana's cheek. " 'Tis turning color already."

Diana wearily motioned Sibeal and the wet cloth away as she sank into the nearest chair. Leaning back, she put a hand to her forehead and stared morosely into the fireplace. In the flames of the hearthfire she could see the face of the tall golden knight as he had been on that day in the glen outside Edinburgh. However, it was not the sight that provided the image; it was her own mind, drawing on memories that were painfully clear, memories she knew would remain with her for always.

Sibeal put the cloth aside, then turned down Diana's bed. Coming back a while later, she viewed her for a moment before she spoke. "Do you wish we could have stayed?" she whispered hesitantly.

Diana lowered her hand to look at her maidservant. There was a long silence before she replied, " 'Tis wishful thinking that it could have been otherwise."

"Like white heather."

Diana tilted her head, not certain that she heard correctly. "What? What is that you said?"

"Nothing, m'lady," Sibeal murmured.

Pushing herself up from the chair, Diana headed toward the bed. "The hour grows late, lass. Let us retire."

But as tired as she was, Diana found herself

too restless to sleep. For a long time she simply thrashed in the bed, finding no position that offered even a measure of comfort.

God! she thought. What was happening to her? Why could she not shake the thought, the image, the touch of the man who had abducted her? She had lain in his arms, felt his kiss, his caress. Was she then forever doomed to seek a replacement? For surely, she could not have the original.

Inside Rath na Iolair, Thorn stood at his brother's bedside, frantic with worry. His hand went to Ian's forehead, but even before he made contact he could feel the feverish heat. Ian was unconscious. Grizel had done all she could.

Thorn tore his eyes from Ian and looked at Grizel. "Will he live?"

"If God deems it so," she replied tonelessly.

Those words were not what he wanted to hear. Even the possibility that Ian might die was a thought not to be borne. He was unable to quell the anguished cry that erupted from him, a cry that resounded through the halls of Rath na Iolair. Then he stood breathing as if he had run for miles.

If Ian had been a man, if he had suffered injury during a battle, Thorn would not have felt this overwhelming sense of remorse and futility. Regardless of their harsh ways, Highlanders were not barbarians. There was a code of honor as real as it was intangible: A man did not strike another when his back was turned; once given, a man did not break his word; a man did not wage war against children.

"The whoreson will die for this!" Thorn muttered, thinking of the man who was responsible for his brother's present condition. His gaze once again fell upon Grizel. "I go to Sidhean to kill a MacLaren."

Grizel arched her brow. "You cannot lay siege to Sidhean," she said. "They have the means to withstand that for years."

"I plan no siege!" he almost shouted. "I plan to attack and slay every MacLaren within those accursed stone walls!"

Grizel gave him a sharp look. "Every MacLaren?"

"Aye," Thorn responded grimly. "They are a curse upon the Highlands."

Grizel appeared about to speak again, but fell silent when the door opened.

Angus came quietly into the room. His eyes immediately sought Ian. "How is he?"

Thorn hung his head. Grief and anger were an unbearable weight on his shoulders. "How would you expect him to be!"

Stepping closer, Angus touched his arm. "What do you want to do?"

"Send the MacLaren to hell," Thorn declared flatly.

Angus nodded. "We will need help."

" 'Twill be no problem," he replied. "The Carmichaels have always answered a call to arms."

255

"I will send word to them immediately," Angus said as he turned to leave.

Though he felt the need for immediate action, Thorn just stood there, reluctant to leave Ian. He watched as Grizel adjusted the blankets, her face anxious as she peered down at the slight figure on the bed.

Gazing at his brother, Thorn was no less anxious. Ian seemed, if anything, more flushed!

Straightening up, Grizel put a hand to the small of her back.

"You should get some rest," Thorn said gruffly. "Summon one of the servants to watch over him."

With a sigh, she sat down in a chair by the bed and stared at Ian. "Nay," she said quietly. "He is child of my heart if not of my body. No one will watch over him save me."

Thorn sat down on the bed and took his brother's small, hot hand. His mind was filled with nothing but thoughts of vengeance. Minutes passed in silence.

"You will have regrets if you do this thing," Grizel said at last.

Startled, Thorn looked at her. She had, he realized, as always, caught his thoughts. It had been ever so, even when he had been a child. "There will be no regrets!" he said firmly.

"Much blood will be shed," she noted.

"And rightly so!" he answered swiftly, casting her an annoyed look.

"I do not question your decision to slay the

MacLaren," she said hastily. "Were it in my power I would do the deed myself." She expelled a deep breath. "Yet not all of them are to blame."

When Thorn did not reply, Grizel frowned. "Is there nothing I can say that will change your mind?"

"Nothing."

"So be it," she murmured in resignation.

As if having made her own decision, Grizel got slowly to her feet. Going to the window, she pushed aside the wooden shutters.

With some curiosity, he watched her. She was staring unblinkingly at the moon. "What are you about, old woman?" he asked in a sharp tone.

She did not answer him; indeed, she seemed not to have heard him. Staring intently, her gaze never wavered.

With a sound of annoyance, he got to his feet. He had delayed long enough. It was time to be on his way.

Chapter Twenty-seven

Miles away, Diana's eyes opened wide, though she had been deeply asleep only seconds ago. For a moment, she lay there, staring up at the dark ceiling. What had awakened her? Dimly, in her sleep-fogged mind, she thought she had heard a cry. A cry of such pain and agony, it shocked her to the core.

She sat up, listening. All was silent. Her brow wet with perspiration, she at last got out of bed and went to the window. Clouds trailed wispy ribbons across a full moon and momentarily obscured stars. In her mind, she could still hear the cry, sounding like an echo that carried long distances across the windswept moors.

Again, her eyes focused on the moon. As she stared, mesmerized, the clouds passed to reveal a clear white globe. And in that almost perfect circle, Diana saw the face of Ian MacKendrick. She tipped her head to the side in puzzlement. She was almost certain that the cry had not been his.

"Oh, God," she moaned then, recalling the boy's fever-bright eyes.

Turning, she went to the chest at the foot of her bed and withdrew a bundle of dried herbs. Only moments later, she was dressed. Fetching a spare arisaid, she stuffed it into a leather pouch, making certain there was enough room for the small amount of food she would need. That done, she awakened Sibeal.

"I must return to Rath na Iolair," she told her maidservant.

Hastily, Sibeal got up from her pallet. "I will go with you."

"Nay, lass," Diana said quietly. "There is need for me to travel swiftly. And there is need for you to explain my absence."

"You've had a vision?"

Diana nodded, though in truth it was unlike any other she had ever had. "Listen," she whispered. "When my absence is discovered, you say that I have gone to the village to assist in a birthing."

Sibeal looked doubtful. " 'Tis a three-day ride and three day's return."

Diana sighed, then brightened. "For the first day or two, you say I am indisposed. When they know I am gone, you tell them about the birthing. I'll wager you have heard of more than one woman who has been in labor for days on end."

Though still doubtful, Sibeal nodded. "I will do the best I can."

Diana planted a light kiss on Sibeal's cheek. "I could ask for no more."

Feeling the need for the utmost haste, Diana left Sidhean. Pushing Banrigh to her limit, Diana raced across the moors, prodded by an urgency she could not explain even to herself. Overhead, the moon was bright, and she prayed that no clouds would obscure the illumination it provided.

Riding hard, she covered the distance to Rath na Iolair in less than three days, sleeping only when she or Banrigh could go no farther.

It was not yet dark when Diana once again approached Rath na Iolair. The long summer gloaming softened the land with shades of lilac, not unlike the color of the heather that would soon be in full bloom.

On the far side of the drawbridge, Diana halted. Nothing seemed amiss. It looked just as it had when she had last seen it.

Prodding her mare forward, Diana crossed the drawbridge warily, uncertain as to what her reception would be. To her surprise, she was immediately admitted entrance.

Leaving her horse in the care of a groom, she walked slowly across the bailey. A glance told her that the earl was not in residency. A mere handful of men milled about, emphasizing rather than decreasing the keep's deserted air.

No one barred her way as she stepped into the entry hall and made her way upstairs. On the landing, she paused. Only one door was opened. She headed for it.

Her step hesitant, she entered the room. Grizel was seated in a chair by the hearth.

"I have been expecting you," the old woman murmured, with only a brief glance.

Diana moved closer. " 'Twas you who summoned me?"

"Aye," Grizel said, not looking at her.

"But yours was not the cry I heard."

A brief smile touched Grizel's lips. " 'Twas Thorn's anguish that reached you. 'Tis ever so between two people who are bound to each other."

"I am not bound to him!" Diana said sharply, remembering how easily he had let her go, remembering the sound of a woman's voice in his bedchamber on her last night in this keep.

When Grizel shrugged, Diana said, " 'Twas Ian's face I saw.

"And 'twas that I wanted you to see," Grizel replied, unperturbed. "Nevertheless, 'twas his brother's cry you heard. I had no part in that."

Confusion marred Diana's brow as she asked, "What is wrong?"

Without answering, Grizel motioned to the bed. Diana crossed the room. "Holy Mary," she gasped as she saw Ian's flushed face. "Did anyone harm him whilst he was at Sidhean?"

Grizel shook her head. " 'Twas a rat bite that caused the infection."

Diana sighed and rubbed her brow. In her mind's eye, she could picture the boy as she had first seen him: proud, vulnerable. Were a few acres of land worth this lad's life? Lowering her hand, she glanced at Grizel. "Does the earl know about this?"

"Aye," Grizel answered. She hesitated a moment, her gaze going briefly to Ian before returning to Diana. "His grief was still upon him when he left."

Diana drew a sharp breath. Was Thorn at this moment on his way to Sidhean? If so, she must go back to warn them. She wet her lips. "Where did he go?" she asked as casually as she could.

"To the south. To the keep of the Carmichaels," the old woman answered truthfully and without hesitation.

Relief flooded Diana. Then, remembering the bundle she had brought with her, she removed it from her pouch, dumping its contents on a nearby table.

Suddenly, Grizel's expression lightened as she viewed the many dried herbs. They were all beneficial in combating fever and infection.

That night, Ian's condition worsened, and he sunk into a delirium so severe that Diana and Grizel despaired of his life. As she sponged Ian's feverish body, Diana could not help but notice how much more delicate the boy appeared than when last she had seen him.

Straightening up, she wiped her forehead with the back of her hand. The fire was burning high, and the room was heated to the point where she was perspiring. Ignoring her own discomfort, she once again dipped the cloth into the basin of water. About to wring it out, she paused when she noticed what Grizel was doing. The old woman was opening every window in the room! Diana gaped at Grizel, who offered a mirthless grin as she came back to the bedside.

"You think the night air dangerous, do you?"

"So I have been informed," Diana declared cautiously, not wanting to offend the older woman.

"Tales told by the ignorant," Grizel declared firmly as she seated herself in a nearby chair.

Taken aback, Diana asked, "By the physicians, as well?"

Grizel waved a hand. "They, more than most. Many have been the times I have tended men who fell on the field of battle where they have lain until they either lived or died." She sniffed. "I have seen no difference in their rate of survival from those who have been nursed in their own bed. There is no difference in the air, be it day or night. Too much warmth is as harmful as too much cold," she concluded with an authority Diana did not dare dispute. "And when a fever is high, snow is of more benefit than a blanket."

The idea was new to Diana, yet she did not

discount it. Once, when she had been a child, she had been in the grip of a ferocious fever. She still remembered the heat, the burning of her young body. She had longed only for the comfort of a cool wet cloth; but all she had been offered was the suffocating weight of blankets to sweat the fever into submission. Wearily, she sank into a chair.

The following day saw little change in Ian's condition. Although Diana had dozed for a few hours, Grizel had remained awake. Diana could only marvel at the woman's stamina.

"You care much for the lad," she said as darkness once again cloaked the land.

"Aye," Grizel said, as she lit the tapers. "I was there on the night he was born, so small and weak." She fell silent a moment, then added, " 'Twas inconceivable that he took the life of his mother." She gave a short, mirthless laugh. "Mary MacKendrick labored long and hard to bring her son Thornton into the world. Yet she survived that first difficult birth." Turning her head, she looked at Diana, her eyes fierce. "Ian was mine from the moment he took his first breath!"

So many things that had puzzled Diana about this woman became clear. "You raised him."

"Aye, and his brother, as well." Grizel heaved a great sigh, and her eyes clouded with worry as she viewed the small figure on the bed.

"He is young," Diana noted, hoping to lift the woman's spirit.

Grizel nodded slowly. "That is in his favor."

Diana could see how weary Grizel was becoming. Exhaustion had deepened the lines beneath her eyes and along the sides of her mouth. Leaning over, she patted the thin hand that was draped limply on the arm of the chair. "Rest," she urged quietly. "I will watch over the lad."

A weary chuckle came from her as Grizel's head fell back on the chair. "And who will watch over you, lass?" she sighed as she drifted off to sleep.

At last, on the morning of the fourth day, Ian opened his eyes. The smile he offered Grizel quickly disappeared at the sight of Diana.

"Where am I?" he cried out.

"You are at Rath na Iolair," Diana said, correctly interpreting the boy's confusion. It was evident the lad had thought he was back at Sidhean.

"Lady Diana was kind enough to bring me some herbs I needed," Grizel said.

Ian visibly relaxed. "I wore your plaid," he said, his smile embracing Diana.

"Then you did it honor," she responded gravely. Her cool hand rested on his brow. No sign of fever. "Are you hungry?"

"Like I've never been before!" Ian declared cheerfully.

With more animation than Diana had ever

seen her display, Grizel sent for a variety of food that would have done credit to a banquet. Laughing giddily, the strain and stress of the past 72 hours taking its toll, Diana ate and joked with Ian while Grizel looked on in approval.

Later, when Ian had fallen asleep, Diana and Grizel sat in companionable silence for a while. The fire was turning to embers when Grizel said, "Go to sleep, lass. 'Tis almost dawn."

On a impulse Diana could not explain then or after, she took a fur robe from the foot of the bed and placed it on the floor in front of the chair in which Grizel was seated. Sinking down into the softness, she placed her head in the old woman's lap. In only moments, she was asleep.

After breakfast the following morning, Diana strapped on her sword belt.

"What are you doing!" Grizel said.

Diana was startled by her sharp tone. "I must return to Sidhean. I have been gone too long as it is. Besides, 'tis best I leave before the earl returns."

Grizel raised her brow. "Did you not expect him to be here when you arrived?"

"I"—Diana shifted uncomfortably—"did not think—"

"Love never does," Grizel observed with a slight smile.

Diana's mouth tightened in exasperation. "I neither love him nor want him!"

"No more than you want to breathe," Grizel said.

"You seem to have a mistaken impression about me and the earl," Diana said. "Just because we—" Pausing, she gave a Grizel a narrow, sidelong glance as a thought occurred to her. "You are not going to tell me that you have never known a man!"

"Hah!" Grizel's laugh revealed a missing tooth. "I would be the last to tell you that!"

Diana relaxed, and her tone was lofty as she said, "Well, then, you obviously know the difference between love and desire."

Solemnly, Grizel inclined her head. "Aye, I know well the difference."

Diana sensed the unspoken question that followed that statement. "And so do I! Love is something that grows between a man and a woman over the years."

"Is it?" Grizel seemed to ponder on that. "Conall and I never had years."

Diana bit her lip, feeling contrite. "I did not mean to imply that it sometimes does not happen sooner." Hastily, she reached for her arisaid.

Grizel took a breath. "I wish you would stay a while longer."

"I cannot do that. My brother might come looking for me. If he finds me here—" Diana did not even want to think about that! She checked the leather pouch to make certain it still contained the spare arisaid, then she closed it again.

"Stay one more day at least," Grizel said, ignoring Diana's questioning look. They both knew that Ian was out of danger.

"Nay." Diana shook her head. "You no longer need me."

Seeing that she could not change Diana's mind, Grizel walked to the table, which still held the remains of their breakfast. "If you must go, take something to eat with you." Using the cloth that covered the table, she began to assemble a bundle of food.

While Grizel was thus engaged, Diana walked toward the bed. "I must say good-bye to you, Ian MacKendrick," she said softly. "I doubt we will see each other again."

Solemnly, he nodded. "I wish you a safe journey, my lady. 'Twas kind of you to come here."

Turning away, she accepted the bundle of food from Grizel. Without further words, she left the room.

Outside, she hastily mounted Banrigh and spurred the horse across the drawbridge. On the far side, she paused for a final look at Rath na Iolair. Raising her eyes, she saw Grizel framed in one of the tall, narrow windows. The old woman was motionless.

Diana raised her hand in a tentative way, but it was not returned. After a moment longer, she tugged on the reins and prodded Banrigh to a gallop.

Chapter Twenty-eight

Rain driven by a severe wind pelted Diana, and she could see only a few feet ahead of her. This was her third night on the road, and she hoped to reach Sidhean before morning. The weather, however, was worsening by the minute.

She clenched her mouth to prevent her teeth from chattering. Her plaid was soaked; her clothes were soaked; and her very skin felt soaked! Banrigh was not faring much better. The animal's step became hesitant as Diana's hand became less certain on the reins. Seeing a stand of trees about a quarter mile away, she nudged the mare in that direction.

"We'll not be going much farther tonight, Banrigh," she muttered, bending her head as a blast of wind nearly tore the arisaid from her shoulders.

It was calmer once they reached the haven of the wood. For a time, Diana sat there, hoping the weather would clear. Then, at last, she reluctantly dismounted. Though she had hoped to cover more miles on this day, she knew it would be imprudent to continue. Best to wait till morning, she decided.

Tethering Banrigh, Diana removed her sword belt, crawled beneath the low-hanging branches of an evergreen, and settled down to sleep. The noisy chattering of birds about their morning business woke her several hours later. She stretched, then sat up.

The rain had ceased. Though the sun was making a valiant effort to penetrate the morning mist, moisture still dripped from trees and hung on bushes.

Diana sighed as she ran her hands over her skirt. Her clothes were still damp, but there was nothing to be done about that. She withdrew the spare arisaid from the leather pouch. It, at least, was dry. Haphazardly, she stuffed the wet one into the pouch.

Then, reaching for the bundle of food Grizel had provided, Diana carefully untied the linen. Though she had eaten most of it, there still remained a slice of oatbread, a wedge of cheese, and two apples, one of which she gave to Banrigh.

When she was through eating, Diana went to

the edge of the small stream. She plunged her hands into the icy cold water to wash them. Then, bending forward, she splashed some of the cold liquid on her face. Pausing, she gazed down into the water and froze, feeling as though her heart had ceased to beat.

"No!"

A low, keening moan escaped Diana as she stared into the burn. Before her horrified eyes the crystal-clear waters began to turn blood-red. Gradually, the color receded, and she saw Robert astride his horse. He was wearing a suit of mail and carrying both sword and shield.

Diana wanted to get up and run as fast as she could from this place. But she was powerless to move, powerless even to turn away.

Robert's destrier moved forward, stride by stride, heading for a golden stallion, whose rider Diana knew all too well. They came abreast of each other. Thorn's sword seemed to move as slowly as Robert's horse. His strong arm rose in an almost casual manner; then it lowered. The tip of his blade found Robert's chest.

Diana watched, paralyzed with dread, as her brother fell from his horse. So slow, so graceful was his descent, it appeared as if he had floated to the ground.

In only the time it took for her to draw a breath, the image at last faded, and she was once again staring into clear water. Shaken, she rose. If what she had seen had not yet taken

273

place she might get back in time to prevent it.

Stumbling toward Banrigh, she hastily mounted. Spurring the mare to a gallop, they sped across the moors.

Less than a mile from Sidhean, in the very wood where he had captured Diana, Thorn stood, his hands on his hips, heedless of his sodden state. The persistent downpour that had besieged he and his men for most of the day was no more than an irritating drizzle.

Angus came to stand beside him. They could see the keep, but knew that if they left the cover of trees, they would be spotted in no time.

" 'Tis hopeless, Thorn." Angus sighed. "To lay siege would be a waste of time. If we attack, we will lose many a good man."

Thorn made no immediate response. Though in the first heat of the murderous rage that had engulfed him it had been his intention to storm Sidhean, he saw how impractical that action would be.

"We neither lay siege nor attack," he replied at last. He turned and viewed his men until he found the one he sought. "Fergus," he called quietly. "Come here."

The young man who approached was the son of a crofter, and his humble dress marked him as such.

"I've a task for you, lad," Thorn said. "Listen carefully. This is what I want you to do. You are to approach the keep and tell the guard that you have a message for the Earl of Sidhean. When you gain entrance, you tell him that the Campbell keep is under attack, and that their assistance is urgently needed. Do you understand?"

"Aye! I will leave now."

"Nay." Thorn put a restraining hand on the man's shoulder. "We do nothing until dawn. By then, I hope the weather will have cleared."

Thorn smiled as he settled down for the night. The plan was a good one, he thought. With a bit of luck it would work.

Dawn had not yet arrived when Thorn roused Fergus and sent him on his way. Then he paced about the wood impatiently. The sun had already tipped the mountains more than an hour later when the MacLaren men-at-arms at last rode out of Sidhean.

"More than half of them, I'll wager," Angus said quietly.

"Is the MacLaren with them?" Thorn asked.

Angus squinted in the hazy sunlight. "Aye, he rides in the lead."

Thorn expelled a breath of relief. Had Robert stayed behind, it would have been necessary to storm the stronghold itself. Now they would be able to meet their enemies in the open.

"Robert MacLaren is mine!" Thorn stated, not taking his eyes from the riders. "Pass the word among the men."

Chapter Twenty-nine

Diana's heart pounded in her chest at the sight that greeted her eyes when she at last arrived at the glen. Robert, astride his favorite mount, was charging across the clearing at Thorn. His sword held high, Robert brought it down in a chopping motion.

The blade struck Thorn's raised shield and threw him off balance. Recovering quickly, Thorn spun Sian around to face Robert, whose horse was once again thundering in his direction. Thorn remained very still, waiting.

Dear God! Diana thought in horror as she watched Robert once again raise his sword. His face contorted with a grimace of hate, he had raised himself up, almost standing in his stirrups. He was leaving himself wide open!

Thorn sat Sian motionlessly. His powerful biceps and broad shoulders seemed enhanced by the coat of mail he was wearing, the links molding his body, yet not restricting it.

Diana's mouth went dry. Had she been closer, she would have recklessly raced ahead to position herself between the two men. But she knew she would never make it. She could do nothing but stand by helplessly while one or the other went down. And in her heart, she knew that she would never forgive the survivor.

The distance between the two men shrank so rapidly, Diana wondered why it seemed to take so long for them to meet. Everything was so sharp in her mind that she imagined she could see Robert's horse lift a hoof, then slowly put it to the ground as the massive body moved forward, stride by stride.

The rest happened just as she had seen it. The blood! she thought in dismay as she spurred her horse forward. It was everywhere, staining the bracken and gorse into an unnatural shade of red. With what Diana considered to be a callous disregard for Robert's fallen figure, Thorn raced to the aid of one his comrades.

Even as Banrigh covered the relatively short distance between Robert and her, Diana saw Thorn's lethal sword cut down two more of her kinsmen. Slipping from her mount, she bent over her brother. His sagging jaw suggested that he had drawn his last breath. Her hand hovered above his throat, but she could not bring herself to touch him. She felt certain that she would find no pulse.

Rage boiled inside her and drummed in her ears. Though she and Robert had never been close, the blood ties that bound them could never be denied. No Highlander ever took lightly the death of a kinsman at the hand of a sworn enemy.

The sound of pounding hoofs caused her to stand. The golden stallion was charging directly at her, and she made no move to get out of the way. Automatically, her hand went to her waist before she realized that she had left her sword in the wood.

"You managed to leave before we came calling," Thorn noted sarcastically when he at last halted Sian.

"Aye." She stared up at him. In her heart, she searched for the feeling he had once stirred within her. She found nothing. Only cold anger had her in its relentless grip. "You should have sent word, and I would not have been occupied elsewhere. 'Twould have been my pleasure to have greeted you upon your arrival." Her eyes bored into him, and her voice held accusing condemnation.

With a howl of rage, Thorn raised his arm. The broadsword, poised directly over her head, glinted evilly. Unflinchingly, Diana met his stare.

"You would do well to show fear," he growled.

Her eyes never wavered. "If I am to die, I will do so with honor. I ask no quarter from you, nor from any other MacKendrick!"

His grip tightened, and her heart chilled; but she never took her eyes from his. Slowly, his arm lowered.

"Your kindness toward my brother has spared your life, lass."

She was not appeased. "Your brother lives! Mine has been murdered. Spare my life if it eases your conscience. 'Twill not change the hatred I feel for you."

Thorn's hand once more tightened on his sword. "Your brother died in a fair fight," he muttered. "There was no murder done here this day!" He returned his sword to its sheath. "That stubborn pride of yours will one day be your undoing, Diana MacLaren!"

Her chin rose. " 'Tis not stubborn, my lord. 'Tis inbred. Something a MacKendrick can never know!" She headed for her mare, then turned to taunt him yet one more time. "Make certain that, when next we meet, I am still without a weapon. I assure you that I will not be as lenient as you, Thornton MacKendrick."

Her shoulders squared in contempt, she deliberately turned her back on him, mounted her horse and rode away. When she approached Sidhean a while later, the portcullis was quickly raised. Dismounting, she raced to the ramparts, where she watched as the MacKendricks took their leave.

Though the site of the ambush itself was blocked from view by a copse of trees, Diana could see the MacKendricks as they rode over the fells in the distance. Then, with no wasted movement, Diana summoned those warriors who had remained behind, among them Lachlan Gilbride. Less than ten minutes passed before she was leading them back to the scene of ambush.

It did not surprise her that the MacKendricks had fled. She had not returned to pursue them; rather it was to claim her brother's body and assist any of those who lived, for by nightfall wolves would gather.

The clearing was as she had last seen it: an idyllic setting of wildflowers defaced by blood and by those who had shed it. The Mac-Kendricks had removed their dead and wounded. Only MacLarens remained.

In the quiet glen, Diana fancied she could still hear the clang of metal against metal, still hear the battle cries of the warriors. In reality nothing broke the stillness save for the mournful whisper of the breeze as it rustled through the bracken.

Diana turned to Lachlan, then pointed to where Robert had fallen. "There!" she said.

A moment later, Lachlan was bending over her brother; then raising his head, he called to her. "He lives!"

When Diana just stared at him, he carefully removed the coat of mail. " 'Tis true! Look here, my lady!"

Moving forward, Diana knelt beside Robert.

She did not touch him. He still looked to her as though he had drawn his last breath.

Lachlan, who had his hand on Robert's chest, looked up at her. "I feel it! He lives!"

Diana's hand went to her brother's chest. There, she felt the slow, intermittent beat of his heart. Tears came to her eyes. "He does live."

Using her fingertips, she drew his torn tunic aside so as to better inspect the wound. It had stopped bleeding. The single thrust of Thorn's blade had apparently angled upward and outward, missing both heart and lungs, but doing great damage to Robert's shoulder.

Lachlan got back on his horse and motioned to his men. "Lift him up to me. Careful now!"

The men did as instructed, and Lachlan held Robert in his arms as if he were a child. Then, at a slow pace, Diana and Lachlan returned to Sidhean, leaving the rest of the men behind to collect their dead comrades and bring them back for burial.

Ellen was in the bailey when they returned. At the sight of her unconscious husband she gave a piercing shriek and rushed forward.

Diana dismounted. "He is alive!" she said shortly, then summoned servants to carry her brother to his chambers.

A while later, having cleaned the wound and bandaged Robert's shoulder, Diana straightened up to find Ellen staring at her with hard eyes.

"Where have you been?" the countess demanded.

Diana arched her brow. "Since when is it your place to question me?"

"For once, you're right," Robert said.

Startled, Diana spun around. Her beginning smile of relief was quickly dampened at the sight of his scowling look.

" 'Tis not Lady Ellen's place to question you," he said. " 'Tis mine! Where were you? And do not be trying my credibility by telling me about a birthing! Inquiries have been made. I'll not be listening to your lies!"

"I'll not be telling any." Diana moistened her lips. No excuse she could have invented would be believed. "I went back to Rath na Iolair."

"You miserable slut!" Robert struggled to sit up, then moaned in pain.

Quickly, Ellen flew to his side and gently pushed him back. "You see what you've done!" she screamed at Diana. "Your lover summoned you away so that he could ambush your brother!"

Diana's chin rose. "I knew nothing of the ambush," she said as calmly as she could. "I did not go to see the MacKendrick. I went to see his brother."

"His brother." Robert sneered, not trying to hide his disbelief.

" 'Tis true! I had a feeling the lad was gravely ill."

"Ah." His sneer grew more marked. "Another

one of your premonitions, was it?"

Diana sighed. It would do no good to say that it was.

"Och! Get yourself from my sight." Robert groaned again.

Gratefully, Diana did so. In her chambers a few minutes later, she smiled wearily at Sibeal. Her smile was not returned.

"I've been so worried about you. I tried to tell them that you were in the village. But—" Sibeal shook her head.

"Do not fault yourself," Diana said quickly. "I know you did all you could."

Sibeal bit her lip. "I heard what happened. I—"

Diana could see that the young woman seemed to be having difficulty in formulating whatever question she meant to pose.

"Speak your mind, lass," she said quietly. "There need be no barriers between us."

Sibeal took a breath. "Well—" She fell silent, and only under Diana's gentle encouragement did she continue. "When the ambush took place, did you see Angus?" Her hands clenched. "Was he harmed in the battle?"

Diana blinked. "Ah, Sibeal." Reaching out, she took hold of the girl's slender hand. "I never thought to look."

Sibeal cast the closest thing to an accusing look she had ever directed at her mistress. " 'Tis of no matter," she murmured at last, withdrawing her hand. "I just thought that you might have noticed."

Diana turned away. After Robert had fallen, she had been aware of nothing and no one save for the man on the golden stallion. Both clans could have left the glen for all she had noticed.

Facing Sibeal again, she said, "Lachlan did not go with Robert. Most likely, the MacKendrick left Angus at Dunmoor. He is, after all, second-in-command. You know as well as I that, if injury befalls a leader, someone capable must be at hand to see to matters."

"Most likely," Sibeal whispered. Aware that her mistress was viewing her with concern, she hastened to explain. "He was kind to me. I would not like to see him harmed."

Diana sighed. How both their lives had been changed! Already, she regretted the heated words she had spoken to Thorn. How was she to live the rest of her life without him? A small cry inadvertently escaped her lips, and Sibeal turned to look at her.

"This time, you should have stayed," Sibeal said softly. Coming closer, she placed a hand on Diana's shoulder.

Diana sighed and patted her hand. "You know that was not possible. If my father was still alive, mayhap—"

Her voice trailed off, and she bit her lip. May-hap what? she wondered. Mayhap he might have allowed her to return to the MacKendrick? And yet, what better way to end a feud than to send one's daughter in marriage to one's enemy.

Useless conjecture. God, how useless. What

evidence did she have that Thornton Mac-
Kendrick even wanted her as a wife? None. Lov-
ers though they had been, no words of love had
been shared, nor were they were likely to be.

"You love him," Sibeal said.

From anyone else, Diana would have taken exception. She was unable to do so with this gentle
girl she knew had only her own interests at heart.

"Aye," she whispered, wondering why it had
taken her so long to put a name to her tumultu-
ous feelings.

"You should have let him know," Sibeal said.

"Why do you harp on things that cannot be!"
Diana cried, growing agitated. Viewing Sibeal's
crestfallen face, she grew still. "You would have
stayed," she said in some wonder.

Sibeal viewed her folded hands. "Aye."

Feeling exhausted, Diana leaned back in her
chair. Sibeal brought her a goblet of wine.

"Drink," she said. " 'Twill help relax you." She
watched a moment as Diana sipped at the sweet
liquid. "Your brother will not give up, you know.
He will not rest until he sees you wed to the son of
the Campbell."

Diana laughed ruefully. "He is insistent," she
said as she finished the wine.

It did soothe her and she felt less stifled. Insistent though he might be, Robert could not force
her to wed. There were alternatives. In extrem-
ity, she could even take the veil, though in all
truth that would not be her choice.

What Robert could not seem to understand

was that she did not just want to marry. She wanted to marry a man she loved.

Diana slammed the goblet down on the table beside her chair, more resolute than ever. "His wishes be damned. I'll not play pawn to his king!"

Chapter Thirty

Thorn returned to Rath na Iolair weary in both mind and body. The usual sense of exultation after a victorious battle was nowhere evident in his slumped shoulders and shadowed eyes. As always, Grizel was waiting, with food, hot water, and whiskey nearby. Thorn availed himself only of the latter.

For the better part of an hour, he brooded and drank while Grizel waited patiently. Finally, as if suddenly becoming aware of her presence, he looked up at her. "How fares Ian?"

"He is well," Grizel murmured.

Thorn accepted that without comment, feeling a bit drunk and welcoming the relaxation.

After several minutes of silence, Grizel again spoke. "Was Lady Diana at Sidhean when you arrived?"

The question was so unexpected Thorn merely gaped at her. "And where else would she be?"

Her head back, Grizel viewed him through narrowed eyes. "You are telling me that she was there, inside the keep?"

"She wasn't inside!" he almost shouted. "The wench was riding about the countryside, just as she was when I first took her."

Grizel's black eyes looked like pieces of onyx. "She was not riding about the countryside. She was on her way back to Sidhean. She was here, caring for Ian."

Thorn got up so fast his chair fell backward. "Here?" he cried hoarsely. "How could she have been here?"

" 'Tis of no importance how she got here! Whilst you were trying to kill her brother, she was trying to save yours!"

Bending forward, Thorn placed his palms on the table to support himself. His head was beginning to swim. Recovering slightly, he again reached for his cup.

"Thornton!"

Forgetting about the cup, his head shot up. He had not heard her use that tone since his childhood!

"You have had enough this night!" Her tone softened somewhat. "What's happened is done and over. You cannot brood on it."

"Hah!" He straightened up with difficulty and spoke with satisfaction. "I do not brood. I have had my vengeance. Robert MacLaren is dead!"

Grizel took a breath. "Robert MacLaren lives."

Thorn did not immediately respond. When he did, his voice conveyed disbelief. "You foolish old woman! He is dead! I was there!"

"But not long enough," Grizel said in a calm voice. "He lives."

With a roar of anger, he hurled his tankard at the wall. "If that be true, I will return to Sidhean; and this time, they will all die!"

Grizel only sighed, and his head lowered. His world seemed to be falling apart. "Damn you, old woman," he groaned. "Leave me be."

Turning, Grizel walked stiffly from the room. Then Thorn sank back in his chair. He could not doubt Grizel's words, for the simple reason that she had never been wrong.

Suddenly, Diana's words flashed into his mind: "Your brother lives!" she had said, and Thorn knew how she had known that.

With a sigh, he leaned his head back. Why did he feel so miserable? he wondered. He had felt this way when he had returned home and thought that Robert MacLaren was dead. If he was not, why then did the feeling persist?

Dragging himself up from the chair, he at last went to bed.

Five days passed before Thorn received confirmation that Robert MacLaren had indeed survived his wounds. Though it was reported that the earl would never again wield a sword due to the severe injury to the muscles in his shoulder.

This news was delivered by a member of the Douglas clan who was traveling the length and breadth of the Highlands in an effort to gather an army of sufficient number to overthrow King James and set the crown upon the head of 15-year-old Prince Jamie.

The uprising was one Thorn had long expected. Putting aside his personal problems, he assembled his men-at-arms and prepared to do battle at the side of the young prince.

Chapter Thirty-one

Diana's step was slow as she ventured from her apartments one summer evening. Accompanied by Sibeal, she descended the stone steps on her way to the great hall.

The evening meal was becoming increasingly difficult to endure. Her brother, fully recovered, was badgering her with renewed insistence to marry Donald Campbell. Why the man still wanted to wed her was something Diana truly could not understand. Even though she had not openly admitted it, there seemed to be no doubt in his mind, nor anyone else's, that she was no longer a virgin; though now, in the first week of July, it was evident that she carried no child.

When they entered the hall, Sibeal moved to her place at one of the lower tables. As Diana approached the dais, a sigh finally escaped her lips. Robert, she could see at a glance, was well on his way to being inebriated, which was happening more and more of late.

Part of his heavy drinking was, she knew, due to the ache in his shoulder. Though the wound itself had healed, his shoulder hurt him each time he moved his arm. Worse, the physicians had informed him that he would never again be able to handle a broadsword, much less a claymore. According to the ways of their people, Robert was to be denied that special place in heaven reserved for a Scotsman who died with his sword in his hand. Diana was very much aware that her brother held her responsible for this state of affairs.

Diana seated herself, grateful that Robert was in conversation with Lachlan Gilbride and did not seem to notice her arrival. The men were discussing the battle of Sauchieburn, which had occurred on June 11, some three weeks ago. James III had been defeated; Prince Jamie was now king.

" 'Twas fierce fighting, I'll wager," Robert said at one point.

"Aye," Lachlan said with a nod. "Many a man fell before it ended." He laughed. "The MacKendrick took a blade in his side. Most thought 'twould be the death of him."

Diana stiffened. The room spun dizzily before her eyes.

"And?" Robert leaned forward expectantly.

Lachlan shrugged. "He survived. The devil takes care of his own."

The room righted as her vision cleared. Shakily, she reached for her wine and drank deeply.

Unaware of her reaction, Robert leaned back in his chair and rubbed his arm. "I confess that I never expected the king to be overthrown, much less murdered!" He turned toward Lachlan. "Does Jamie plan retribution against those who sided with his father?"

Slowly, Lachlan shook his head. "I think not. But then, one never knows."

"Well, we cannot be counted among them, in any event," Robert said with more conviction than he felt. "We fought for neither side."

"Aye." Lachlan drained his cup. Then he gave his earl a long look. "But the Campbells fought for the father, not the son. Our friendship with them is well-known."

The observation caused a worried frown to appear on Robert's forehead. "Then we must make certain that Jamie is aware of our allegiance," he mused. His brow cleared. "We will invite him here to Sidhean."

Lachlan raised a brow. "On what pretext?"

Robert thought a moment, then gave Diana a sidelong glance. "Why, for a wedding, of course."

She stiffened and put down her knife. "I will not wed Donald Campbell!"

Robert's fist slammed onto the table. "I am through putting up with your disobedience!" he shouted. "I have already given my word to Donald that you will wed him!"

Her stomach clenched at the news. "You should not have done that."

"How dare you take exception to my wishes!" Robert shook his head. "God's bones! What manner of woman are you that you do not want to wed!" Leaning over, he grasped her wrist and twisted it cruelly, as if by so doing he could gain her attention, but Diana said nothing.

Enraged, Robert released her, then smiled thinly. "I'll not waste any more time with you. I've a wedding to prepare. You will do as I say!" he concluded as if that were the end of the discussion.

"And you will not go against the word of our father!" Diana shot back. "If you make the attempt, I will present my plight before the Council."

"And if they judge in my favor?" her brother responded silkily. Beside him, Ellen smirked.

Diana raised her head. "If they were so unjust, I should refuse to respond during the ceremony."

Robert glared at her, his expression growing sly. "Father Alasdair is old, and his wits are failing him day by day. If after the ceremony he was told that the intended bride responded, he would forever believe it."

" 'Twill do you no good," she said. "Everyone here tonight has heard my words. I will not wed Donald Campbell!"

Robert's hand moved in an expansive gesture. "Who among you here has heard my father's supposed last words?"

No one stood up, but Diana did not expect anyone would. Only she and Robert had been present at their father's demise. It was her word against his.

"You are the worst of scoundrels, Robert MacLaren," she gritted. "A man who does not respect the last wishes of his father is no man at all!"

" 'Twould be as you say," Robert replied smoothly. "However, as I did not hear our father speak the words that you have placed into his dying mouth, then I am not guilty of your charge."

Diana stared at him in amazement. Robert had been there! He had heard the same words that she had heard. Sickened, she turned away.

"I will not marry unless I agree to the union, Robert," she said in a quiet voice that was more effective than a shout heard throughout the Highlands. The large room was silent as she added, "There is nothing you can say—nay, there is nothing you can threaten me with— that will change my mind."

Getting up, she hurried from the room, only to pause when she heard Ellen's voice once she reached the corridor. The countess had followed her.

"You realize that 'tis your brother's right to throw you out, don't you?"

Diana viewed her sister-in-law coolly. "Then why does he not do so?"

Ellen gave a short, nasty laugh. "Only because Donald Campbell is daft enough to want you! You don't know how fortunate you are. You are a fool not to accept the first proposal that comes your way!" Ellen said as Diana began to ascend the stairs. "Not many men will want you now!"

Diana turned back again and arched a taunting brow. "Mayhap my experience will appeal to them, Countess," she noted sweetly. "Obviously, yours is not enough to keep your husband in your bed."

Ignoring the gasp of outrage her remark produced, Diana continued on her way up the stairs.

Chapter Thirty-two

The great hall at Holyrood was festooned with flowers and lit with candles that played on frescoed walls. Present were members of those clans who had supported young Jamie in the recent uprising, as well as those who had rushed forward to swear allegiance to their new sovereign. Young as he was, Jamie was no puppet, and he gave every indication of becoming a decisive leader.

Standing just inside the doorway next to a malachite vase whose deep greens were enhanced by candlelight, Thorn shifted from foot to foot. The festivities had not yet begun, and already he was bored. Court life had never appealed to him. He was unused to the protocol that seemed to dictate everyone's slightest move.

Outspoken and honest, he was also unused to the hazards that even the most casual remark held. Was the weather dreary? Probably. But not if the king had pronounced it a fine day. Was it a happy occasion? If His Majesty laughed, it was. Otherwise a person smiled at his own risk.

Thorn accepted a drink from a passing servant. At Rath na Iolair, no such restrictions prevailed. A man spoke his mind as he saw fit. He laughed when he was amused and fought when he was offended.

Thorn wanted to return home. Even the sight of the beautiful women who, collectively, appeared as an enchanting bouquet left him unmoved. So engrossed in his musings was he that the voice of the king took him completely by surprise.

"You appear morose, Thorn!"

Startled, Thorn took a moment to collect himself. " 'Twas not my intention to appear so, my liege," he said hastily, then forced a chuckle. Knowing the king's sensual inclinations, he added, "With so many lovely lasses around, a man's mind tends to stray."

"Indeed." Jamie took the time to survey the hall. Then he smiled in satisfaction. "Not even the Courts of England or France have women to compare with ours."

"I would not take exception to that," Thorn murmured.

The young king again looked at Thorn, and a

glint of mischief lit his blue eyes. "You would be the last, from what I have heard."

"Your Majesty has me at a disadvantage," he noted modestly.

That remark drew a delighted laugh. "We must see you wed, Thorn," Jamie said jovially. "Now, let's see." His eye traveled the room.

"Your Majesty," Thorn said lamely.

But the king's attention was elsewhere. "Ahh, there!" He made a subtle gesture. "Barbara, Lady Drummond."

Reluctantly, Thorn glanced at the lady in question. About 17, she was lovely enough, but her eyes were blue, not gray. She was petite, not tall. She appeared docile; no hint of fire sparked her demeanor. Just then the young woman spoke, and Thorn drew back at the sound of her voice. It was piercing, almost childlike in its shrillness. Unbidden, came the echo of another voice: low and well modulated, even in anger. Hearing his king speak, Thorn returned his attention to Jamie.

"Her father has most recently become a lord. The family is old and of good standing." Receiving no response, Jamie frowned. "Well, then. Cast your eye upon Eileen Lindsay. She is the daughter of the Duke of Montrose."

Thorn cleared his throat. "Both lovely lasses, Your Grace. But—"

"But the Earl of Dunmoor is not yet ready to settle down," Jamie said with another laugh. "Well, we cannot fault you for that. 'Twill be many a year before we do." He clapped Thorn on the shoulder. "You came to our aid when needed, suffering an injury that almost took your life. We will not forget. If there is anything we can do—"

"There is one thing, Your Majesty." Thorn took a breath. "I would request permission to return to Rath na Iolair."

Jamie nodded, pleased with the simple request. "You may take your leave whenever you wish, Thorn."

Gratefully, Thorn gave a deep bow, ignoring the pain in his side as he did so. "I offer my gratitude."

Jamie did not smile as he said, "Rather would we have your loyalty."

Thorn looked up before he rose from his bow. "That you need not ask for, Your Grace," he said quietly. " 'Tis yours as long as I live."

Solemnly, Jamie inclined his head as once again Thorn stood erect. "We will not forget your support," he murmured quietly as he moved away.

At dawn the following morning, Thorn, flanked by Angus and trailed by those men who had accompanied him into battle, was on his way back to Rath na Iolair. Though what he would find there beyond despair he did not know. They had ridden a distance before Thorn became aware of Angus's silence.

"You're glum," Thorn noted after a while.

"You're not as happy as I've seen you," Angus

snapped in a disgruntled tone.

Taken aback by the short answer, Thorn said no more.

In the predawn darkness a week later, Angus sat in the quiet great hall, shadowed by candlelight. His elbow on the table, Angus cupped his chin as he stared morosely at his chief.

Certainly he had tried to keep up, Angus thought to himself, stifling a yawn. He really had, matching Thorn drink for drink until his stomach had at last rebelled in protest, after which he had fallen asleep in his chair.

Now, he felt fine. He wondered how Thorn felt. Never had he seen his cousin drink as much as he had in these recent days since their return from court. Oddly, the fiery liquid seemed to have little effect. Angus marveled at how Thorn remained steady on his feet, how his voice remained unslurred, and how his vivid blue eyes never lost their haunted look.

With a sigh, Angus planted his feet firmly on the floor and tipped his chair back on two legs as he scanned the empty hall. The evening meal had long since ended, and the hour was approaching four in the morning—an hour when any civilized man should have been in his bed. Becoming bored with the deafening silence about him, Angus cleared his throat.

"Mayhap I should organize a hunt for tomorrow," he suggested to Thorn.

An unintelligible grunt came from his cousin.

With the perception that comes from a long relationship, Angus was certain that Thorn had answered in the negative. Still attempting to bring Thorn out of his black mood, Angus adopted a bantering tone. "Have you decided to grow a beard?"

Thorn gave him a blank look, then rubbed his chin. He grunted again. "Go to bed."

"After you," Angus said.

Watching Thorn, Angus sighed. All attempts at levity fled. In truth, Angus was not in a much better mood himself. The image of a certain bonnie lass with fiery red hair was one he could not seem to banish.

"You will have to get her back!" Angus declared, not putting a name to the woman. He knew that Thorn would assume that he was referring to Diana. In fact, it was Sibeal who was on his mind. He knew perfectly well that, if Diana returned, Sibeal would be with her.

"What makes you think she wants to come back?" Thorn asked.

Angus's chair hit the floor as he leaned forward. "You'll not be knowing the answer to that until you ask her!"

For several minutes, Thorn stared into space. A deep, vertical line appeared in his brow above his nose. A definite mark of displeasure.

Angus ignored it. If his earl became angry enough to deliver a blow, Angus was prepared to accept it, whether it was delivered with a fist or a sword, for he was steadfast in his loyalty.

A man, however, had a right to speak his mind; and Angus felt justified in doing so.

The moment lengthened; the silence deepened. Thorn shifted restlessly in his chair. Slowly, he turned to look at Angus. "You speak with more wisdom than I possess. Yet—" He shook his head, displaying a futility that was not lost on his companion.

Angus took a deep breath. If ever he was to receive a blow, his next words would occasion it. " 'Tis boldness that's needed now! I have never known you to be lacking."

Anger flooded Thorn's face. "No man questions my valor!" he growled. "If you are suggesting that we storm Sidhean, then it is suicide you propose!"

"I am not speaking of a raid," Angus said hastily. He sighed and shrugged his shoulders. "You would not want her back on those terms anyway."

"I would not!"

Angus cleared his throat. "Well, then"—he adopted what he thought was a reasonable tone—"you must get word to her."

Thorn stared in astonishment. Then he raked a hand through his hair. "Word! Christ's bones, you are in your cups! Do you propose I send a message under the seal of Rath na Iolair? Or mayhap I should deliver it in person?"

Angus shifted uneasily. He did not know how! All he was doing was offering an idea. It was Thorn's place to find the path! "To be sure, the messenger would have to be unknown to those at Sidhean."

"Aye," Thorn said jeeringly. "And he will walk up to the gate, simply ask for Diana, and promptly be admitted by that gargoyle Lachlan Gilbride. That man would not admit his own mother without cause!"

Silence returned. But the seed of an idea had been planted, and Angus knew that Thorn was studying all the angles to make it succeed.

"Subterfuge," Thorn said at last. "It worked once. It could again. The peddlers," he murmured nodding his head as the idea began to take shape.

Angus bent forward, at first puzzled. Then his brow cleared. Aye, he thought with a grin. The peddlers! "When are they scheduled to arrive?"

Thorn sat up straighter. "Find out!" The barest hint of a smile touched his lips as he added, "I'll wager both of us have unfinished business at Sidhean."

In the age-old gesture of comradeship, Thorn's large hand reached out to grip Angus's wrist, as almost simultaneously the other man's hand wrapped around the equally powerful wrist of his earl.

Chapter Thirty-three

The late-morning sun danced in and out of the clouds as Diana and Sibeal approached the outskirts of the village of Sidhean, which had taken on the appearance of a hamlet.

Twice a year merchants from Inverness and as far away as Edinburgh brought their wares to the outlying villages and isolated keeps, and quickly as their stalls were erected, the villagers and crofters congregated to inspect the merchandise.

Diana and Sibeal drew near to one of the stalls, and people stepped aside for Diana; however, they did not move away. Their smiles beamed their pleasure at her return.

Her answering smile never faltered as she sternly refused to allow the memories of the past months to intrude on her outing: memories that nevertheless invaded her dreams and played havoc with her waking hours. Sibeal's enthusiasm was the one thing that drew a genuine response from Diana as she watched the lass look through the wares. But Sibeal took so long to make a decision, Diana became restive.

"Sibeal!" she said with a rueful smile. "You have been looking at both of those items for ten minutes! Which one do you want?"

Sibeal sighed and examined the length of blue ribbon, then the delicate piece of lace she had been holding for several minutes.

"Och!" Diana said at last. "Take them both!"

"I have money to pay for only one," Sibeal said.

"Then pay for one, and I will buy the other!" Ignoring the forthcoming protests, Diana paid the peddler and smiled when she saw Sibeal clutching her coveted purchases to her breast.

As they continued on their way, Diana could not help but notice the happy expressions of those about her. She said to Sibeal, " 'Twould be nice if they had food and drink to cap their celebration."

Sibeal gave her a worried look. "The earl would not approve."

Diana grinned. "You are right. He would not approve." She decided that she would give the order as soon as they returned home. By the time her brother discovered the unauthorized largess, it would be too late for him to stop it.

An hour later, their arms filled with bolts of

material, ribbons, and laces, Diana and Sibeal were ready to return to the keep. They were approaching the bridge when a lad sidled close to Diana. He wore no plaid, and she thought he was a member of the caravan. Draped over his lower arm were lengths of velvet ribbons.

"Buy a ribbon, m'lady?" the lad said.

Diana's glance was only superficial, both for the boy and the merchandise. "Thank you, lad. However, we have all we need."

About to move on, Diana was startled when the lad stepped in front of her, effectively halting her progress. Her annoyance was quickly replaced by puzzlement. She thought she recognized him; but she was uncertain. Then, suddenly, she knew. It was Richard, the young groom from Rath na Iolair! Diana's heart began to pound as she searched the crowd. Was Thorn here?

The groom seemed to know for whom she was looking. "The earl is not here," he said in low tones, then he nodded in the direction of the woods. "He waits there and hopes you can come to him."

Diana's first instinct was to run in the direction of the wood. Then she noticed that Ellen, who had also come to shop, was looking at her with curiosity.

"I cannot go there now!" she whispered as she hastily turned away from her sister-in-law's piercing blue eyes.

The groom sensed her disquiet. In a casual

motion, he held up a red ribbon as if for her inspection.

" 'Tis no matter," he murmured, viewing the ribbon. "His lordship will wait. He said to tell you that he will wait as long as it takes."

With that, the lad moved away and lost himself in the crowd. On trembling legs, Diana continued onward.

"Will you go?" Sibeal asked in a voice only barely above a whisper.

"I don't know."

But she did. She knew she would go when the first opportunity presented itself.

In her room, Diana immediately ran to the window, her eyes scanning the wooded area beyond the glen. Though she could not see Thorn, she knew he was there. The idea was at once thrilling and frustrating.

Her eyes lowered to the throng of people still milling around the wagons. There was absolutely no chance of her getting through that crowd undetected. A long sigh escaped her when she realized that she would have to wait until morning.

About to turn away, Diana remembered her resolution to offer refreshments. She motioned to Sibeal. "Go to the kitchen and tell the cook to have food and drink sent to the villagers."

After Sibeal hurried from the room, Diana sank into a chair and stared at the clock, willing the hands to move swiftly.

That night, Diana could not sleep, though she

wished she could, if for no other reason than to pass the hours. Why did Thorn want to see her? She vividly remembered their last meeting. In the darkness, she winced and groaned as she remembered her last words to him. What man would want to come near a woman after she had expressed hatred for him!

A thought struck and chilled her. There was always the chance that the Earl of Dunmoor still sought vengeance. She buried her head in her pillow. She would rather die at his hands than live without him.

Diana at last fell into a fitful doze and was awake at first light. Donning her riding habit, she and Sibeal went down to the great hall for breakfast. Diana fidgeted through the meal, grateful that neither Robert nor Ellen had yet gotten out of bed. Back in her room less than an hour later, she started to remove her riding habit.

"What are you doing?" Sibeal asked in consternation.

Diana paused, surprised by the question. "I thought I would wear the dark blue velvet."

Sibeal's eyes widened. "For the crofters!" She shook her head. "Nay, 'tis best you look as you always do. Besides," she added with a smile, "somehow I think he'll not be caring about your clothes."

"Och," Diana murmured as she realized what she had been about to do. She gave Sibeal a rueful smile. "You see so much more than I do."

Quickly, Diana removed her courtly raiment, then hugged Sibeal. "What would I do without you, lass?"

Moments later Diana was again arrayed in the tan chamois outfit she always wore while on her rounds. Just before she left the room, Diana looked at Sibeal, and she knew her cheeks were flushed. "I may be a while. Please don't worry. And I promise I will inquire about Angus."

Holding her impatience in check, Diana leisurely made her way to the stables and just as leisurely rode from Sidhean. She made her rounds faster than she had ever done before, thankful that no problems arose to detain her. Then, responding to Diana's urgings, Banrigh cantered across the glen at top speed.

Had Thorn waited for her? Diana would not allow herself to believe otherwise.

Entering the shelter of trees a while later, she slowed her horse to a walk. Foliage was thick, and the sun dappled the emerald ground with splashes of gold. She hadn't gone very far when she saw him. Her heart skipped a beat, then another at the sight of his tall figure. Halting Banrigh, she dismounted.

Across an expanse of wildflowers, they looked at each other. Diana never knew which one of them moved first. But in an instant they were in each other's arms. No words were spoken before they kissed, for none were necessary. Breathlessness from that kiss alone forced them finally to part.

Together they sank down onto a soft bed of flowers whose fragrance enveloped them with their seductive scent. They were reluctant to release each other even for the time it took to remove their clothes, and they assisted each other with clumsy, impatient hands. But at last they were together, side by side, flesh against flesh, with only the birds to witness their searching kisses.

The feel of Thorn's muscular body was at once familiar and new beneath Diana's questing touch. Had his shoulders always been so broad, his flesh so solid, his stomach so flat and lean? Nowhere did her fingers encounter softness. Certainly not in that most intimate part of him, which pulsed and throbbed in anticipation of joining her body to his.

Parting her lips, Diana welcomed the demanding thrust of his tongue, and when his lips moved to her neck, she gasped as he trailed moist kisses to her breasts.

She could wait no longer. "Take me now!" she cried, clutching at his shoulders as a feverish passion engulfed her.

His muscular body pressed eagerly against hers. She shivered in delight as his hands moved seductively, teasingly, over her body. Then he entered her, and the world faded away. Reality fled as it always seemed to do with his closeness. Her legs wrapped around his waist and tightened as she sought to draw him deeper within her. Diana gave herself up to the surge of excitement that spiraled her body to peaks of ecstasy until at last she shuddered in fulfillment. Sated for the moment, they both lay quietly, entwined in each other's arms. Unable to keep from caressing him, Diana let her hand play across his body until it came to the wound on the side of his hip. She winced, touching the puckered skin.

"You were injured," she murmured.

" 'Tis nothing," he said.

Diana suddenly remembered her promise to Sibeal. "And Angus? Was he harmed?"

Thorn shook his head. "Not even a scratch!" he said emphatically.

Her hand again caressed the wound. "Does it hurt?" she whispered.

"No." He laughed and deposited a kiss on her chin. "But if it did, I would not admit to you. A warrior does not complain about a nick such as this."

She sighed, distressed by his levity. "There were those who thought it fatal."

Again he laughed. "Wishful thinking on their part!"

Her lips found the corner of his mouth. "I'm glad that I did not know about it until it was over. 'Twould have caused me endless worry if I had."

Thorn's hand rested on her cheek, and his thumb moved to caress her lips. "Diana Mac-Laren, I love you more than life itself."

She kissed him fiercely. "Then you love me

half as much as I love you!"

His eyes searched her own. " 'Tis true? You do love me?"

Her fingertips lightly moved across his lips. "Though I never thought it possible," she said quietly, "that word seems suddenly inadequate for what I feel."

She clutched him tightly. Idyllic as this reunion was, nothing had changed. Their love was impossible before; it was impossible now. The thought was so depressing Diana relaxed her hold. Her eyes brimmed with tears as she saw his questioning look.

"Ah, Thorn," she whispered, drawing away, "it can never be. Our love is a curse upon us both. Were I to wed you, our clans would know no rest till one or the other was destroyed. I cannot put my people through that. Nor can you. You know as well as I that the situation would be worse than ever. This feud has gone on for such a long time."

"Aye." Sitting up, Thorn gazed into the shadows cast by the trees. "One can hardly remember the names of the two who started it."

Diana raised her head to look at him. There was truth to that, she realized. And she further realized that the dispute of two long-gone ancestors had laid a mantle of hate and war upon the shoulders of their offspring. Yet how to overcome it?

"I'd give you the land, if it were mine to give," she whispered.

His hands sought the softness of her hair, and he bent toward her. " 'Tis not the land I desire."

His warm kiss sparked a renewed hunger, and she responded eagerly. She would not give voice to the thought that this might be their last encounter.

Grasping his hand, she placed it on her breast. "Feel my heart beat," she whispered. "And know that each time it does, it says I love you."

He frowned. "I know that your brother will try to keep us apart." he said earnestly. "But he will not succeed! You must believe this. We will be married as soon as we reach Dunmoor."

Slowly, she shook her head. "My brother—"

Thorn made a sound of disgust, interrupting her. "Your brother cares not who you wed!"

She sighed. There was so much that Thorn did not understand. "He does care. A great deal."

Drawing back, he gave her a sharp look. "You would discard what we have?"

Her heart wrenched at just the thought. "There's no way, beloved. There's no way!"

"I'll not give you up, Diana," he vowed grimly. His brows dipped, giving his face a hard look. "Wed another and he will die before he leaves the altar!"

Diana shivered, knowing he spoke the truth. "I'll not wed another, Thorn," she whispered softly. "If my life depended on it, I'd not give myself willingly to another man." She sighed deeply. "But as for the two of us being married—"

Thorn was silent. "There is one way," he said after a moment. "If the king were to sanction our union, none would dare gainsay him."

"Jamie?" she breathed, her eyes wide. "Why would he involve himself in our affair?"

"While our new king has not punished those who did not support him, he has bestowed favors upon those who have."

"You fought for Jamie?" Though Lachlan had mentioned Thorn's injury, he had not said on which side Thorn had fought.

"Aye." Thorn nodded. "And Jamie well knows it."

A glimmer of hope flared within Diana. If the king would indeed give his blessing—"Oh, Thorn!" She threw herself into his waiting arms.

"We will go to him together," he whispered as he clasped her close. "Once we are in Holyrood, we will be safe. We will be married there."

Releasing her, Thorn began to dress in a hurried fashion. Diana, however, dressed slowly, not wanting this interlude to end. When she was at last dressed, he took her hand and began to head for their horses.

Diana hung back. "I cannot go now. I must return for Sibeal. She would not be safe were I to leave her at Sidhean." She bit her lip, knowing that her words would be unwelcome.

Thorn, however, quickly nodded his agreement. "You are right. We will send for her."

He started to move forward again, but Diana shook her head and stood her ground. "I must go back."

"Nay!" he said quickly. "I do not want you to return!" He tightened his hold as if the pressure alone would keep her at his side.

She placed her hand on his tanned cheek. "I must, beloved," she said softly, willing him to understand. "I gave Sibeal my word that, when I left, I would take her with me."

Thorn raked a hand through his hair. "She followed you once before."

Again Diana shook her head. "She will know that this time I left of my own free will. If I do not tell her, she will assume that I have deliberately left her behind. I cannot do that. Please understand."

He sighed. "Very well, fetch her. I'll wait here for you."

"Nay! 'Tis too dangerous. You return to Dunmoor." As he was about to protest, she put a fingertip to his lips. " 'Tis not so long. Tomorrow, when I make my rounds of the crofters, I will take Sibeal with me. We will ride directly to Dunmoor and meet you there."

To forestall any further protest, Diana kissed him.

Chapter Thirty-four

Responding to Diana's urgings, Banrigh cantered across the glen at top speed prompting birds and small animals to quickly flee from her path. When she at last reached the drawbridge, Diana slowed Banrigh's pace to a more sedate trot and hoped that the excitement she was feeling was not evident in her face. If Thorn was correct in his assumption that the king would sanction their marriage, then no one, not even Robert, would dare take exception.

As Diana approached the stables, a groom came running forward to assist her in dismounting. When she handed the reins to the groom, she said, "Walk her, I fear she is overheated."

With difficulty, Diana managed to adopt a calm demeanor and refrained from running across the courtyard. She couldn't wait to tell Sibeal the good news. Sibeal, she knew, would be just as elated as she had been when she'd learned that they would both be leaving in the morning.

Still holding herself in check, Diana ascended the stairs and walked along the corridor until she reached her chambers. Opening the door, she paused at the sight of the empty room.

"Sibeal?" she called out, thinking the lass might be in her alcove, but there was no answer.

She sighed in exasperation as she went back into the hall. No doubt Sibeal was in the kitchen, chatting with the cook. She motioned to a passing servant. "Have you seen Sibeal?"

"Not since this morning, m'lady," the man replied with a deferential smile.

She frowned. She wanted a bath, and she did not want to wait. "Have hot water sent to my chambers, and fetch someone to assist me."

The man hurried to do Diana's bidding as she returned to her room. Going to the wooden chest, she opened it and surveyed its contents, trying to decide on which of her personal belongings to take with her when she left in the morning. Unfortunately, clothing could not be among them. It would never do for her to leave the keep with a noticeable amount of luggage in tow.

At the knock on her door, she hastily closed the chest. "Come in."

Servants entered with her bathwater, and a

short while later her tub awaited her. Diana disrobed and sank into the scented water, allowing the servants to wash her hair and scrub her body until her flesh gleamed. By the time she stepped out of the tub, she was becoming annoyed with Sibeal's extended absence. She waved away a hovering maidservant.

"I will dress myself. Fetch Sibeal and send her to me."

The young woman picked up the towels strewn on the floor. "Gladly, m'lady," she murmured, then straightened up. "Where is she?"

Diana made an irritated gesture. "I do not know where she is! Find her and send her to me!"

When the servants departed, Diana hastened back to the chest. An hour later, uneasiness lay in her stomach as heavy as an undigested meal. The servant had returned to inform her that Sibeal was nowhere to be found.

Her knuckles pressed to her lips, Diana listened to the clock as it ticked away the minutes. Sibeal knew where Diana had gone. She would very much want to know the outcome. Whatever else she was, Sibeal was not frivolous. She would not absent herself without reason.

Diana allowed another half hour to pass. Then, panic-stricken, she left her chambers to conduct her own search. She had no destination in mind. She simply felt the need to move, to do something!

Slowly, she walked along the hall. Torches

blazed flickering light that scampered up and down the walls, highlighting gilt frames and finding nooks and crannies that would otherwise be hidden.

Diana was unaware that she had halted before the door that led to Ellen's chamber until she found herself staring at the carved wood. This door had once led to her mother's apartments. Within, resided the present Countess of the Sidhean—the woman who had once tried to kill Sibeal.

Her mouth tight, Diana threw open the door and entered the room she had not seen since Ellen took possession of it five years ago. It was not the way she remembered. Her mother had favored soft colors. Ellen preferred crimsons and bright yellows. The combination was garish. Yet in a way, Diana welcomed it. No memories lingered here.

Ellen was seated in a high-backed chair before a tapestry board. She seemed unprepared for the abrupt entrance and gaped at Diana as she crossed the room with purposeful steps.

Keeping herself in check, Diana confronted her sister-in-law. "Where is Sibeal?"

Though taken by surprise, Ellen quickly recovered. Her hand was steady as she took another meticulous stitch. "One wonders what you were taught as a child," Ellen said as she carefully drew the thread through the material.

Ignoring that remark, Diana repeated her question in a stronger voice. Ellen took another stitch before she said, "I neither know nor care."

Diana's patience was fast leaving her. "Heed me, Ellen," she said in a low voice, "and heed me well. If you have harmed Sibeal, you will answer to me!"

Looking up from her handwork, Ellen offered a cool smile. "My word as a Douglas, Diana. I have not harmed your precious maidservant."

"Then where is she?"

Ellen's slim shoulders rose and fell in a delicate motion. Diana took a step forward, and the countess raised a hand in alarm. "Ellen!"

"Leave me be!" Ellen exclaimed, dropping her needle. "If you have questions as to the whereabouts of your servant, ask your brother!"

Diana froze. God, she thought, Robert could not have summoned Sibeal to his bed again! Turning on her heel, Diana hurried next door to Robert's chambers. He was not there. His servants informed her that the earl had left the keep.

Thoroughly confused, she stood uncertainly in the hall for many minutes, trying to collect her thoughts. She had no idea what to make of this situation. Sibeal had never before left the keep without first informing her.

Mayhap she followed me to the wood, she thought. Then she shook her head. Had that been the case, they would have met on the way back.

Unwilling to give up just yet, Diana went to the end of the hall and opened a narrow door.

Quickly, she made her way down a winding flight of stairs used mostly by servants. Before she reached the bottom step she could smell the mutton and barley broth that would constitute the evening meal.

Hot, steamy air enveloped her as she stepped into the kitchen. Only servants and the cook were in evidence. The cook, a wiry man in his early fifties named Ewen, looked up in pleased surprise. "Milady!" He wiped his hands on a towel, then proudly pointed to a slab of mutton roasting on a spit. "Plenty of mace, just like you said 'twas made at court."

She nodded absently. "Aye, you make it better than they did." Ignoring his puzzled look at her distracted manner, she asked, "Have you seen Sibeal today?"

He shook his head. "I've not seen the lass since yesterday morning."

Glancing out the window just then, Diana saw Lachlan striding across the courtyard. If anyone knew the answers to her questions, he would. With no further words, she headed for the door, leaving the cook looking more puzzled than before. A few minutes later, she confronted Lachlan.

"Where is the earl?" she asked, a bit breathlessly.

"Off on a hunt, m'lady," he replied. "He left just after you did."

"Have you seen Sibeal?" Her voice was growing frantic.

The knight shook his head. "Not today."

"She is not in the keep!" she said sharply. "If she left, you must have seen her!"

"I did not," Lachlan replied stiffly, upset with having the veracity of his statement questioned.

Observing his roughhewn face, Diana knew he spoke the truth. Lachlan Gilbride had no knowledge of Sibeal's whereabouts. But Robert did. And so did Ellen. Diana knew that with as much certainty as she knew day would follow night.

Expelling her breath in a despondent sigh, she returned to her room. Shadows lengthened. She ate a solitary meal and finally went to bed.

Tomorrow, she thought as she drifted off to sleep, she would return to Thorn. Nothing and no one would keep her from him.

Chapter Thirty-five

The next morning, Diana opened her eyes and stretched, filled with a sense of euphoria. Thorn! Today she would go to him. And remain with him forever.

Sitting up, she swung her legs over the side of the bed, momentarily surprised that Sibeal was not there with her robe. Then she remembered, and the disquiet that overcame her left her for the moment powerless even to move. Sibeal would never have left of her own free will. That fact recognized, the possibilities were not those Diana wished to face.

She was still sitting there moments later when a sharp cry drew her to her feet so suddenly that she stumbled and almost fell. Righting herself, she ran to the window.

Nothing in her wildest nightmare, her wildest

visions, prepared her for the scene that greeted her eyes. There, in the courtyard below, was Sibeal, her slim body bound to a stake, around which were clumped faggots, waiting only to be ignited by the man who stood to the side, holding a lit torch.

Her breath seemed to have been pressed from her chest, and Diana gasped for air. Preoccupied she never noticed that Robert had entered the room.

"It surprises you, does it not," he said cheerfully as he came toward her, "that your faithful Sibeal has been found to have Satan's mark upon her?"

It took a second for Diana to recover her senses enough to face her brother. "What have you done!"

He looked affronted. "Done? I've done nothing." Going to the window, he glanced down, then at Diana again. "Sibeal spent yesterday with Father Alasdair. Unfortunately, the good father became suspicious during her confession."

Diana swallowed and backed away. "What are you saying, Robert?"

"He gave her the test."

For a moment, Diana just stared at him. The test to which he was referring, though seldom used, was simple enough. After being blindfolded, the priest, using an ordinary pin, poked at various parts of a person's body. If, at any time, the person did not produce a reaction to the prick of the pin, it was said that place was where Satan had put his mark.

Diana put a hand to her breast, as if she could still the pounding of her heart. "I do not believe you! Why would Father Alasdair even consider such a thing?" Robert did not answer. Her eyes narrowed as her suspicions solidified. "You told him to do it, didn't you?"

Robert took a moment to view his nails before he made a response. "Ellen has always considered Sibeal to be a witch. Naturally, I told her it was all rubbish, but—" He waved a hand in a gesture that conveyed how futile it was to argue with his wife.

At that moment, another cry reached her ears, and Diana raced back to the window. "My God, Robert! What are you doing?"

Robert's frown was disapproving. "Sibeal did not pass the test, Diana. I was as grieved to learn of it as you are," he said with a false sympathy that was not lost on her.

He attempted to put his arm around Diana, but she pushed him away. At her rejection, Robert's lip curled, and his tone became brisk. "Very well, Diana. Which means more to you: Sibeal's life or your continued refusal to marry Donald Campbell?"

As the full realization of what was happening washed over her, she trembled. Numbly, she could only shake her head in disbelief. She looked down to see the man, the lighted torch in hand, bending forward. Quickly, the small faggots caught fire, sending a thin column of smoke into the air.

Leaning on the sill, Diana began to pant, her breath coming in tortuous gasps. She must not faint! she told herself even as the courtyard began to blur and swim before her eyes. If she did, Sibeal would be dead before she recovered her senses.

"Robert!" Diana screamed.

"Nay! The time for discussion is over! I would have your word that you will wed Donald."

Diana could only stare at him. This was her brother! This was the man who came from the loins of her own father. "You cannot ask me to make such a promise!"

"I can and have," Robert replied coldly. Then he pointed. "Look there! Will you see her burn to satisfy your pride?"

Diana sank weakly to her knees. Pride! she thought wildly. No, not her pride. Her heart! Her soul! Her reason for living!

Her thoughts too much to bear, Diana pressed her hand to her mouth to keep from screaming. If my life depended on it, I would not wed another man, she had said to Thorn. But what if it were not her life? Could she be responsible for Sibeal's death? Mother of God, no! She could never go to her Maker with such a sin on her soul.

Raising herself slightly, she peered out of the window. The flames were higher. Sibeal's slender body strained at the bonds that held her secure to the stake; her terrified eyes rose to Diana's window.

Diana shook her head sharply, trying to rid herself of the image she was seeing so clearly. It had to be a nightmare—a vision that would pass. Horrified, she tried to speak, only to find she did not have the strength to do so. Her mind was seared with the sight of Sibeal's suffering face.

"Stop it!" Diana screamed. "I will do anything you ask!"

Robert bent forward. "What? Am I to understand that you will comply?"

Diana took a breath that came from her soul. "Aye," she whispered. Her fingers slid from the sill as she collapsed to the floor. "I will comply."

Throwing open the window, Robert waved an impervious hand. "Set the wench free!" he called out. "I am no longer convinced that she is a witch."

"But you are Satan's henchman, Robert," Diana said through clenched teeth. "I will yet see you in hell."

"If you live long enough," he said offhandedly, then sneered. "Mayhap you will join me there after your husband has his way with you. I know well how a man can occasionally lose control of his more civilized inclinations when inflamed by lust and, God knows, Donald has kept his contained for a long, long time."

Whistling a small tune, he left her room.

Why couldn't she cry? Diana wondered distractedly. If ever in her life there was time for tears, it was now. Yet the pain and loss she was feeling seemed beyond the solace of that simple release. She felt as though she would never laugh or cry again.

She was still on the floor sometime later when a servant opened the door to admit the man who had held the lighted torch. In his arms, he carried Sibeal.

"Just fainted, she has," he remarked cheerfully.

Crossing the room to the alcove, he deposited Sibeal's limp body on her mattress. Coming back, he paused, looking at Diana, expecting her to speak. When she did not, he shrugged and left the room.

Minutes passed before Diana roused herself sufficiently to get to her feet. Her limbs felt heavy, as if invisible chains had been wrapped around them. She gazed at Sibeal. The lass had not moved, though the rise and fall of her breast indicated she was alive.

Diana moved closer. The acrid smell of smoke assaulted her. Kneeling beside Sibeal she brushed the hair from her white face. Though the hem of her skirt was singed, there were mercifully no burns in evidence.

By sheer effort of will, Diana forced her personal problems from her mind as she began to tend to Sibeal. Wetting a cloth in the cold water in the basin on her dressing table, she gently sponged Sibeal's face. Sibeal's eyelids fluttered, then opened. A smile began, then fled as awareness coursed through her.

"Hush," Diana murmured softly. " 'Tis all over. There is nothing for you to be afraid of now."

"Father Alasdair said I had Satan's mark on me!" She struggled to sit up, but Diana's hand gently pushed her back.

"He has realized that he was in error," Diana said soothingly. Seeing that Sibeal was still frightened, she added, " 'Twas all a mistake. You know I would not say it if 'twas not true."

Gradually, Sibeal relaxed, her trust in Diana implicit.

"You rest," Diana said as she straightened up. "I will bring you food. You are to do nothing this day."

With a sigh, Sibeal closed her eyes. When Diana returned a while later, followed by a maidservant carrying a tray of food, she found Sibeal asleep. Not wishing to disturb her, Diana instructed the servant to place the tray on a table. When the woman left, Diana sat in a chair to wait until Sibeal awakened.

Though the hour was still early, Diana felt exhausted in body and mind. Thorn was waiting for her that minute, and she could not go to him.

Closing her eyes, she said a prayer that he would not come here searching for her. Suddenly, the door opened, and Robert entered. Diana did not look at him.

"Is the wench all right?"

"She is asleep."

Robert nodded and narrowed his eyes as he looked at Diana. "Even though you are bound by your word, I feel it prudent that you remain within the keep until the wedding."

The restriction did not surprise her. "When is it to be?"

"Two weeks from Sunday."

She sat up. "So soon?"

Robert laughed at her dismayed look. "Your bridegroom is anxious. You should be pleased. I will brook no more foolishness from you, Diana. You have agreed to wed Donald Campbell, and I shall hold you to your word! If you break your promise, your pretty little maid won't have you to save her again."

Turning on his heel, Robert left the room.

Chapter Thirty-six

Inside her windowless alcove, Sibeal raised herself up on her elbow, having been awakened by the voices coming from Diana's room. She had heard Diana and Robert's entire conversation, and she was shaken that Diana had forfeited her own future to once again save Sibeal's. She, more than anyone, knew how much Diana detested Donald Campbell.

Though weak, having had no food for the past 24 hours, Sibeal got to her feet. As soon as she was certain that Robert had left, she went into Diana's chambers.

"You agreed to marry him for my sake!" she cried out, unable to quell her tears. "That's the truth of it, isn't it?"

Diana turned away. " 'Tis of no matter now,"

she said quietly sitting in the chair in front of the hearth. " 'Tis done, and there's an end to it."

Through her tears, Sibeal cast an anxious look at her mistress. In all the years she had known Diana, she had never seen her so subdued; Diana appeared almost defeated.

"You did not agree of your own free will!" Sibeal said.

Diana did not answer as she stared into space. The sadness on the beautiful face of her mistress was more than Sibeal could bear. Her knuckles pressed to her lips, she tried to marshal her thoughts. Everything she had—including her life—she owed to Diana. There had to be something she could do!

A week before the wedding, Sibeal and her mistress sat in Diana's chambers, stitching Diana's wedding gown. The gray weather outside matched their mood. Accompanied by rain that produced a sharp staccato rapping on the closed shutters, thunder rumbled across the sky. Wind made its presence known by demanding entrance through cracks and crannies.

A particularly loud crash of thunder startled Sibeal, and she paused to listen to the rain. Normally a comforting sound, it seemed that day to chastise her for her inability to aid her mistress.

Turning her head, she gazed at Diana, whose

hands had also fallen idle. She seemed lost in thought.

Sibeal hesitated a moment, then murmured, "Have I given you my thanks?"

Roused from her musings, Diana appeared surprised. "For what?"

"For everything."

"Och! You speak nonsense more often than you should," Diana grumbled as she resumed sewing.

But Sibeal's hands remained motionless. As she had been doing for the past week, she was frantically searching for a way to assist her mistress. Surreptiously, she glanced at Diana, who was sewing mechanically. In accordance with the orders from the Earl of Sidhean, Diana had not left the keep in the past seven days. Sibeal well knew how difficult the restriction was for her lady.

And what would it be like when Diana was at last in her husband's keep? Sibeal shivered. A prison would be preferable!

" 'Twill be a large gathering, I'm supposing," Sibeal murmured in reference to the wedding.

"Aye," Diana said listlessly, "even the king will be in attendance."

Her hands still in her lap, Sibeal stared into space, imagining she could see Angus's face. "If you are ever in need," he had said. Well, she could think of no other time when she needed him more than now, she decided.

Thoughtfully, Sibeal plunged the needle into

the fabric. An idea was at last forming in her mind. Never adventurous, she at first rejected it. But like an irritating gnat it would not go away.

Almost an hour passed, and finally she became aware that the thunder had ceased. The rain had become no more than a fine mist. She put aside her sewing. Casually, she stood up and stretched. Then she walked to a corner, studying the bolts of material Diana and she had purchased when the caravan had come to Sidhean.

"You know, m'lady," she said quietly, "a length of this gray satin stuffed with down would make a handsome blanket for a bairn."

Diana blinked as she raised her head. "What bairn?"

"I was thinking of Ranald, the crofter. Cook told me that his wife has recently birthed a son. I know you always like to give a gift when one of the crofters has a bairn. This time, of course, you could not go, and what with everything else—" She made a vague gesture.

"Och!" Diana exclaimed, momentarily roused from her lethargy. "Why did you not tell me of this sooner!"

"Well, 'tis a small matter to set right," Sibeal said. " 'Twould take little time for me to deliver it." She looked hopefully at her mistress.

Diana immediately got up. "And you must do so right away!" Taking the bolt, she proceeded to cut off a generous portion, then folded it neatly. She handed it to Sibeal. "See to it that this reaches them today."

Sibeal cleared her throat. "Mayhap 'twould be a good idea if I rode there," she said glancing out the window. "The weather is still threatening."

"Aye," Diana said readily. "Take Banrigh. I'll wager she has not had a run in this past week."

Hurriedly, Sibeal fetched her arisaid and made her way down to the courtyard. Though the sky still remained gray and threatening, the rain had ceased altogether. Though it was August the weather was cool, and Sibeal tightened her arisaid as she headed for the stables.

To Sibeal's vast relief, neither the earl nor Lachlan was in evidence. She was uncertain whether she could brazen it out if questioned by either one of them.

Without hesitation in her step, she approached one of the grooms. The young man viewed her in surprise when she instructed that Banrigh be brought to her.

"What ails you!" she demanded sharply. "Saddle my lady's horse, and be quick about it! I've not the whole day to do a simple errand."

The groom took what seemed to her to be a long time to consider. "No one rides Banrigh but Lady Diana," he said at last.

Sibeal pursed her lips. "And who has ridden her in this past week? She will grow stiff with disuse!"

The groom scratched his head in indecision.

"Mayhap I should ask Lachlan."

"And mayhap you should have your ears boxed for questioning the wishes of Lady Diana!"

A sigh greeted that retort. "Well, Banrigh has been in her stall for almost a week now."

Concealing her relief, Sibeal watched as the groom at last brought forth the horse. When Banrigh had been saddled, the groom assisted Sibeal in mounting. But he still looked doubtful. "I don't think you should go beyond the village."

Sibeal raised her brow in apparent surprise. "And where else would I be going?" She prodded the horse forward before the groom could offer any further argument.

As soon as they cleared the bridge, the mare went from a walk to a trot of her own accord. With some trepidation, Sibeal tightened her grip on the reins.

"Quiet now, you little beast!" she muttered. "You'll not be trying out any of your fancy steps with me on your back!"

Arriving at the crofter's small house a while later, Sibeal dismounted and walked along the dirt path to the front door. She knocked, then waited.

Ranald opened the door. Tall, thin, and stooped shouldered, he appeared older than his 30 years. The initial smile on his face died at the sight of Sibeal. With a sharp gasp of fright, he crossed himself.

Sibeal was more hurt by the gesture than she displayed. She had no doubt that everyone in the village knew that she had been branded a witch.

" 'Tis not necessary for me to enter your house," she said stiffly, then thrust the bundle at him. "My lady hopes you can make use of this as a blanket for your son."

The crofter had the grace to blush. " 'Twas no disrespect intended." He stepped back and opened the door wider to admit her entrance.

Sibeal's gaze flicked past him into the interior of the cottage. Fruits and vegetables hung from the ceiling, drying for winter use. By a table, two giggling girls pushed and shoved each other as they placed wooden trenchers on the rough-hewn surface.

From within a room Sibeal could not see, she heard the wail of an infant. Unexpectedly, her arms ached to hold the child. More than anything else in this life, she wished for a child of her own.

Ranald still held the door ajar. Though Sibeal would have dearly loved to enter, to see the bairn, mayhap to hold him, she knew it was not to be. If she came within five feet of the baby, Ranald or his wife would attack her with all the fury they would display toward a demon who had approached their child.

She did not move. "I've not the time to visit," she said with dignity. "You may convey your thanks to my lady when next you see her."

With no further words, she retraced her steps down the dirt path and untethered Banrigh. Thoughtlessly, she attempted to mount the horse from its right side instead of its left. Banrigh neighed and skittishly moved away.

"Stand still, you little beast!" Sibeal muttered in exasperation. After several more attempts, she at last managed to again seat herself on the mare. Grabbing the reins tightly, she heaved a great sigh. "Now, listen to me! I know that mine is not the hand you're used to, and if time was not of such importance, I would gladly walk to my destination. But as matters stand, you will have to take me there." Bending forward, she tapped the horse on the neck. "Do you understand me, you little beast?"

Banrigh twitched her ears, but made no further acknowledgment.

For the next quarter of an hour, Sibeal rode through the village, glancing back now and then at the stone walls of Sidhean. She saw nothing amiss.

Allowing the mare no more than a walk, Sibeal headed for the wood, expecting any minute to hear a cry of alarm. None came.

When she was within the cover of the trees, she turned Banrigh loose. The speed with which the animal traveled took her breath away. Putting her confidence in the mare's ability to keep its balance, Sibeal hung on, directing the spirited animal with a tug of the reins when necessary.

It was midafternoon when Sibeal at last stopped to rest Banrigh. Dismounting, she stretched out on the grassy cover and pressed her ear to the ground, knowing that the sound of thundering hooves could be heard in such a fashion. With relief, she heard nothing.

Getting up, she went to a nearby burn to quench her thirst, not caring that the horse was beside her doing the same thing. A few minutes later, she was again on her way.

Dawn had not yet lighted the sky when Sibeal at last reached Dunmoor. The trip, most of which had been across MacLaren land, had been uneventful. Crofters in the fields had paused at their labors to view her, but none had spoken to her.

Tugging on the reins, Sibeal halted Banrigh. If nothing else, the beast was obedient, she thought as she slipped to the ground.

The earl, she knew, had been in residency a week ago, which meant that Angus would be here as well. If they had returned to Rath na Iolair, she was prepared to ride the distance. By now, she knew the way.

Feeling weary and stiff, Sibeal awkwardly patted the horse on the neck. "You're a good beastie."

Glancing up at the ramparts, she could see no movement, though she was certain that the guards were on duty. She opened her mouth to call out, then closed it again when her mind conjured a vision of arrows descending upon her.

Sibeal leaned against the horse. Her head began to nod. Exhaustion was robbing her of the ability to think clearly. Summoning the last of her strength, she tethered the mare to a bush. Then she sank to the ground. It felt as inviting as a feather mattress. In only seconds, she was asleep.

A sword prodded her awake some hours later, and Sibeal screeched in terror. Swallowing her panic, she pushed herself to her feet and glared at her attacker. His plaid told her he was a MacKendrick.

"You'll be taking me to Angus MacKendrick!" she declared with as much authority as she could summon with a sword pointed at her chest. "And you will be doing it now or be answering to him for your lax ways!"

She expected an argument, but the man just grinned at her. It was only then that she noticed that he was the same man who had accosted her on her second night at Rath na Iolair.

"Come on then, lass," he said with a chuckle. "I'll not be facing Angus again if you're not treated proper."

Sibeal swallowed, feeling a relief that threatened to send her sprawling to the ground. She untethered the mare and docilely followed the guard across the drawbridge.

A while later, Sibeal stood before Angus in the great hall, and he noticed that she absently rubbed her palms on her skirt.

"You said I could come to you if I needed help," Sibeal said hesitantly.

He immediately moved toward her. "I said only what I meant."

Seeing her agitation, he led her toward a chair and gently pushed her into it. Going to a sideboard, he poured a glass of wine and handed it to her. She took a deep draft; then the words poured from her.

"You say your lady is being forced to marry Donald Campbell?" Angus asked when she was through.

With difficulty, he had held his anger in check while Sibeal related that she had been bound to a stake and condemned to be burned for being a witch. But he knew that, if ever again the MacKendricks and the MacLarens met on the battlefield, he would kill Robert. Not even Thorn himself would deny him that satisfaction.

"Aye, 'twas only to save me. I know it!"

"Things of this nature would never have happened when the old earl was alive," Angus muttered. He made no mention of the tales he had heard of Robert MacLaren's conduct during a battle or even during a friendly joust. Whatever honor the father had been endowed with had not been passed on to the son.

"You must tell the earl what has happened!" Sibeal said in a strong voice.

Angus sighed, more disturbed by the news than he displayed. Thorn had expected Diana to arrive there within a day or two of their meeting. When a week had passed with no sign of her, Thorn had been like a man possessed. He was convinced that Diana was being held against her will. And from what Sibeal said, Thorn had indeed been correct in his assumptions.

Only the combined urgings of both Angus and Grizel had prevented Thorn from rushing to Sidhean. Finally, he had decided to seek assistance from the king. Whether he had been successful or not was something Angus had no way of knowing.

Aware that Sibeal was watching him with concern, he said, "Thorn has gone to Edinburgh to see the king."

Sibeal's green eyes widened, and her voice was edged with panic as she exclaimed, "The king is not there! He is on his way to Sidhean for the wedding!"

"When is it to be?"

"This Sunday at the kirk in the village."

Angus groaned. Five days hence.

"Couldn't you go after him?" Sibeal cried.

"Nay. Even riding hard, I could not make it there and back in time. All we can do is wait and hope that Thorn is by now on his way back. Meanwhile, you will stay here. When Thorn gets back, he will know what to do."

Sibeal shook her head until her curls bounced. "I cannot stay! I've been gone too long already."

"That's the point," he said. "If you return now and the MacLaren questioned you, what would you say? You don't want him to discover that you have been here. After what he did to you at Sidhean, 'twould be only natural that he thought you ran away."

"But my lady Diana—"

"She will know soon enough. Trust me, Sibeal. 'Twould be better for all concerned if you stay here." Turning from her, he instructed the servants to see to her comfort. Then he looked at her once more. "You're still a brave lass," he noted quietly.

Sibeal averted her eyes. "You say that because you don't know me," she whispered.

He smiled. "I know you. And I like what I know."

Chapter Thirty-seven

Inside her chambers, Diana sat listlessly in a chair. On the floor before her was her wedding gown. She had finished stitching the hem, but could not bring herself to complete the work on the bodice. Each stitch she took was like a blade thrust through her heart.

Finally, getting up from her chair, Diana went to the hearth and began to stoke the fire. Thoughts swirled around in her mind like the tiny embers beneath the poker's proddings.

More than a week had gone by since she had seen Thorn. A lifetime! What had his reaction been when she had not arrived at Dunmoor at the appointed time? She had not sent word to him, would not have sent word even if she had been able to do so.

If she had sent word to him, he would have

come to her. But at what cost? Her blood ran cold at the possibilities. No. Their relationship had been impossible from the start. It was impossible now.

The clock struck the hour.

Startled, Diana glanced at the timepiece in disbelief. Seven? Sibeal had been gone for hours!

Putting down the poker, Diana stood there for a moment, trying to quell the fear that suddenly washed over her. The trip to and from Ranald's house should have taken no more than an hour. Where was the lass?

In a quick movement, Diana headed for the door. Down the stairs she raced, running until she reached the stables. Seeing one of the grooms brushing a destrier, she headed in his direction.

"Has Sibeal returned from her errand?" she asked, trying vainly to catch her breath.

The lad tugged on his forelock before he answered. "Nay, m'lady. She took your horse and left, she did. But she's not come back."

"She may be hurt!" Diana cried, cursing herself for her thoughtlessness. Sibeal had little experience handling a horse, much less one as spirited as Banrigh. She could have been thrown off and right now could be lying beside the road, injured!

The groom shrugged. "If she is, Lachlan will find her. He's in the village now, making inquiries."

That, at least, was comforting. Diana nodded, then returned to her room. From her window, she watched as Lachlan rode into the bailey more than an hour later. Neither Sibeal nor Banrigh were with him.

It was Banrigh's absence that told Diana that Sibeal had left Sidhean. If her maidservant had been thrown from the horse, Banrigh would have returned to Sidhean of her own accord.

And why shouldn't Sibeal have fled? Diana thought resignedly, turning away.

Finally, though she had little appetite and no desire for the company that awaited her, Diana made her way downstairs to the great hall. She had no sooner seated herself at the table than Robert turned to speak to her.

"Lachlan tells me your wench left the keep with your horse! Where did she go?"

Diana lowered her head. "I do not know," she answered truthfully. A servant put a bowl of broth in front of her, but Diana made no move to touch it.

"I'll not hear your lies!" Robert's cheeks flushed with quick anger. "Where did she go?"

"She delivered a gift from me to Ranald. After that, I do not know." A faint smile touched her lips as she added, "Why does it come as such a surprise to you that Sibeal would want to leave Sidhean after what you did to her?"

"I did nothing!" Robert protested. "And you well know it. 'Tis no fault of mine that the priest saw fit to punish her."

"Sibeal was punished for my disobedience," Diana remarked coldly. "And you well know that."

Robert snorted. "Well, small loss, after all." He looked at her, then at her untouched broth. "Eat! You are as thin as a skeleton and as pale as a ghost!"

Picking up her spoon, Diana dutifully dipped it into the barley soup. But there it stayed. She had neither the energy nor the inclination to raise it to her lips.

"God's bones, Diana!" Robert exploded. "I insist you eat. I'll not turn you over to Donald looking like a wraith!" About to rail at her again, Robert faltered at the defiant glance she threw him. "Well, go hungry then!" he muttered as he applied himself to his food.

Unable to bear any more, Diana got up and left the hall. Alone in her room again, she sat at her dressing table and stared into the mirror.

A mirthless smile barely lifted the corners of her lips. Robert had been right. She was beginning to resemble a wraith. Her hand went to her hip, feeling the prominence of the bone there. Her smile, such as it was, disappeared.

Futility had robbed Diana of her appetite in this past week; despair had taken the color from her cheeks. Now, added to that, was a growing sense of loneliness. She had not realized until this moment how much she had counted on Sibeal's comfort and companionship.

Chapter Thirty-eight

The portcullis was lowered to allow Diana to ride forth from Sidhean on this sunny afternoon. It was a small victory for her. Robert's initial command to keep her a prisoner in her own keep had been withdrawn.

The crofters had been badgering the Earl of Sidhean to settle their squabbles, and they were becoming fractious when he declined to do so. That, combined with his conviction that Diana would never renege on her word, had prompted Robert to withdraw the restriction.

Diana made her rounds and was greeted with an enthusiasm that warmed her heart. Finally, she arrived at Ranald's small cottage. Both he and his wife were profuse in their thanks for her gift.

" 'Twas my pleasure," she responded sin-

cerely. "I know how much you were both looking forward to the birth of a son." She was
amused as she watched the four young girls
across the room, all of whom were standing in
respectful silence.

"A joy and a relief!" Ranald said with a laugh.
Despite his words, his eyes held affection as
they swept over his daughters.

Diana headed for the door, where she paused.
"My maidservant was the one who delivered the
material?"

"Aye," Ranald said readily. "A lass with red
hair and a sc—" He broke off and flushed.

Diana merely nodded. "And when she left,"
she said, careful to keep her voice casual, "did
you happen to notice in which direction she
rode?"

Ranald shook his head, then looked at his
wife and daughters. They, too, professed no
knowledge as to where Sibeal had gone when
she had left the house.

With a sigh, Diana thanked them and left.
Again, she mounted her new horse. The animal
was not as well trained as Banrigh and had a
tendency to be skittish, even under Diana's firm
hand.

With difficulty, she kept him to a walk as she
made her way slowly back to Sidhean. She was
in no hurry to return. What awaited her was
despair and what she considered to be the end
of her life.

She was but a mile from the village when,

from the corner of her eye, she suddenly caught sight of a horse and rider bearing down on her with great speed. It seemed to her at first glance as if they were on a collision course! Startled, Diana jerked on the reins with such force that the horse reared on his hind legs. Only her years of riding experience prevented her from falling.

Thorn said nothing as he angled Sian beside Diana's horse. He merely took the reins from her unresisting grip and led the animal into the wood. Coming to a halt in a small clearing, he dismounted, then assisted her from her horse.

"What are you doing here?" she asked in a tremulous voice.

"I might ask you the same thing!" he growled. Concern etched his handsome features as he reached for her.

Summoning every ounce of willpower she possessed, she managed to disengage herself and step back to what she considered to be a safe distance.

"Why haven't you come to me?" he demanded.

She avoided his question by asking, "Have you seen the king?"

"No, he was not in residence."

"I did not think he would be." She studied him a moment, only then noticing how weary he looked. His face was lined with weariness, his clothes dusty and travel worn. "You are just now returning from Edinburgh?"

"Aye," he said, "with little rest in between the

coming and going." His look was both condemning and accusing. "I was racing at full speed, hoping that when I reached Dunmoor, you would have arrived in my absence."

Diana nodded, knowing that, to reach Dunmoor, he had to pass Sidhean.

"Instead, I find you riding about the countryside as if you had nothing better to do!"

"I was making my rounds."

He looked at her intently, his brow creasing in perplexity. "How would you be knowing that the king was not in residence?" he asked, as if her words had only registered.

She hesitated a moment, then replied, "Because Jamie is on his way to Sidhean to attend a wedding."

His brow furrowed. "Only the wedding of the earl himself or a member of his family would prompt such a royal visit!" he scoffed. His eyes narrowed. "And unless I am misinformed, the earl is already married! Then whose wedding is he to attend?"

"Mine."

In a quick motion, Thorn grabbed her arms and shook her. "What are you saying!"

She waited a moment until he seemed to calm. "I am to marry Donald Campbell."

"You are to marry me!" he exclaimed forcefully. "And no other." Of a sudden, his tone softened and his touch gentled. "Och, I see it now. Robert has acted without your consent, and you feel trapped. No need!" he quickly added before she could speak. "Once we have the king's permission, Robert would not dare gainsay him. Come." Releasing her, he began to walk toward the horses. "We will go to Rath na Iolair right now. We will be safe there until the king returns to Edinburgh."

She drew back. "I cannot go with you."

He spun around, not for the first time startled by her disobedience. "You will come with me!"

Diana smiled sadly. How well she recalled his arrogant, authoritative behavior. At the time, her virginity and her pride were in question. Now, something more important was at stake. Though it was the last thing in the world she wanted to do, she knew she would have to send Thorn away.

And she must make certain that he would not follow her. To do so could easily result in his death. If that happened, her own life would be forfeit, for she would have no reason to go on living.

Turning away from him, she extended her hand and began to toy with a small branch of a tree, effecting a casualness that was odds with the turmoil in her heart.

"And if I do not choose to go with you, are you going to abduct me again, as you did once before, to live as a prisoner in your keep?"

"What?"

Appearing determined, Diana faced him squarely. "I do not wish to return with you, nor do I wish to marry you."

Thorn blinked and rubbed the back of his neck. God, he needed sleep, he thought. He could not focus on her words, which were at odds with their last meeting.

"What manner of nonsense is this!" he thundered. "Last time we met, you said—"

"I know what I said," she said smoothly. With a snap, she broke off the branch and absently twirled it between her fingers. "I have changed my mind. I no longer wish to wed you."

"You can say you no longer love me?" He watched her closely.

That was the one question she had wished he would not have asked. Even under these trying circumstances, she found it difficult to answer.

"I meant it when I said it," she replied carefully.

He stepped back, eyeing her from head to toe. "Meant it when you said it?" he echoed, dumbfounded. His eyes narrowed.

Diana could see that he did not understand, did not believe her.

"Diana," he said softly, "you must tell me the truth. Is Robert forcing you into this marriage?"

She raised her eyes to look at him. Options flashed through her mind. She could return with him to Rath na Iolair now. That would result in bloodshed which she did not want to contemplate, much less be responsible for.

She could run away. To where, she could not fathom. Clans did not easily accept outsiders.

Court was out of the question. She was well-known there.

Or she could marry Donald, and thereby keep the peace for all concerned. And although it was her last choice, she knew she had no options after all.

What remained, then, was to convince Thorn that the choice was her own. And she would have to do it in a decisive manner. No doubt must remain in his mind.

"No man forces me into marriage, my lord." Having crushed the little branch, she threw it to the ground. "It is a known fact throughout the Highlands that my father gave me his word that I would not be wed without my consent."

Thorn's blue eyes glittered dangerously. "What sort of game is it you play now?"

"No game, my lord," she countered swiftly. "I state merely the truth. Marriage to you would be against the wishes of my clan."

He came toward her, his rage evident. His manner held the menace that Diana once knew and feared. She faltered, but she quickly caught herself. She feared nothing but the crumbling of her own resolve.

"Never think to best me, my lord," she said coolly. "Better men than you have tried."

The cold bleakness in his vivid blue eyes tore at her. In them, she could see a reflection of her own pain, made worse because he was suffering.

How she loved him! No one in her life had

called forth such emotion, nor such potential for bloodshed! Had she had only herself to consider, she would not have hesitated for a moment. But there were more, many more, lives to consider.

Robert—How foolish that she should think of him and his men in battle at this time. But she did. She could easily recall Dunmoor when she had first seen it: ransacked, devastated, homes destroyed, blood needlessly spilled.

Thorn was still staring at her. She turned from him so that he would not see the tears that glistened in her eyes. Clasping her hands at her waist, she clenched them until her nails dug into her palms. She welcomed the pain, but it was not enough to override that which she felt so heavily in her breast.

"I have known you for a prideful wench from the first moment I set eyes on you!" he lashed out.

Diana forced herself to speak with anger. "Do you seek to parry words with me, my lord? Or will you accept the end of something that was never meant to begin?"

"I could take you now, you know," he said, his voice tight with anger.

"I do know," she answered, marveling at how she managed to keep her voice even. From somewhere deep inside her, she never knew where, she summoned a small laugh. "But you can never force me to say the words before a priest that will make me your wife."

He gave her a mocking smile, and her stomach lurched at the sight of it. "No priest has thus far sanctioned our union."

"True, my lord." Her eyes were level. "But at the time I had no say in the matter. Now I do."

Silent a moment, Thorn asked, "Is Donald Campbell aware of what has taken place between us?"

"He is. 'Tis of no matter to him. He realizes that I was taken against my will."

"How considerate of him," Thorn said. "Is that because he has also taken you against your will?" He watched her carefully.

She gasped, and outrage heated her cheeks. "Donald Campbell has never—" She came to an abrupt halt, again seeing doubt in his eyes. She could almost read his thoughts: Why would a man restrain himself when he knew his bride-to-be had nothing to lose? Even so, she could not bring herself to say that!

She moistened her lips. "Donald is a gentleman and very considerate." The lie almost choked her. She could only hope that Thorn did not know Donald personally. Her hopes were quickly dashed with his next words.

"I have met him," Thorn stated flatly. "He has neither quality you attribute to him."

She raised her chin. "With me, he does."

Thorn fell silent again. "And when is this auspicious wedding to take place?" he finally asked.

"Three days hence, on Sunday."

"So a MacLaren is what you are and what you

will always be!" he muttered.

"Aye," she said. At least in that she spoke the truth.

"Very well, Diana MacLaren," he said in a cold voice that touched her heart with frost, "go to your betrothed and be damned!"

Turning, Thorn strode away. A moment later he was on Sian and riding away from her. But not from her heart or her thoughts. Within those confines, he would remain forever.

Numbly, she watched him go. Feeling incredibly weary, she rode back to Sidhean beneath skies that were turning gray with clouds.

On a rise, Thorn halted Sian and turned to look back in the direction whence he had come. He could see Diana riding slowly across the fells. In three days she would be lost to him forever.

Mayhap he should have tried harder to convince her to come with him! he thought. Then his shoulders slumped. And to what end? he wondered despondently. He wanted her only on his own terms. And they were stringent! Diana MacLaren had to be his of her own free will. He would have her no other way.

Tensing, he gripped the reins, his eyes still on the rider. Strong, she was. But was she strong enough to withstand his physical prowess? He could easily take her. He had, once before.

But now it was different. He wanted her for

his wife. Only a fool abducted a wife. And he was no fool.

At last, he turned away. How could he have been so wrong, so bewitched?

Well, she had made her choice, he thought grimly as he spurred his stallion forward. And it was one they would both have to live with.

Chapter Thirty-nine

When Diana entered the bailey some time later, lights were blazing from almost every window of Sidhean, sending flickering shafts of amber through the misty rain. Every stall in the stables was filled to capacity and those horses that could not be accommodated within that shelter stood stoically beneath the chill drizzle.

She sighed at the sight. Everything pointed to the early arrival of the king, and Lachlan, who assisted her from her horse, confirmed her suspicions.

Inside, she swiftly ascended the stairs, hoping that Robert had not noticed her extended absence. Having changed his mind once regarding the restrictions he had imposed upon her, it was not beyond him to change it yet once again.

Reaching the landing, she had to step around

the pallets that lined the hall, placed there for those servants and knights for whom no better lodging could be found.

At last in her chambers, she hurriedly rummaged through the wooden chest for a suitable gown. Though she was disinclined to primp, the presence of the king demanded she look her best.

"Och, Sibeal," she murmured to the empty room as she selected then discarded a gown. "Which would you have chosen?"

She at last decided on the green one. As quickly as she was able, she dressed and, a short while later, entered the great hall.

It was crowded. Not only had the king arrived, accompanied by a contingent of men who constituted a small army, the Campbells, too, had arrived in great numbers.

For a moment, Diana paused on the threshold. A feeling of pride momentarily overshadowed her grim state of mind. She could see at a glance that everything had been done to make the king feel welcome.

The great hall had never looked so elegant. Pewter and silver had been polished to a brilliant sheen. Fresh rushes covered the floor. Tapestries had been brushed; torches had been lit; and all tables had been covered with snowy linens and bowls of rambling roses.

Diana planted a smile on her face and hoped it would remain in place for the evening. Her smile became genuine when the young king, whom she had not seen in almost three years, came toward her. He was no taller than she; however, since he was 15 years old, it was to be assumed that he had not yet reached his full height.

"Your Grace." Diana dipped a curtsy, looking up at him as Jamie paused before her. His doublet was a work of art so richly decorated with crimson and gold thread it was impossible for her to guess at the material that formed the basic garment.

Although the king was young, Diana could see in Jamie's eyes a new maturity tinged with a sad awareness. His mother, Queen Margaret, had died in 1486, the year after Diana had left Holyrood. And not two months past, he had lost his father as well. Diana wondered how true were the tales that he wore an iron chain beneath his clothes as a reminder of the price he had had to pay to gain the throne of Scotland. Knowing the sensitive, intelligent nature of the man who was her sovereign, Diana decided the rumors were indeed true.

The king extended a ringed hand to raise her to her feet. " 'Tis difficult to believe that a lass could grow more fetching with the years," he said, gazing at her with admiration. "Yet you prove it so."

"You are kind, Your Grace."

"Kindness has nothing to do with it, my lady," Jamie said gallantly, then laughed. "Indeed I fear your assessment of our being kind would be challenged by more than one member of our realm."

Diana gazed at him seriously. "If so, they would be mistaken."

About to speak again, Diana fell silent when she saw Robert and Donald approaching. Robert's eyes as he looked at her glittered with warning. She knew that her brother assumed that she had been seeking the king's aid. She smiled grimly. How little her brother knew her. He continually judged people by his own standards.

A spurious smile curved Robert's lips when he paused before them. "I hope my sister has not been boring you, sire." He laughed nervously. "A woman's prattle will ever bend a man's ear."

"We have yet to find a beautiful woman who bores us!" Jamie replied curtly.

Taken aback by the sharp retort, Robert recovered quickly. He motioned toward Donald, who was standing at his side. "If I may be permitted, I would like to present Donald Campbell to Your Majesty."

Donald gave a sweeping bow. "And I would like to take this opportunity to once again avow the allegiance of the Clan Campbell to Your Majesty."

With a slight nod, the king accepted the avowal. "We have been informed of the allegiance of the Clan Campbell—however tardy it may have been." He raised his hand in a gesture of dismissal, and both Donald and Robert hastily retreated.

From the expression on Jamie's face, Diana could tell that the king disliked Donald. His speculative gaze fell on her. She saw a flicker of disappointment darken his eyes. Doubtless, she thought wryly, the king had thought her to be more perceptive, more discriminating in the choice of a husband.

She could not blame him. Even the king was aware that the old Earl of Sidhean had given his word that his only daughter would have to agree to any marriage presented to her. The only assumption he could make was that she had indeed chosen Donald for a husband.

Jamie rubbed his chin and moved closer to her. "This wedding," he said carefully. "You have agreed to the union?"

She hesitated only a moment. "Aye."

If he caught the hesitation or the lack of enthusiasm in her reply, he made no comment. Looking at her, he smiled broadly and spoke jovially. "Then 'twill be a happy affair, and one which we are pleased to attend."

Diana only wished she was of the same mind as the king led her to the table. Somehow, she got through the tedious evening, but her head ached, and her jaws felt stiff from smiling when she was at last permitted to leave.

To her acute annoyance, Donald insisted on escorting her from the room. This, she permitted, but only until they reached the entry hall.

There, she turned to face him, her bearing and manner indicating that he could accompany her no farther.

"Get your rest this night, my lady," he said to

her in a mocking voice. "There will be little of it once we are wed. Since you already know what is expected of you, be warned that I will not countenance a rebellious female in my bed."

Her cheeks flamed at his boorish manner. As always, pride came to her rescue. "Rest assured, I am aware of my duty."

A wintry smile came to his lips. "I hope so, my lady." He brushed at his belted plaid. "It would distress me to be responsible for the dishonor that would befall the Clan MacLaren if it became necessary for me to return the earl's sister to him in disgrace."

A chill raced through for she knew he was not referring to her behavior in or out of his bed. If on his wedding night, a man discovered that his bride was not a virgin, he was well within his rights to return her to her clan. Banishment was the best a woman could hope for under those circumstances. Incarceration and even death were possibilities for a woman who so disgraced herself.

Then Diana relaxed. Whatever plans Donald had in store for her, returning her to Sidhean was not among them.

"Mayhap you would like to withdraw your offer of marriage?" she suggested quietly, her composure returning.

His smile turned even colder. "I would never consider such a dishonorable course, my lady. Indeed, I think we will have a most enjoyable union. However, be forewarned! There is more that I, as your husband, will demand of you. 'Twill be necessary for you to humble that pride of yours!"

"That is something I would not do even for a man I loved!" she said icily.

Donald's mouth tightened, then relaxed. "I once possessed a young mare," he said in a casual tone that did not deceive her, "who was fractious and unbiddable. She, too, was proud of spirit and refused to bow to the will of the man who owned her." The smile that Diana so disliked returned. "However, after a few beatings she learned her lessons well enough." Donald swept her a bow that was as deep as it was mocking.

Shakily, Diana hurried up the stairs to seek a privacy she knew that henceforth would be denied her. Depression followed her, relentlessly trailing her footsteps like a shadow cast in bright moonlight. In her chambers, she closed the door, then leaned against it, suddenly aware of how alone she was.

Sibeal was gone. In her heart, Diana could not fault the lass for running, as she had apparently done. She herself would have run had she been able to do so.

Removing her jewelry, she dropped it carelessly on a table, then cast an eye about her empty room. How odd, she thought. She felt more like a prisoner in her own keep than she had in her enemy's stronghold. And before too many more days passed, she would truly be a prisoner.

Despair took such a hold on her, she began to tremble. Crossing the room, she flung open the window, inhaling deeply of the cool air. Her hands gripping the sill, she looked down into the courtyard. Almost of its own accord, her body leaned forward, and she stared down at the flagstones. One move on her part would be all it would take. Then, horrified by her own cowardly inclination, Diana hastily straightened up.

Just before she drew the shutters, she glanced up at the sky. There was no moon. It was clearing. Only a few thin ribbons of clouds trailed along the carpet of stars that decorated the blackness.

Thorn was beneath those stars. Did he, at this very moment, raise his head to gaze at the twinkling brilliance? Was he thinking of her? Diana did not know, and as always, what she most desired to know was withheld from her.

"I wish you peace and happiness, my love," she whispered. "Neither of which I can share with you."

Chapter Forty

An overcast sky muted the delicate colors that normally accompanied the gloaming, and alone on the ramparts of Dunmoor Castle, Sibeal anxiously scanned the fells to the south. She paid no mind to the capricious gusts of wind that whipped at her hair and billowed her skirt. Her hands gripped the stone wall, and she ignored the heavy despair that made her want to cry out in helpless frustration.

Only two days left! And one of them needed simply to travel to Sidhean!

Her brow gathered in concentration as she strained to see through the gloom. With all her might she tried to will the appearance of the Earl of Dunmoor, astride his golden stallion.

Without warning, the moon pierced the cloud cover, touching the land with its ivory glow and creating wavering shadows as branches swayed and dipped. For an instant, her heart lifted, then plummeted when a movement proved to be no more than a shadow.

The moon retreated again, and the wind quickened. Beneath her gaze the fells were an unbroken expanse of green. There was no sign of the earl.

Unable to remain still any longer, Sibeal hurried down the narrow steps to the bailey. She was so engrossed in her thoughts she collided with Angus when she entered the keep a few minutes later. Quickly his hands reached out to steady her.

"You can knock a man off his feet like that, lass." He laughed, then added, "Not that I would mind."

Her eyes brimmed with tears, and Angus brushed a tear from her cheek. "You must not weep, Sibeal," he chided softly. "You must keep your hopes high! All is not lost yet."

" 'Tis no use!" she cried and tried to break away, but his grip was too strong. "The earl will never get here in time. I must go back!"

Despite her struggles, Angus tightened his hold. "You will do no such thing!" he said sternly. "There's still time. You must be patient."

She shook her head. She had never had much patience to begin with, and she had none left now.

"Come with me," Angus said before she could

again speak. "I've something to give you. I was going to wait until these matters were settled, but it seems as though now would be the proper time."

Diverted, Sibeal obediently followed him up the stairs, pausing abruptly when he opened his bedroom door and eyeing him warily.

"I don't want to see that look in your eye!" he admonished in a sharper tone than she had ever heard him use.

"Can't you show me here?" she asked cautiously, scanning the hallway. No one, not even a servant, was in evidence.

He pursed his lips. "I could, but that would tell me that you don't trust me. I'd not like to think that would be so, lass."

Turning from her, Angus entered the room. After a moment, she warily followed. The room was not unlike the man who occupied it. Large, plainly furnished, unpretentious. Only the bed looked comfortable. She gave it a cursory glance, then hastily averted her eyes.

Angus was standing by a bookshelf, his back to her, and she could not see what he was doing. Facing her then, he said, "I've a present for you."

"For me?" she asked, surprised. She could not recall a time when anyone had given her anything. When she saw the book in his hand, she frowned in disappointment. She could not read.

But Angus did not offer her the book. Instead, he put it on the table. Then, with what she considered to be an inordinate amount of care, he parted the pages. When he at last withdrew what had been hidden between the pages, she gasped and put her fingertips to her lips. Even though she saw it, she did not believe it.

"Och! And where did you find it?" she exclaimed in wonder.

Taking her hand, Angus placed the sprig of white heather on her palm. Though dried and pressed, it still retained its sweet scent.

"In the glen that borders Loch Maree," he said. " 'Twas almost hidden in a clump of wildflowers. But I knew what it was as soon as I saw it. And I"—he seemed embarrassed for a moment—"saved it for you."

Displaying the same care that he had, Sibeal placed the sprig back on the pages of the book, fearful that the flower would crumble.

" 'Twas kind of you to think of me," she murmured. Her fingertips caressed the sides of the volume, but she refrained from touching the heather. It was too precious to be handled.

"Nay," he said quickly. "I've done little but think of you since you left."

Looking up at him, she smiled. "You must have had better things to do," she protested teasingly, then fell silent at the expression on his face.

"You should smile more often, Sibeal," he said in a quiet voice. "You look so bonnie when you do."

Her smile slipped. " 'Twould be foolish for a person to smile without reason."

Angus rubbed his chin. "Most women I know seem to smile all the time."

"Then they must be daft!"

Angus nodded, and an awkward silence ensued, as he wandered about the room.

"Would you like to sit down?" he said at last, motioning to a chair.

"Nay!"

From the corner of her eye the four-poster took on a menacing shape. First the chair, then the bed! Sibeal thought, knowing a man's ways.

"Would you be caring for a glass of wine?" Angus said. "Or mayhap a wee dram?"

"You'll not be getting me in your bed with that one!"

His brow wrinkled with exasperation. "Why is it that you think a man has no other objective than to get you in his bed?"

A feeling of guilt made her turn away. In all the time she had known him, Angus had never acted improperly. "I'll be having a glass of wine then," she said in a low voice.

He moved to the table and uncapped a decanter. She watched him in silence. For a big man he was very graceful.

Sibeal grew pensive. She was being less than honest and knew it. Angus thought he knew everything about her. Yet there was one thing he did not know. She took a deep breath.

"Did you know I'm a bastard?" she remarked casually.

Angus started, spilling the wine. He glanced

around helplessly. "Are you?" he murmured, moving the glasses from the red puddle in which they rested.

"Aye," she said with a solemn nod as Angus filled two clean glasses.

"Well, then," he said as he handed one of them to her, "I would imagine that the man who weds you will not be bedeviled by his in-laws. 'Tis something a man can live without." He downed his wine in one swallow.

Sibeal sipped the red liquid, then placed her glass on the table. Angus placed his empty glass next to it. He stared at her for such a long moment, she became restive. At last, he bent forward to kiss her.

Like a startled doe, she tensed. But she made no move to draw away. He did not embrace her as his lips gently caressed her.

Beneath the feathery, seductive movement of his mouth, Sibeal began to relax. She wasn't aware that her arms crept slowly about his neck, she wasn't even aware of the exact moment when she began to return his kiss. But suddenly, she was, with an intensity she had never before felt. Strong arms encircled her— arms so powerful she felt they could shield her from the world.

It was Angus who first drew away. "You would tempt a saint, Sibeal," he whispered hoarsely.

She was so stunned by her own emotional reaction to what was, after all, a simple kiss, she made no immediate response. Yet in truth, it was no ordinary kiss. It had been her first real kiss. She discounted those disgusting episodes with Robert, whose tongue had ravaged her mouth and left her heaving with nausea.

In some wonderment she stared at the man before her. Auburn hair flecked with gray at the temples framed a face that was tanned and as yet unlined. His warm brown eyes were gazing deeply into her own. His expression sobered. "I know I'm not like the young man you dreamed might come courting you."

"And what would you be knowing about my dreams?" she said swiftly.

"Are they so different from the dreams of any other young lass?"

"Mayhap not," she said, then added quickly, "but I've never dreamed about a man, young or not!"

"And just what did you dream about?" he asked.

Her cheeks flushed. "Bairns," she whispered in such a low voice he bent toward her.

"Bairns?"

"Aye." Her chin rose defiantly.

"And just how did you think you would get them?" he asked.

"With my husband!" she answered promptly. "My children will have a father—one they know and respect."

Uncomfortable with his flippancy, Angus fell silent. He ambled back to the table. Most of the wine had sunk into the grain of the porous wood, looking like tiny red rivers going nowhere, just as his life had been in recent years. He tried to recall the women he had had since his wife had died. Ill-defined faces flashed before him—some bonnie, some not, all forgettable.

Angus tilted his head to the side, but did not turn as he inquired, "Do you think they would respect a knight such as myself?"

"Do you have children?" she asked, not answering his question.

Slowly, Angus turned to face her and shook his head. His words came with difficulty. "I did have a daughter. She was less than two months old when she died."

Sibeal bit her lip. "I think you would make a good father."

"But of course you would not be wanting an old man like me." He waited quietly for her response.

Her head shot up. "And since when did you take to speaking for others?" she demanded.

His eyes widened. "Would you be thinking to consider me?"

She drew herself up. "I might," she said noncommittally. After a moment's hesitation, she moved her shawl to her shoulders and deliberately presented the left side of her face to him. "Of course, you might tire of looking at me. And there's none who would say you were wrong."

"Oh, yes, there would," he said in a strong

voice. "And I'd be among the first." Then he grinned. "I don't suppose any bairns you may have would bear the scar you're so ashamed of."

"I'm not ashamed!" she protested quickly. " 'Tis just that—"

"You suppose a man cannot see beyond your scar," he said softly, then took her in his arms. "Well, I can. And you're the prettiest lass I've ever seen."

She raised her head to look at him. "You mean that?"

His hands slipped to her well-rounded buttocks, and he drew her against him. "Oh, lass," he whispered. "You must know how much I care for you."

" 'Tis only because I remind you of her," Sibeal said in a small voice.

"At first that was so," Angus said. "But Adele had neither your strength nor your courage." His arms drew Sibeal closer. " 'Tis you I love! Whatever your decision might be, that much I want you to know." He bent his head so that he could look deeply into her emerald eyes. "Many traits in a woman capture a man's eye, lass. But only a few capture his heart. I've not much to give you, but I offer my sword and shield to protect you forever."

Her eyes glistened with tears. " 'Tis enough, Angus," she said softly, resting her head on his chest. " 'Tis enough."

After a moment, Sibeal stepped back. She had questions and no one to give her the answers. She had, in effect, agreed to marry Angus. But marriage, she knew, entailed more than kisses.

Was there always pain to accompany the act that would follow? Robert had driven his fist into her stomach on one occasion. On another he had bitten her breast so severely he had drawn blood.

She cast a furtive glance at Angus. Older than Robert, Angus probably had even more experience in mistreating a woman than Robert. Oh, aye, he was gentle now, but when the moment came. . . .

"You're having seconds thoughts, are you?"

She wet her lips. "Not exactly." Her hands worked against each other. "But there's something I want you to do before we wed. I want you to bed me."

He gave her a quizzical look. "You want me to?"

"I do!" She raised her chin, daring him to take exception.

Angus shook his head, then cleared his throat. "Well, then"—he waved his hand in the direction of the bed—"mayhap you would like me to leave whilst you disrobe?"

"You don't want to watch?" she asked, astonished.

"The choice is yours."

She smiled at that, feeling more confident. Then, modesty intervened. "Well, mayhap you could just turn around."

He did so, and she stared at his broad back with some trepidation, wondering what she had gotten herself into. Her spine stiffened. She was not about to wed a man who rutted like an animal! Hastily she removed her clothes and slipped beneath the covers. "I'm ready," she said bravely.

He turned. Covers drawn up to her chin, she watched him warily. Walking toward her, Angus sat down on the edge of the bed and gazed at her. She began to tremble, sorry for having made such an insane suggestion.

"Your hands are shaking, lass. I told you once, you would never be in my bed unless it was of your own choosing," he said quietly, making no move to touch her. "You can still leave it."

She swallowed. Her fingers plucked nervously at the sheet. Memories assailed her, none of them pleasant. "Mayhap I should."

He started to get up, and her hand grasped his arm. "I didn't mean that," she cried tremulously. "I am ready."

He smiled ruefully. "For what?"

She blinked. "For whatever 'tis you want to do."

Angus hesitated a long moment; then his motions deliberate, he got up and slowly began to undress.

Sibeal's trepidation grew. Lord, he was big! she thought in amazement mixed with dismay. Every part of him was big! By the time he crawled into bed beside her, Sibeal was numb with fear. She wanted to tell him that she had changed her mind about everything! But she knew if she opened her mouth she would scream.

Closing her eyes, she waited for the agony to be over. A moment passed, but nothing happened. She opened her eyes to find Angus staring at her.

"When I kissed you a few minutes ago, you didn't tremble like this," he remarked softly.

"That was different," she said. " 'Twas just a kiss."

He smiled tenderly. "Mayhap we could try one more."

Dutifully, she raised her face toward him. His lips were softer than any she had ever known. They did not demand; rather, they sought to entice.

The pressure on her own lips was light, and she could feel his warm breath on her skin. His powerful arm held her firmly, but not tightly. She knew she could break free whenever she wished.

Still tense, Sibeal made no move when his mouth moved to her chin, then slipped to her throat. He reached her breast, and his tongue swirled around her nipple. She gasped as he suckled it. Then she began to relax as a languid feeling crept over her.

Time had no meaning as Sibeal sighed and gave herself up to the gratifying sensations that relaxed her muscles, one by one. Her arms lay limply at her sides as if all strength had left them.

When his mouth moved to her stomach, she was at first disappointed. Then his tongue began to move in circles along her lower abdomen, and she again tensed. But it was not fear that caused her muscles to tighten.

She moved restlessly against the pleasurable onslaught, and she was startled when his knee gently prodded her legs apart. She made a move to push him away, only to find her wrists held fast.

She bit her lip and squeezed her eyes closed. Now it would begin.

When his mouth fastened on the sensitive bud, her eyes opened, and she drew a sharp breath, feeling as though a bolt of lightning had immobilized her.

"No." She breathed and tried to free herself. But she was held fast by the powerful man who loomed over her.

Gradually, her struggles ceased as the sweet torment continued. Her head thrashed on the pillow, and her voice was a whimper that was ignored.

Releasing his hold on her wrists, Angus grasped her buttocks and raised her so that his questing tongue could plunge deeper inside her. She felt as though her senses had fled. Her hands clenched the sheets, and she crumpled them in her fists. When she thought she could bear no more, he raised himself, straddled her, and gently entered her.

So intoxicated was she by the unexpected sensations that flooded her she clutched at his back and pulled him closer to her, liking the feel of the crisp hair on his chest against her breasts.

Slowly at first, then more rapidly, he thrust into her. Suddenly, a pinpoint of sensation grew within her and began to swell to unbearable proportions. Her head back, she cried out as the climax took hold of her, shaking her body with tremors that left her weak as they subsided. A moment more, then Angus at last experienced his own release and settled at her side.

Sibeal's breasts rose and fell as her breath at last returned to normal. When she was finally in control of herself, she turned her head on the pillow and saw Angus watching her.

He smiled and gently brushed her nose with his lips. "Mayhap you would now like to kiss me?"

He gave a low, throaty chuckle as she came willingly into his arms.

Chapter Forty-one

The sun was shining brightly, pouring in through the window in buttery rays of golden light. Feeling weary from a night of restless slumber, Diana dragged herself from the bed. She stared accusingly at the clear blue sky. Today was a day it should have rained! she thought resentfully.

A sharp knock sounded on the door. Before Diana could respond, her brother strode into her room. This morning, the unsmiling Robert looked every inch the earl. His kilt and trews were of the distinctive MacLaren tartan. His black velvet jacket was adorned with silver buttons, and beneath it, he wore a scarlet silk vest.

The sporran buckled around his waist Diana recognized as one belonging to their father. Made of sealskin, it was highly ornamented with gold stitching. His shoes were of leather with silver buckles. He was not yet wearing his bonnet or dress sword.

His arms folded across his chest, her brother glared at her. "Why weren't you down to breakfast? 'Twas necessary for me to make excuses to the king for your absence!"

"I have only now gotten out of bed." She shrugged her arms into her robe. Her eyes felt gritty, and she blinked to clear them.

"How could you oversleep on your wedding day?"

He moved toward her, as if to capture her attention. To her amazement, Robert sounded incredulous. Did he, she wondered crazily, actually think she was looking forward to becoming Donald Campbell's bride?

She kept her voice calm as she replied. " 'Twas not so difficult. I was awake most of the night."

Robert gave a short laugh. "Too bad, for 'tis a certainty that you will be awake most of this night as well."

Diana made no retort. Tonight was something she did not even want to think about. Apathetically, she went to the window and stood there, gazing outside.

Robert came to her side. "Stop mooning about! You've wasted half the morning as it is. Get dressed."

She did not move, and Robert grabbed her arm. She quickly shook free of him. His anger was visible in the pulse that throbbed at his temple, and she watched as he made an effort to control himself.

"Get dressed, I said. The wedding is in less than an hour!"

Less than an hour! she thought in dismay. The force of reality hit her hard enough to take her breath away. She managed to keep her voice even as she said, "I'll not need an hour to put on my dress."

Robert's nostrils flared. "You will not be shaming me by not appearing at your best!"

She turned to him, quizzically arching her brows. "Is that what it would take to shame you?" She regarded him with a certain interest.

"If you do anything to upset the ceremony, I'll—" He raised his hand as if to strike her, but then he paused.

Diana knew that her height, which was the same as his, had always been something he'd hated her for. She had also shown him that she was not a docile woman who would tolerate being stricken. She would fight back, and there was no one else in the room. Slowly, his hand lowered.

"There's nothing more you can do to me, Robert," she stated in a scorn-filled voice.

The door suddenly opened again, this time to reveal Ellen. She, too, was dressed for the occasion. Her silk dress was of a yellow so bright that it resembled a dandelion. Pearls were entwined in her blond hair, and diamonds blazed at her throat.

Behind her were servants carrying pails of hot water. The countess waved her hand at her husband, and with her words, Diana knew that Ellen had been listening to the conversation from the hall.

"Take your leave, my lord," the countess said with a nod. "I will see to it that Diana looks her best. Of course," she added with a condescending smile at her, "I'm certain you feel that no one can attend you as well as your maidservant. Unfortunately, the ungrateful wench decided to leave you and run away to God knows where."

"If Sibeal ran away, she did so with good cause!" Diana said heatedly. She knew she was being baited, but time was pressing inexorably, each minute drawing her closer to what she considered to be the end of her life.

Ellen put a white hand on her own bosom. "If? I cannot believe that any doubt still lingers in your mind!"

Robert grunted. "Sooner or later I'll find her. And when I do, I will hang her for the common thief she is! No one gets away with stealing one of my horses!"

Diana moistened her lips. "May I remind you that Banrigh belongs to me," she said. "Sibeal did not steal her. She took the horse with my permission."

"And did you give her leave not to return?" Robert demanded. "Hah! You would sooner give away your jewelry than your precious mare!" he added when Diana made no immediate response.

"If you do not believe me, then ask Lachlan," she said. "Sibeal took Banrigh with my permission!"

Robert's eyes narrowed. "Suit yourself!" he muttered, growing bored. "In less than an hour you will be answering to your husband, not to me."

Diana turned away. Despair washed over her in waves that threatened to submerge her. She was hardly aware of Robert's leaving the room or of Ellen's insistence that everything be perfect about Diana's appearance.

Offering no resistance, Diana allowed herself to be bathed, coifed, and dressed. Nothing about her appearance interested her. Finally, Ellen stepped back to view her. "Your cheeks are pale!" she said. Turning, she roughly poked one of the maids in the ribs. "Fetch the pot of rouge on my dressing table. Be quick, you lazy wench!"

The lass scurried from the room, returning a few minutes later with the pot of rouge. Ellen watched closely as a bit of the color was applied to Diana's cheek.

"A vast improvement," Ellen muttered with satisfaction. Once more, she stepped back to assess her creation. "You look positively virginal," she purred, then gave a scornful laugh. Ellen's smirk was not lost on Diana as she further exclaimed, "Donald Campbell will be pleased at the sight of his bride!"

Diana closed her eyes as she sought to find the sharp retort she would have normally delivered to the countess. She found nothing, not even anger. It did not matter what she said or what she did not say. It would not change this day's outcome.

A brief glance in the looking glass told her that she did indeed look her best. Her gown was of ivory satin, the skirt full and looped at the hem at intervals to reveal the cream-colored underskirt. Each loop was caught and decorated with clusters of pearls. The bodice was pointed at the waist and tight fitting around her breasts. The sleeves molded her arms to the elbow, where they fell in delicate folds that were fringed with lace. Her hair was free of adornment or covering. Its unrelieved blackness was in stark contrast to the ivory of her gown. Unbound, it fell to her waist.

Diana was unimpressed. She turned away from the sight of her image. A memory of something Sibeal had once said touched her mind, and Diana put a hand to her lips to stifle an hysterical cry.

"What is wrong with you!" Ellen demanded in alarm. She took a step closer to peer into Diana's face. "Your brother will be furious if he sees you in tears!"

Lowering her hand, Diana drew a deep

breath. "Nothing is wrong with me." A greater lie she had never told.

Muttering to herself, Ellen clapped her hands smartly, and the servants hastily departed.

Diana stole another look at herself, her conversation with Sibeal echoing in her mind with frightening clarity: "Of course I want to look my best," she had said. "What woman would not?"

"Only a woman who did not want a man to think her beautiful—and desirable," the wise Sibeal had said.

Ah, Sibeal, Diana thought, tears springing to her eyes, I do not know where you have gone, lass. But I hope you are happy and safe.

Ellen's harping voice intruded on her thoughts, and Diana reluctantly turned toward her.

"In the absence of your mother," Ellen was saying, "I feel I must remind you that you must obey your husband." She paused a moment to collect her thoughts. "A dutiful wife is a jewel to be treasured," she said with a pious nod that would have done credit to a nun.

Diana raised her eyes to look at the ceiling. She felt as though she should either laugh or cry. She did neither. Lethargy blanketed her as warmly as an arisaid.

Ellen's smile was as thin as a sliver of ice as she said, "However, I don't suppose I will have to prepare you for what will take place in your wedding bed. Doubtless, you already know about a man's desires."

A bit of Diana's spirit returned as she faced her tormenter. "I know very well, Countess! Mayhap I should be the one to impart that information to you so you could satisfy those desires enough to keep a man in your bed."

Ellen's eyes widened in rage. "You will be singing a different tune on the morrow!" She took a few steps toward the door. "Come along! 'Tis time."

Numbly, Diana stood there as if she had been planted into the floor. A moment later she caught the heavy scent of roses as Ellen returned to stand at her side. Putting her hand on Diana's shoulder, the countess pushed her toward the door.

"Everyone is waiting, Diana!" Ellen glared at her. "The earl will never forgive me if you are late!"

Sick apprehension engulfed Diana as she reluctantly made her way downstairs. Robert was waiting for her at the foot of the stairs. As she descended, he looked up at her.

"By God!" he muttered, viewing her with a dispassionate eye. "I begin to understand Donald's obsession."

Diana reached the landing and gave him a cold look. The admiration she saw in her brother's eyes was, for some reason, extremely distasteful to her, most especially on this day.

"I must say, sister dear, that you do look lovely." He gave a rueful laugh. "If only you could keep your mouth shut, you would be a paragon among women!" He took her arm. " 'Tis a fine day for a wedding," he said cheerfully as he led her outside.

Chapter Forty-two

Diana moved as if in a dream. She heard the admiring murmurs of the villagers and crofters, who had been given a holiday, as she walked slowly through the crowd. But they all left her as cold as the bracken beneath a December frost. Lethargically, she allowed Robert to guide her toward the priest.

" 'Tis not a wake I escort you to! Smile!" he muttered beneath his breath.

"You smile, Robert," she said in a low voice. " 'Tis a happy day for you."

His hold tightened on her arm until her soft flesh protested. Her face remained impassive. As they approached Father Alasdair, the old man watched Diana with watery blue eyes, and his thin lips stretched into a smile.

When they stood before the priest, Donald

came to her side, and Robert moved away—
with relief, Diana thought sardonically.

The priest began to intone words. They
washed over Diana as would the water at high
tide in the fish pond. Standing quietly, she felt
the warmth of the late-summer sun on her
shoulders and wondered what the coolness of
the night would bring.

Donald's response broke through her
numbed state of mind, and she sighed, knowing
that her own would have to follow. But even
after the priest addressed her, the words caught
in her throat. Father Alasdair bent toward her,
concern deepening the lines in his face. Then
his expression changed to displeasure.

Diana did not care or react until, beside her,
Donald's hand went to his sword. For a wild
moment, she thought he was going to use it on
her! Then he spun around, his back to Father
Alasdair.

Her brow furrowed, Diana turned and her
breath caught in her throat when she saw
Thorn. He wore no armor or suit of mail. He
carried no shield, and his sword was sheathed.

But how splendid he looked! Diana thought.
His doublet of gold satin was vivid beneath the
sun's rays. His hair gleamed and glinted as Sian
took a few dancing steps forward, then halted.

Behind him, Diana saw Angus and Sibeal,
and she smiled ruefully, knowing where her
maidservant had gone. Then Thorn's forceful
voice rang out across the glen.

"Diana MacLaren is promised to the Earl of Dunmoor! I have come to claim what is mine!"

The silence that followed his announcement was unnatural, and with deep trepidation, Diana glanced at the king. She wondered what his reaction would be to the unexpected intrusion. He was, at the moment, standing very still. She could see his eye travel the assemblage, as if assessing the situation.

Glancing around her, she felt that the atmosphere was fraught with danger. Men were subtly shifting their stance to protect their women. And every man upon whom Diana's eye fell had his hand on his sword.

Still holding her breath, Diana watched as the young king stepped forward, his casual attitude suggesting that he only wanted a better view of the proceedings. As his gaze swung from Thorn to herself, and back again, she saw a small smile of awareness curve his sensual lips.

Diana at last released her breath. Jamie was, she had no doubt, very well aware that she had been a captive of the MacKendrick. His informants kept him advised of all troubles throughout his kingdom. Highlanders, she knew, accounted for the majority of these problems. Jamie interfered only when the situation might be to his own detriment. Such was not the case here.

Diana tensed again when the king, appearing to have made a decision, took a few steps forward, then halted. At first confused, Diana suddenly became aware of what he was doing. Jamie had positioned himself in such a way that no one could make a move. He did it with such aplomb that, at first, no one except Diana realized what he had done.

She smiled slightly at the scene. To the left were the MacLarens. To the right were the Campbells. Behind each of them were the king's men. To the rear of all, were the MacKendricks. No one could let loose an arrow without hitting either the king's men or, worse, the king himself.

At first startled by the king's actions, Diana knew that, without uttering a word, Jamie was offering her the opportunity to make her own choice. Turning her head slightly, she looked at her brother. In angry conversation with Ellen, he was not looking at her. Diana turned away. Not even Robert would dare to defy the king.

Thorn had paused about 60 feet from where Diana was standing, and he made no move to come any closer. He was staring at her as if they were alone in the meadow.

She wanted to run, but her legs would not move. Nor, she noticed, did Thorn move. Having halted Sian, he was sitting upon the stallion as if he had turned into a statue.

Sunlight glinted off Sian's trappings. Both horse and rider appeared to be cloaked with a nimbus of light.

Diana then became aware of what Thorn was doing. He had come to claim her, but he would not abduct her. She would have to go to him of her own free will! In plain view of all those assembled, she would have to renounce publicly her clan. No longer would she be identified as a MacLaren, as she would have been even if she had wed Donald Campbell.

Across the expanse of purple heather, their eyes met. You will have to make the choice, lass, he seemed to be saying to her; then he smiled.

Although her lips did not move, an answering smile warmed her heart. Her beloved golden knight had come for her; and she could no more refuse him than she could the breath of life.

He was asking her to give up everything that was dear and familiar: her home, her family, her clan. All would be lost to her with her first step. She would forever be an outcast among her own people.

Her chin rose a fraction. When all was said and done, there was no choice at all. From the first moment their eyes had met, she had known in her heart that she belonged to this man. Many times her lips had betrayed that fact; but her heart had never been fooled.

In the continuing quiet, Diana glanced around her, seeing grim faces. And suddenly, she found herself not caring. They all had their feuds, their wars, their disputes. Let them fight their battles. She wanted only to be held in Thorn's strong arms.

Her back erect and her head held at a proud

angle, she slowly began to walk forward. Though she could hear the angry murmurs from the gathered MacLarens and Campbells, her step never faltered.

Astride the golden stallion, Thorn paid no heed to the angry discussions that swirled about the glen. His attention was fastened on the figure of the woman who was walking proudly in his direction. She was thinner than when last he had seen her. Yet never had she looked so lovely to him as she did at this moment.

When Diana at last reached Sian's side, Thorn looked down at her. "You broke your promise to me, lass," he murmured in a low voice.

She blushed, but held her head high. "Nay, my lord, I promised you I would not wed another if my life depended on it. 'Twas not my life that was at stake."

"So it wasn't," he said solemnly, having been informed of what took place at Sidhean. Bending forward, he reached down and easily lifted her up onto his saddle.

When Diana was settled, he spurred the golden stallion forward.

Turning, Diana glanced at Sibeal. Riding beside Angus, the girl was not looking in her direction. Instead, she was looking at Angus. Indeed, she could not seem to take her eyes from the knight, who was resplendent in tartan and trews. On his bonnet was fastened a sprig of white heather. Diana saw all she needed to know, and she was content.

Aware that Thorn was returning to the gathered assemblage, Diana gave him a questioning look.

He grinned at her. "They are expecting a wedding. 'Twould be a shame to deprive them of the festivities."

Halting Sian before a thoroughly confused Father Alasdair, he dismounted and assisted Diana to the ground. Taking her hand, he led her in the direction of the priest.

Before words could be spoken, Diana saw Jamie approach Robert. Standing only a few away, she could easily hear their conversation.

" 'Twould appear that a long-standing feud will soon be laid to rest," Jamie said conversationally to the Earl of Sidhean.

Robert's face was red and mottled. Diana had never seen him so furious. He appeared, at the moment, unable to speak.

"The dowry for the lady," the king said, ignoring the look of rage.

"Dowry?" Robert choked. He stared in astonishment. "No one need dower a used wench! One breathes a sigh of relief to be rid of such a one! Your Grace, I cannot allow you to condone this!"

Jamie's gaze was cold. "Cannot?"

"I mean no disrespect, Your Grace," Robert stammered.

" 'Tis pleased we are to hear that." Jamie nodded solemnly. "We would not like to think that the support of the Clan MacLaren was in question."

" 'Tis not!" Robert said hastily.

"The dowry," Jamie said again. " 'Twould please us greatly if it included the disputed territory."

When Robert gaped at him, Jamie fixed the Earl of Sidhean with a hard eye. "Do you take exception to our suggestion?"

"Ahh—"

"We did not hear your answer, my lord!" Jamie straightened up. His men moved closer.

Robert floundered for a moment. Then, apparently, prudence intervened. " 'Tis an excellent suggestion, Your Majesty."

"You will of course see to it before this day is gone?" The king's amiable smile reappeared.

"Aye," Robert murmured in defeat.

Jamie then raised an imperious hand. "You may begin the ceremonies."

Diana gazed up at Thorn, basking in his smile of approval. She then turned her attention to Father Alasdair. This time, there was no hesitation in her responses.

When the ceremony was over, Thorn again helped Diana to mount the golden stallion and swung himself up behind her. Pausing, Thorn raised a hand in a gesture of homage to his king. Then he spurred the stallion forward. In only moments, Angus and Sibeal followed at a discreet distance.

Faster and faster Sian sped, surefooted on the familiar terrain. The wind whipped at Diana's hair and lashed at Thorn's bronzed cheek. His arm held her securely, and she reveled in the strength and possessiveness of it.

Once before, Diana had ridden in front of the man who had captured her. How long ago it seemed. And now she was captured in the truest sense of the word. Every part of her belonged to him. Nor would she have it any other way.

Tilting her head to look at the face of her beloved, Diana was rewarded with a kiss that left no doubt of his mounting desire.

When he pulled away from her, Thorn chuckled and tightened his hold. "You're a proud minx, lass," he said with no little pride. " 'Twill be my pleasure to show you who is your master."

Diana rested her head against his broad chest. "Aye, my lord," she said softly. Her deceptively docile tone belied a spark of amusement inside her. " 'Tis a lesson we both will benefit from learning."

Passionate Historical Romance by Love Spell's Leading Ladies of Love

Sheik's Promise by Carole Howey. Whether running her own saloon or competing in the Rapid City Steeplechase, Allyn Cameron banks on winning. Sent to buy Allyn's one-of-a-kind colt, Joshua Manners makes it his mission to tame the thoroughbred's owner. But his efforts to win Allyn for his personal stable fail miserably when she ropes, corrals, and brands him with her scorching passion.

__51938-0 $4.99 US/$5.99 CAN

The Passionate Rebel by Helene Lehr. Passionate in her support for the American patriots, Gillian Winthrop is determined not to give her hand—or any part of herself—to the handsome Tory her grandmother means her to wed. Will Philip's false identity as a Tory sympathizer cost him Gillian's love? Or can he convince Gillian that he, too, is a passionate rebel?

__51918-6 $4.99 US/$5.99 CAN

Love Comes Unbidden by Marion Gwyn. It will take more than a king's ransom to win Frances Clifford's family manor back after Queen Elizabeth accuses her dead father of having stolen a priceless jewel—and awards the estate to a foreign courtier. Gaston de Vere is determined to make Frances the mistress of both his heart and his home, but only when the past is laid to rest can he hope to conquer the rebellious beauty who stirs a hungry passion within him.

__51942-9 $4.99 US/$5.99 CAN

Dorchester Publishing Co., Inc.
65 Commerce Road
Stamford, CT 06902

Please add $1.75 for shipping and handling for the first book and $.50 for each book thereafter. NY, NYC, PA and CT residents, please add appropriate sales tax. No cash, stamps, or C.O.D.s. All orders shipped within 6 weeks via postal service book rate. Canadian orders require $2.00 extra postage and must be paid in U.S. dollars through a U.S. banking facility.

Name _____

Address _____

City _____ State _____ Zip _____

I have enclosed $_____ in payment for the checked book(s).
Payment <u>must</u> accompany all orders.☐ Please send a free catalog.

DANCE of the FLAME

ELAINE BARBIERI

Elaine Barbieri's romances are "powerful...fascinating...storytelling at its best!"
—Romantic Times

Exiled to a barren wasteland, Sera will do anything to regain the kingdom that is her birthright. But the hard-eyed warrior she saves from death is the last companion she wants for the long journey to her homeland.

To the world he is known as Death's Shadow—as much a beast of battle as the mighty warhorse he rides. But to the flame-haired healer, his forceful arms offer a warm haven, and he swears his throbbing strength will bring her nothing but pleasure.

Sera and Tolin hold in their hands the fate of two feuding houses with an ancient history of bloodshed and betrayal. But no matter what the age-old prophecy foretells, the sparks between them will not be denied, even if their fiery union consumes them both.

_3793-9 $5.99 US/$6.99 CAN

Dorchester Publishing Co., Inc.
65 Commerce Road
Stamford, CT 06902

An Angel's Touch

Time Heals
SUSAN COLLIER

Tired of her nagging relatives, Maeve Fredrickson asks for the impossible: to be a thousand miles and a hundred years away from them. Then a heavenly being grants her wish, and she awakes in frontier Montana.

Saved from the wilderness by a handsome widower, Maeve loses her heart to her rescuer—and her temper over the antics of his three less-than-angelic children. As her angel prods her to fight for Seth, Maeve can only pray for the strength to claim a love made in paradise.

_52030-3 $4.99 US/$5.99 CAN

Dorchester Publishing Co., Inc.
65 Commerce Road
Stamford, CT 06902

Please add $1.75 for shipping and handling for the first book and $.50 for each book thereafter. NY, NYC, PA and CT residents, please add appropriate sales tax. No cash, stamps, or C.O.D.s. All orders shipped within 6 weeks via postal service book rate. Canadian orders require $2.00 extra postage and must be paid in U.S. dollars through a U.S. banking facility.

Name _____

Address _____

City _____ State _____ Zip _____

I have enclosed $_____ in payment for the checked book(s).

Payment <u>must</u> accompany all orders.☐ Please send a free catalog.

ᴛʜᴇ ROSELYNDE CHRONICLES

ROSELYNDE

Roberta Gellis

"A superb storyteller of extraordinary talent!"
—John Jakes

In an era made for men, Alinor is at no man's mercy.
Beautiful, proud and strong willed, she is mistress of
Roselynde and her own heart as well—until she meets Simon,
the battle-scarred knight whose passion and wit match her
own. Their struggle to be united against the political obstacles
in their path sweep them from the royal court to a daring
crusade through exotic Byzantium and into the Holy Land.
They endure bloody battles, dangerous treacheries and
heartrending separations before their love conquers time and
destiny to live forever.

_3559-6 $5.99 US/$6.99 CAN

Roberta Gellis

"A superb storyteller of extraordinary talent!"
—John Jakes

Ravishing, raven-haired daughter of a Welsh prince, Rhiannon is half shy and half wild. It is said she can cast a spell over any man, but she is no man's prize.

Notorious for loving—and leaving—the most beautiful women in the realm, Simon is the court's most eligible—and elusive—bachelor.

Then the handsome nobleman meets Rhiannon, who drives him mad with fury and delirious with desire. While bloody rebellion rages through England, Rhiannon and Simon endure ruinous battles and devastating betrayals before finding a love so powerful no enemy can destroy it.

_3695-9 $5.99 US/$6.99 CAN